THEIRS TO CORRUPT

ENTICING BILLIONAIRES

SIERRA CARTWRIGHT

USA TODAY BESTSELLING AUTHOR

THEIRS TO CORRUPT

Copyright @ 2024 Sierra Cartwright

First E-book Publication: October 2024

Line Editing by GG Royale

Proofing by Cassie Hess-Dean

Layout Design by Once Upon an Alpha

Cover Design by Once Upon an Alpha

Photo provided by Depositphotos.com

Promotion by Once Upon an Alpha, Shannon Hunt

All rights reserved. Except for use in a review, no part of this publication may be reproduced, distributed, or transmitted in any form, or by any means, electronic or mechanical, including photocopying, recording, or by any information storage and retrieval system, without prior written permission of the author.

This is a work of fiction. Names, characters, places, brands, media, and incidents are either the products of the author's imagination or are used fictitiously, and any resemblance to any actual persons, living or dead, is entirely coincidental.

The author acknowledges the trademarked status and trademark owners of various products referenced in this work of fiction. The publication/use of these trademarks is not authorized, associated with, or sponsored by the trademark owners.

Adult Reading Material

Disclaimer: This work of fiction is for mature (18+) audiences only and contains strong sexual content and situations.

It is a standalone with my guarantee of satisfying happily ever after.

All rights reserved.

DEDICATION

Thank YOU.

CHAPTER ONE

Link

"The first time I saw him kill a man, he was balancing a tray of champagne." I tip my head to the side, indicating Paxton Gallagher, my trusty bodyguard and the man I can't imagine not having by my side.

My words hanging in the air, Johnson frantically looks at the man who is blocking his way out of the booth.

Pax shrugs. "And I didn't spill a drop."

In the most satisfying way possible, Johnson's face contorts with fear.

Men like him are all too predictable. Swaggeringly brave when bullying others but crumbling under real pressure.

I lean back in my seat at the Rusty Nail, the fabric of my suit whispering against the cracked vinyl upholstery.

The man across from me—the latest in a long line of disappointments—squirms. Beads of sweat form on his balding head, despite the way the air-conditioning is valiantly struggling against Houston's summer humidity.

The stench of Johnson's fear clogs my nostrils.

He should have carefully considered his options before betraying my trust.

Allowing myself a cold smile, I continue the story. "We were at a charity gala. Black tie. Pax was undercover as a waiter." I pause, savoring the growing terror in Johnson's watery eyes. He can't look away. "Whole thing was over in less than two seconds."

Even now, though he appears relaxed, Pax is a mountain of barely restrained violence in a tailored suit. His gaze constantly scans the room, ever vigilant.

Johnson's Adam's apple seems to be convulsing. "Mr. Merritt, please. I swear I didn't know about the discrepancies in the books. If you'll just give me a chance to explain—"

"You've had chances, Johnson." I keep my tone conversational. "Three of them, to be exact. I don't appreciate being lied to, especially not by someone I trusted to manage one of my investments."

As I speak, movement catches my eye.

A server approaches our table, and for a moment, I'm caught off guard.

She's young, early twenties perhaps, with a mane of chestnut hair pulled back into a sleek ponytail. Her jeans are a little loose, as is her shirt. The caution in her eyes speaks of hard-won experience beyond her years.

And I'm intrigued.

Pax notices her too.

I continue addressing Johnson, but my attention is divided. "You have twenty-four hours to produce the real financials, or my friend over there might have to provide another champagne service." I lean forward, allowing steel into my voice. "Do we understand each other?"

The woman is close enough to have heard my thinly veiled threat.

Her composure slips, her hand trembles, and the glasses on her tray clink together precariously.

She avoids my gaze as she fights to steady the beverages.

Why, I'm not sure, but I reach out to stabilize a teetering glass.

My fingers brush against hers, and a surprising burst of electricity jolts through me. Her hand is small, a stark contrast to those I shake in boardrooms and back alleys.

"Thank you," she murmurs, refusing to look in my direction as she continues to a nearby table.

I track the sway of her hips as she walks away, noting the feminine grace in her movements despite her obvious nervousness.

She doesn't belong in a dive bar.

So why is she here, waiting tables?

Shaking off the momentary distraction, I refocus on Johnson. "You've got twenty-four hours."

"I'll get you what you need, Mr. Merritt. Just…please…" he stammers, his pudgy fingers leaving damp prints on his glass of untouched whiskey. "My family—"

"Be grateful I'm being generous. Same time tomorrow. Same place. You'll be here." It's not a question.

As he attempts to flee, he knocks over his drink. "I'm sorry. I'm…" He grabs a napkin and tries to mop up the mess.

"Get out of here," Pax snaps.

Tripping over his own feet, Johnson scurries away like the rat he is.

Moments later, the server is back, smelling of jasmine, vanilla, and sweet innocence—something I'm surprised I can still recognize.

She hasn't missed a thing, and within moments, she's leaning past me to wipe away the liquid and pick up the discarded glass.

Pax slides into the seat that Johnson has vacated. As

always, my bodyguard has his back to the wall and his face to the door. Nothing will ever get past him.

"Your server had to leave." After clearing her throat, she goes on. "I'll be taking over your table."

Quickly she glances toward the bar and the owner, Marge. "If you'd rather have someone else wait on you, I can arrange—"

"No." My interruption is swift. No way in hell am I letting her get away after what she overheard.

After what she overheard?

As if that has anything to do with it.

No way in hell am I letting her get away while her scent is still tantalizingly wrapped around me.

"In that case... Can I get you anything else? Another round?"

There's no reason to stay.

We'd planned to go to the Braes—the exclusive country club I belong to—but I'm reluctant to leave. "Another round." I nod.

Pax arches a single, dark eyebrow.

"Thank you..." Looking at her, I tilt my head, inviting her to supply her name, which she doesn't.

That makes me lean back in my seat to regard her more closely.

Though Pax and I don't come here often, I know all the bartenders and most of the servers. "You must be new here."

"Relatively."

Her vague reply only intrigues me more.

"I'm Pax." My bodyguard has more charm than I do, and he smiles disarmingly at her.

"Hello." Once again, she keeps her features neutral.

So much for charm.

"Link," I offer.

"I know who you are." She barely hesitates before moving off.

I scowl, and Pax clears his throat, no doubt to cover his laugh. I'm not caught off guard often.

No doubt she asked Marge about me.

What the hell had the owner said?

Pax makes a motion that imitates a plane crashing, and he makes a whistling sound to accompany it.

"Asshole," I snap, but I can't take my gaze off our innocent server as she moves to a small terminal to key in our order.

Someone feeds the jukebox, and a classic country tune drowns out casual conversation as she disappears into the back room.

What's your story?

And why the fuck is my dick hard?

"Think Johnson will come through?" Pax asks.

His question drags me away from musings, and I can't say I'm happy about it. "He'd be a fool not to."

Pax shrugs. "And he's already proven himself to be exactly that."

But until now, he hadn't heard that story about Pax.

The object of my interest finally appears from the back room, and she walks around to the bar where she leans forward, waiting for the order to be filled.

The view of denim stretched over her rear holds me speechless.

I continue to take her in as Marge pulls our bottle from the top shelf behind the bar. It's the only thing we drink. But we hadn't ordered the same for Johnson.

"You didn't hear a word I said," Pax notes, a hint of amusement in his voice.

When I don't respond, Pax follows my gaze. "She doesn't belong."

His words echo my earlier observation.

"Want me to find out who she is?"

For a moment, I consider my response.

The smart move would be to have Pax dig up everything he can on this mysterious woman. But there's a part of me—a part I thought long buried—that relishes the challenge of unraveling the puzzle myself. "No," I decide. "Let's see how this plays out."

As if on cue, she starts to walk our way, a fresh round of drinks balanced on her tray.

I note the way she squares her shoulders before approaching us. *Feeling as if you're stepping into the lion's den, little dove?*

If so, she's not far from wrong.

Without a word, she delivers our whiskey.

"Thank you," I reply, then pause deliberately before adding, "I didn't catch your name earlier."

A flicker of something—caution? defiance?—crosses her face before she answers. "That's because I didn't give it." She dazzles me with a smile.

Pax clears his throat.

I sweep my gaze over her, and her face heats. "What are you running from?"

"Running?" She shakes her head. "Nothing."

"Hiding, then."

She balls a hand into a fist, then shoves it into her apron pocket as if to hide it.

My guess is closer than she's willing to admit.

"Nikki," she says.

Though she doesn't blink, I taste her fib on the air.

Interesting.

"Well, *Nikki,* I noticed your interest in my business discussion. Dangerous habit, that. Eavesdropping."

Though a pulse frantically flutters in her throat, she doesn't blink. "Didn't hear a word."

She lies easily but not convincingly.

I tilt my head, studying her with care. "You did. And you'd be well advised to forget that you did."

At my pseudothreat, momentary fear flashes through her wide, light-blue eyes. Almost instantly, she blinks it away and she tips her chin back.

She's not as adept at hiding her emotions as she'd like to think.

"I'll bring your check."

After pivoting, she hurries away and is flagged down by the occupants of another table.

As she stops, she gives them an actual smile—which is much more than the fake one she offered me.

I scowl in a way that makes grown men cower.

Fuck me.

I want that attention directed at me.

At the bar, she confers with Marge once more. And the older woman flicks a frown in my direction. A warning not to mess with this particular employee?

"What's your interest?" Pax asks.

With a sigh, I shake my head to clear it.

"Boss?"

Judging by the small grin on Pax's face, he's asked the question more than once. "You're enjoying this."

"Yeah." He nods.

Pax and I are more than bodyguard and protectee. He lives in a guest house on my River Oaks estate. Not that he spends much time at his own place.

He was assigned to me as a bodyguard when I hired Hawkeye Security. Now only he will do.

We're no longer employer/employee. He's my closest confidant and friend. We're inseparable to the point that now we share women. Neither of us dates unless the lady in question understands the score in advance.

"You generally charm the pants off any lady you're interested in."

I take a drink of the finest single malt on the planet.

"She's not interested."

Yet.

"Is that her appeal?"

Pax knows I love nothing more than a conquest, no matter how short-lived the relationship—be it a night or a week.

But this is about much, much more than the challenge she presents. The wariness she struggles to hide intrigues me.

I want to get to know her.

Intend to get to know her.

She returns to drop the check on the table.

Without glancing at the total, Pax pulls out a credit card and slides it in her direction.

Then I produce a crisp hundred-dollar bill and offer it to her.

Her eyebrows furrow as she glances between me and Pax. "Would you like me to use this instead of the card?"

"No," I reply before Pax can. "This is your tip." The amount is not ridiculously out of line, given the cost of the drinks.

She shakes her head.

"I insist."

Annoying me, she looks in Pax's direction.

"Take it," he encourages.

Still, she hesitates.

"For your excellent service," I add. "Along with your discretion." And because she fucking looks like she needs it.

"I told you I didn't hear anything."

"So you did."

"Take it," Pax repeats. "For putting up with him. You deserve it."

"I…"

For the first time, the ice queen thaws.

"Thank you." She accepts, and our fingers brush once again.

This time I note that her skin is slightly calloused from hard work. *Fuck.* I want to save her from that.

Once more, she moves off, and I can't look away.

"Obsessed, boss?"

I don't obsess over anything but business.

Yet my gaze is riveted on her. "She's going to be ours," I reply.

He knows me too well to argue. "Do you want me to let her know?"

CHAPTER TWO

Two Weeks Later
Tessa

What is wrong with me?

Frustrated with myself, I tighten my grip on the steering wheel as I near the Rusty Nail.

Even though I haven't seen Link or Pax since that fateful evening, memories of their intense gazes still send shivers down my spine.

I should be grateful they haven't come in, at least not while I've been at work.

They see too much, and they are far too dangerous. And it's not just my intuition telling me that.

After they left, Marge confirmed just that.

And what I overheard Link say—about Pax shooting someone at a charity event—is evidently more than just a story to scare the pants off the man who'd betrayed him.

When I arrived home at the run-down apartment that I share with my friend Natalie, we dug into a bowl of spaghetti with meatballs, poured some sweet tea, and dropped down on the couch, and I told her the story about Pax killing that man.

"Makes you wonder why he needed to shoot someone at a charity event, doesn't it?"

Her words fascinated me, and I couldn't get them out of my head.

Later that evening, while I was babysitting overnight for a nurse who lives on the other side of the complex, I scrolled to *Scandalicious*, my favorite online gossip rag, one that isn't afraid to spill juicy details.

There, I learned that Link is richer than God. Because of his cutthroat business practices, he was once called a vulture capitalist, and now that moniker has been shortened to Vulture.

He's rumored to belong to the Zetas, a secret society.

From there, I fell deeper into an internet rabbit hole.

Though there's never been an official confirmation that such an organization exists, there's plenty of rumor and conjecture, including assertions that it's been around for generations, and that the group's headquarters is somewhere in Louisiana.

They supposedly have bizarre rituals, including a yearly bonfire.

One article called members Titans, which seems fitting. They're rumored to have a symbol so they can recognize one another—Athena's owl. On one page there was a mockup. Framed by laurel leaves, the bird was ordinary, but had terrifying, unblinking green eyes.

Having read too much already, I went back to *Scandalicious* to see more pictures of the drop-dead gorgeous, movie-star handsome Link. Many of the images showed him with various women. Never the same one twice.

Some of the ladies had not-very nice things to say about

him. One called him a manwhore who notched his bedpost and discarded conquests without a backward glance.

Unsurprised, I placed my phone onto a coffee table, facedown.

But every day since then, I've wondered if he'll show up at the bar.

And today's no different.

I turn into the Rusty Nail's parking lot and glance at the time.

I'm early for my shift, but instead of going inside and clocking a few extra minutes, I park the car beneath a lamppost, then open my phone to the *Scandalicious* page, wondering if there are any new stories about him.

Why am I doing this?

The man's an alleged murderer and confirmed womanizer. He is the last person I should be interested in.

But a traitorous part of me understands how Link is able to effortlessly charm women.

With his chiseled, angular features and searing blue eyes, he's gorgeous. And every time I approached his table, all his attention had been focused on me.

Factor in multiple commas in his net worth, he probably has women throwing themselves at him.

At least I'm too smart to ever be one of them.

Not that he'd be interested anyway.

Suddenly an alarm chimes on my phone, jolting me, letting me know I have one minute to get inside or I'll be late.

No time for sitting here thinking about the billionaire and his bodyguard.

I turn off the ignition, but the vehicle keeps rattling for a few more seconds.

Every day, the beat-up sedan makes a valiant effort to avoid the junkyard, and I appreciate its efforts. One day it will lose the battle, but unfortunately I can't afford anything better.

Still, I count my blessings that I have any form of transportation and that the AC blows semicool air.

As I hurry across the parking lot, the sticky Houston heat clings to my skin like a second outfit.

I'm so ready for summer to be over.

When the door closes behind me and my eyes adjust to the dimness, my steps falter.

They're here.

Link and Pax sit at their usual booth, an island of power in a sea of rowdy regulars.

My heart does a terrible little flip in my chest.

"Nikki!!" Marge's gravelly voice cuts through the twangy sounds of Blake Shelton lamenting lost love on the jukebox.

Grateful she's remembered to call me by my fake name, I glance her direction.

"Table five just got here, and they need service."

Table five. That's not Link and Pax.

Grateful, I nod, then go into the back room to put my purse away for safekeeping.

As I emerge, Link catches my eye, and he crooks a finger at me, a small smile playing at the corners of his mouth.

My stomach performs a gold-medal-worthy somersault.

"They got their first round from the bar," Marge says. "But it looks as if they want you to wait on them."

No way. "Are you sure they don't want Cheryl?" I ask, glancing at my bubbly blonde coworker.

Unfortunately she's on the far end of the bar, and there's no way he means anyone but me.

"If you don't want to take care of them, I'll handle it."

I sigh, remembering the hundred-dollar tip, which I probably hadn't deserved with my outright hostile behavior.

As much as I would have never admitted it, the money

had been a lifesaver. That day, my cellphone bill had been due, and my car needed gas. Oh, and it had been my turn to buy a few groceries from the supermarket.

"Nikki?" Marge prompts.

"I'll take care of them." *When I get around to it.* "Thanks, though." I take my time tying my apron into place and grabbing my order pad.

Marge laughs. "Like living on the edge?"

"Something like that." I grin at her.

With practiced ease, I weave through the space, dodging the occasional grabby hand. And I help table five before making my way over to Link and Pax.

Still, I can't help but smooth the front of my apron into place, which is ridiculous. After all, I'm not nervous. They're just customers. Like all the others.

When I stop near them, I'm nearly knocked sideways by the aura of lethal command they both radiate.

How wrong I'd been a minute ago.

These men are anything but *just* customers.

Link rests against the back of the tired booth like it's a throne, his classic, tailored suit a stark contrast to the bar's shabby decor.

Even in the dim light, I notice the hint of stubble that makes him look devilishly appealing.

Stupid to notice.

And Pax... *Dear heavens.*

A black leather motorcycle jacket is on the seat next to him, leaving his broad chest and sculpted arms on full display. The fabric of his black T-shirt hugs every ridge and valley of his upper body, and it's all I can do not to stare.

I force politeness, hoping not to betray the butterflies dancing in my stomach. "What can I get for you?"

Link's eyes, dark and intense, never leave my face. "The usual, little dove. And a round for everyone in the bar."

"For everyone?" *What game are you playing?*

"You heard me."

"Got it." I turn to head back to the bar. But the sound of Link's voice reaches me.

"Nikki?"

I consider pretending I didn't hear him.

But I have no doubt he'd make a scene if it suited him, so I stop and glance back.

Then I wish I hadn't because I'm caught in his gaze, like a mouse to a cat.

"You're ours for the evening."

The undercurrent of authority makes me swallow hard. Then I hurry back to the relative safety of the bar top.

"They're buying a round for all the customers," I tell Marge.

"I see." Saying nothing else, she nods, then rings a big brass bell.

When she has everyone's attention, she calls out, "Your next drink is on the gentlemen in that booth!" She points.

People cheer and clap, and Link laps up the adoration.

Asshole loves being the center of attention.

Even mine.

As Marge pours their stupidly expensive drinks—Bonds whiskey that is kept tucked away on a top shelf, reserved exclusively for them—I lean against the wood, trying to calm my racing heart.

Why am I letting these men affect me like this?

"You sure you're okay, sugar?" Marge asks, her weathered face creased with concern.

I force a smile. "Yeah. Fine."

She nods, understanding in her eyes. "They're a handful."

"Nothing I can't deal with. It's…" I come up with a story that's really close to the truth. "I babysat all night, so I'm tired."

She nods.

Cheryl and I are kept busy delivering drinks to all the patrons, and I have to walk by Link and Pax's table several times.

Now I begin to see the method to his madness.

Keeping me near?

The thought is ridiculous, and I shake myself to rein in my galloping thoughts.

Why would two insanely gorgeous men want something to do with a woman who is barely scraping by with this job and the occasional babysitting gig—anything that pays under the table so I don't have to show identification or file taxes. *So that no one knows who or where I am.*

At one point, I might have had the opportunity to meet Link at a party or something, but that was when my—

This time, I shake my head, ruthlessly cutting off my ruminations.

That part of my life is over.

Tessa has vanished.

And Nikki is determined to be a survivor.

In a small act of defiance, I deliver their order last. And I slide the first drink in front of Pax.

Then Link reaches for his glass and intentionally touches my hand.

Sensual awareness crashes through me.

If he hadn't been paying attention and caught the glass, I would have dropped the whiskey.

"Thank you, little dove," he murmurs, his voice soft and intimate, husky.

Not trusting myself to speak, I hurry away.

The rest of the evening passes in a blur of drink orders and country ballads. Every time I approach Link and Pax's table, I feel their gazes on me, assessing, evaluating. Their scrutiny unnerves me.

Finally Pax signals for the bill.

Like last time, Link offers me an enormous tip.

Though the money is nice, I wonder about his motivations. "I don't need to be bought."

"For the conversation you didn't hear?" He smiles, knowing I've inadvertently revealed the truth.

Damn it. I have to be more careful. If Nikki is to get away with this ruse, I can't afford slipups.

"Once more, you earned it," Pax says, ignoring his boss's jab. "For serving the whole bar."

Well, except most people tipped me when I delivered their drinks.

Still, I pluck the crisp bills from Link's fingers, taking care not to touch him. I've had enough of that unnerving experience.

If he wants to shove hundred-dollar bills at me, who am I to complain?

With a smile in Pax's direction, I tuck the money into my apron pocket.

When they leave, the bar seems strangely quiet.

I shake my head, telling myself I should appreciate the break.

Because it's almost time for me to leave, I turn over a couple of tables to Cheryl and make sure my area is clean, ready for the next customers.

"You did a great job today, sugar," Marge says, startling me.

She presses a wad of cash into my hand—tips that were added via credit card. There's more than expected, and I exhale with gratitude.

"Now get on home and get some rest. You look dead on your feet."

I am. But my night is far from over. "Thanks."

Marge—and this job—are a lifesaver.

The parking lot is eerily quiet as I make my way to my car, keys clutched between my fingers. The flickering streetlight casts long shadows, and every rustle of leaves sends my heart racing.

I practically dive into my beat-up Honda, locking the doors before I even start the engine.

As I pull out of the lot, I can't shake the feeling that I'm being watched. But a quick glance in the rearview mirror shows only empty darkness.

I'm far too jumpy.

Leaning back against the worn fabric seatback, I turn up the radio and sing along to the eighties tune.

By the time I climb the rusty exterior stairs to my second-floor unit, my eyes are ready to close.

But as I push open the door, the smell of home-cooked food makes my mouth water. "Nat?" I call out, kicking off my shoes.

With a smile, she pokes her head out of our tiny kitchen. "Hey, girl!" Her mismatched earrings glint in the fluorescent light. "I made enchiladas."

The quick meal is one of our go-tos. We make them out of cheese, and if one of us has a particularly good week, we splurge by stirring in some ground beef. "You're amazing. Thank you."

"Go sit down."

"I can help," I protest.

"You'll be in my way."

The galley kitchen is barely big enough for one person, let alone two. "I'll wash the dishes."

"You can handle it another time. You have to babysit tonight, don't you?"

"Yeah." Again. Grateful for Natalie, I make my way into the living room and collapse on the threadbare couch.

We grab every opportunity to catch up that we can. I

watch Miguel when his mom works the night shift at the hospital. Nat also recently picked up a second job, cleaning office buildings after hours. And since we're not scheduled together at the Rusty Nail very often, we cherish our time together.

I've barely had a chance to roll some tension from my shoulders when she places our dishes and silverware on the coffee table. Then she plonks down next to me.

"Anything interesting happen this evening?"

"It's the Rusty Nail." I shrug, and we both laugh.

That's become one of our favorite sayings.

There's always something going on at the Rusty Nail, from hookups to breakups, arguments, people belting out terrible songs on karaoke night, occasional fights, people breaking pool cues because they lost, customers needing to be poured into rideshares because they're too drunk to stand up, and well, Link Merritt threatening someone's life.

We each grab a plate, and I settle back. I have barely enough time to relax for a few minutes. "Link and Pax came in. They bought a round for the bar."

"No shit?" She's about to take a bite, but she pauses, hand in midair. "I don't think they've ever done that before. He's trying to impress you."

"Me?" I laugh. "No."

"Why else would they do it?"

"Celebrating something?"

"Sure." She presses her lips together. "Mmm-hmm."

"They're not interested in *me*," I promise her. "I mean, seriously. The idea is ridiculous."

"Why not you?" she demands loyally.

"I've seen pictures of him and his harem." Beautiful women. Tall. Willowy. Rich.

"And where have you seen such a thing?"

"Uhm…"

"You've been checking him out!"

"No! I mean…" I put down my plate and sigh. "You're the one who told me to look him up. Remember? The first night I met them?"

She takes her bite and considers me. "And that's the only time you googled him?"

I blush.

"Ah-ha!"

Shaking my head, I push hair back from my face.

"They *are* gorgeous. And rich."

Without a doubt. "And scary."

She nods, but she's smiling.

"We've both had enough of that," I remind her.

"True."

I'm lucky to have Natalie in my life.

Months before, she escaped a brutal, controlling relationship.

When I got off the bus in Houston, I found a local women's shelter to hide out in while I made sure I wasn't followed.

The counselors running the place put me in touch with Marge, who didn't ask questions or check references. Better yet, I was told she paid weekly and in cash.

Nothing comes up that she can't handle. Rumor has it that some guy came in one night. He was strung out on meth, waving a knife, and he attempted to rob her. She grabbed the trusty sawed-off shotgun that she keeps behind the bar and blasted a hole in the floor right next to where he was standing. Then she calmly went back to pouring a cold Bud.

Not only did she take me under her wing, she introduced me to Natalie and suggested I move in with her.

Because Nat had some credit, she had found an apartment. It's not in the best area of town, but we have somewhere to call home.

Marge is part heroine, part savior, always looking out for us.

Realizing Natalie is still talking, I drag myself back to the conversation.

"I was saying…there's the kind of shitty situation we both escaped, but Link and Pax are a totally different kind of dangerous."

True. "But I don't have any desire to be a rich man's plaything." After all, that's part of why I ran away.

Resolved, I change the subject.

After dinner, I take a quick shower and dress in shorts and a T-shirt. Then I say goodnight to Nat and walk across the complex to Serena Rodriguez's apartment.

The young single mom greets me with a harried smile. "I don't know what I'd do without you."

I wave off her thanks. This job is easy. After all, I mostly get paid to sleep. "It's no problem. How's Miguel doing?"

"Finally asleep," she says. "Three bedtime stories tonight."

I grin. One time, he managed to get four out of me.

Miguel is a great kid. But he's five, and he has way more energy than I do.

"I should be home in the morning around seven thirty. If you can feed him breakfast and get him ready to go, I'll drive him to school."

"It's a plan." Occasionally something comes up at work, and she can't get out in time. "Just let me know if that changes."

Since the apartment is blessedly quiet, and I don't have any immediate obligations, I lock the door, then drop onto the couch and turn on the television.

Maybe because of the conversation with Natalie, or the fact I'm imagining Link's masculine, spicy scent, I can't stop thinking of the men.

Even though I don't mean to, I pick up my phone.

Within seconds, I've opened the *Scandalicious* site.

To my surprise, I see a photo of him, snapped last night at some high-society gala. He's gorgeous in a tailored tux, his longish black hair brushing his collar.

Eventually I realize he's with another man.

My eyes widen as I read the caption.

Link is speaking with Matteo Moretti.

Heir apparent of the infamous Moretti crime family.

An icy chill skates down my back.

Mob connections? No wonder Link needs a bodyguard.

I wonder if the man they threatened that night is still alive.

My God.

And yet...

I never felt threatened, even when challenging Link—which my instinct for self-preservation should have stopped me from doing.

Unnerved, I close the article and instead google Pax.

There's frustratingly little information about him online, but I'm not deterred. After all, I have nowhere else to be.

So I spent the next hour digging.

The few things I discover are intriguing. Former special forces, highly decorated, accustomed to violence and danger.

The information about him and Link tells me that I'm out of my mind for continuing to look them up.

But as I drift off into an uneasy sleep, my mind filled with images of them, one question burns in my mind:

Will I be able to resist them if they come back?

CHAPTER THREE

The Next Day
Link

The sun dips below the Houston horizon, painting the clouds in vibrant streaks of orange. The stunning view is one of the reasons I have office suites on the fiftieth floor of my downtown building. This evening, I barely notice it.

My mind is consumed by thoughts of *her*.

Nikki.

The door to my office opens silently, and Pax strides in. His face is grim, a thick folder tucked under one arm.

"You found something," I state, not bothering to phrase it as a question.

Pax nods, dropping the folder onto my glass-topped desk with an ominous thud. "You're not going to like it."

I'm behind my desk, and I lean back in my chair, gesturing to the folder.

But before I can reach for it, Pax moves to the sleek chrome-and-glass bar cart in the corner. The clink of crystal and the quiet gurgle of pouring liquid fills the silence.

"You're going to need this," he says, returning with two tumblers of amber liquid and offering one to me.

Bonds whiskey. *What else?*

I accept the glass, raising an eyebrow. "Bad?"

Pax drops into the seat across from me, his muscled frame dwarfing the modern leather chair. "Worse."

With a deep breath, I flip open the folder. The first thing I see is a driver's license photo. It's her—Nikki—but the name reads "Tessa Tremaine."

My blood runs cold. "Tremaine," I mutter. "As in…"

"Axel Tremaine's little sister," Pax confirms.

Axel Fucking Tremaine.

I down half my whiskey in one swallow, welcoming the burn.

The man's name conjures a mixture of disgust and fury.

Almost a year ago, he'd come to me, begging for a loan to finance some "can't-miss opportunity."

Because his father was a man I'd known and respected, I considered the idea.

Though my better judgment advised against it, I'd been persuaded.

He hasn't made a single payment since.

"There's more," Pax says quietly.

I force myself to look back at the file. Police reports. Bank statements. And then…

Fucking hell.

No.

"He's trying to sell her?" My grip on the glass tightens dangerously.

Pax nods grimly. "He's in deep with some seriously bad people."

Because a tic is ready to explode in Pax's temple, I flip the page and see a candid shot of a Tessa I don't recognize.

Her figure is a little fuller, and she's less guarded, actually smiling. She's wearing a sundress and floppy hat.

Then I scan the text.

In it, she's referred to as a virgin, and bids to fuck her are being solicited. The opening minimum is one hundred thousand dollars.

The amount Tremaine owes me.

Rage, raw and primal, threatens to swallow me, and I shove the file folder, sending the contents scattering.

I've dealt with all manner of motherfuckers in my line of work, but this...this is a new low.

"What you didn't read... Emiliano Sartori offered one hundred fifty to stop the auction so that he could claim her and marry her."

"Fuck." I stand abruptly and pace the length of my office like a caged animal. "No fucking way."

Pax studies me carefully. "Is this just about Axel?"

Ready to lash out, I turn and snarl.

But the knowing look in Pax's eyes stops me cold. There's curiosity and compassion, not judgment. Regarding him, I counter, "Tell me you don't feel it too."

For a moment, he says nothing. Then he raises his hands in a placating gesture. "Just asking, boss."

Somewhat mollified, I sink against the back of my chair. "You know damn well it's more than Axel." Which is why we've stopped by the bar at least three times a week, why we drive past the bar almost every night, why we follow her home.

Pax remains silent.

"She's not like anyone else." Women angling for money or prestige or both. But Nikki—Tessa—wants nothing to do with me. With either of us.

"Interesting." He takes a drink.

I picture Tessa's face. The wariness in her gaze, the determination in the set of her jaw. Her quiet strength and resolve.

"The idea of anyone hurting her…" I clench my fists, the rage bubbling up again.

Not happening. Not while there's breath in my body.

I fix Pax with an intense stare. "What about you?"

"Yeah. There's something about her." He rolls his glass between his palms. "Vulnerability with a core of steel."

My response to her is primal.

I stand and pace to the floor-to-ceiling windows.

Tessa's out there, alone.

And we know Tremaine won't rest until he gets his sister back and whores her out. "He's going to pay." And he'll never come near Tessa again.

Pax nods. "Consider it done."

Then he turns to stride across the room.

"Pax," I call out, stopping him at the door. "Have someone drive by the bar, see if her car is still there."

"Planning a visit?" he asks, eyebrow raised.

I nod. "Soon. Very soon."

Once I'm alone again, I return to my desk and press my palms together thoughtfully.

I'm going to make Tessa Tremaine ours.

And my plan starts now…

CHAPTER FOUR

Three Weeks Later
Tessa

The neon sign of the Rusty Nail flickers in the humid Houston night, casting an eerie red glow over the cracked asphalt of the nearly empty parking lot.

I swipe away a bead of sweat as I push the bar's heavy back door just a little farther open. The two a.m. air hits me like a wall, thick and heavy with the promise of an approaching storm.

For moments I stand there, surveying the parking lot, glancing at the shadows, watching for any hint of movement or unexpected vehicles, making sure I'm safe.

My beat-up car is beneath the parking lot's only lamp, and I see nothing out of the ordinary.

"All clear, sugar?" Marge asks from behind me.

I glance back and force a smile. "Yeah. Looks good. Thank you." I appreciate her so very much. "Good night, Marge."

"Be safe out there, honey. Call if you need anything."

Going home this late unnerves me.

The door clicks shut behind me, and she turns the lock, leaving me alone in the stifling darkness.

I dart toward my vehicle, clutching my small purse tightly, keys threaded between my fingers—a makeshift weapon I pray I'll never have to use. Of course, I also carry pepper spray, but I'm afraid of pointing the nozzle in the wrong direction.

How is this my life?

I ask that question daily.

My parents loved me and supported my dreams of going to college, having a career, and eventually getting married. Two years ago, my future was bright and shiny. I'd enrolled in college, and I was thriving.

Now I'm scraping by, barely able to buy groceries, jumping at shadows, all to escape the cruelty of the one person my parents counted on to protect me.

The image of Axel's cold, calculating eyes flashes through my mind.

Once, he'd been my hero.

Until greed turned him into an unrecognizable monster.

I'm so lost in my thoughts that I almost miss the sound of approaching footsteps. *Almost.*

Keys raised to strike, I whirl to find myself face-to-face with two men who've detached themselves from the shadows.

My blood ices as I recognize one of them. He works for Axel.

A wave of nausea hits me. This is my worst nightmare come to life.

"Well, well." He sneers. "What have we here? The boss's runaway sister."

My heart thunders as I bring up my keys, my hand shaking so badly I can barely hold them. "Stay back!" Despite my best efforts, my voice is squeaky and weak. Inside, I'm screaming at myself to run, to fight, to do something, but terror rivets me to the spot.

The men laugh, a cruel, mocking sound that sends chills down my spine. Suddenly I'm small, helpless.

"Time to come home, little girl. Your brother's been worried sick about you. And Emiliano is getting impatient."

The name almost makes me heave. *Emiliano.* The man my brother sold my virginity to.

Run!

How close am I to my car? Can I make it? My mind races, calculating distances, but panic muddles my thoughts. A knife blade flashes, and my world narrows to that glinting point of metal.

He takes another step.

"I said no!" The words burst from me, fueled by desperation, determination, and a surge of adrenaline. *"Help!"* I scream.

Nearby, a motorcycle roars.

As they advance, I stumble, my back hitting the cold metal of my car. The contact jolts me, and I grab for the door handle. Only seconds from safety...

"Drop the fucking blade."

My gaze swings toward the newcomer, and the assailants look behind them.

Two men emerge from the shadows, their presence commanding and intimidating.

Link and Pax.

Pax steps forward, his eyes cold and focused. "Do I need to repeat myself?" His voice is low, dangerous.

Axel's men hesitate, their confidence wavering.

"The lady's under my protection," Link says, his voice equally menacing.

The knife glints in the dim light, and the man flashes a

grin, a silver tooth shining. "Don't mind cutting you up either."

Paxton and Link exchange glances.

"Get her out of here," Pax nods at Link.

Then everything happens at once.

Pax lunges, a blur of motion as he disarms the knife-wielding attacker with a swift, precise strike. The weapon clatters to the ground.

Before the second man can react, Paxton has him pinned against the car, his arm twisted painfully behind his back.

"Let's go." Link grabs my elbow, jolting electricity through me, and I drop my keys.

Not slowing down, he pulls me toward a sleek black SUV parked nearby.

"Wait!" I gasp, my voice hoarse. "My keys—"

"Forget them," he snaps, practically lifting me off my feet as he yanks open the car door and shoves me inside.

The sudden shift from danger to relative safety leaves me dizzy and disoriented.

Through the tinted windows, I watch Pax take down the remaining assailant with brutal efficiency. A part of me is horrified by the violence, but another part—a part I'm not proud of—feels a grim satisfaction seeing my would-be attackers subdued.

Just when I think it's over, a van screeches into the lot, and more men pour out, heading straight for Pax. "We've got to help him!"

Ignoring me, Link slides into the driver's seat, the engine roaring to life

Pax doesn't hesitate. He meets the new attackers head-on, his movements precise, powerful.

Each strike calculated and effective, he takes down one after another.

One of the men gets a punch in, and I scream in horror.

Pax barely flinches, retaliating with a blow that sends the attacker sprawling.

Sirens pierce the night air, growing louder with each passing second.

The men freeze, their gazes darting toward the source of the noise.

Link glances back at me. "Stay down." He revs the engine, ready to move at a moment's notice.

Through the rearview mirror, I watch Pax finish off the last of the attackers, his chest heaving slightly from the exertion.

The remaining men retreat, jumping into the van and gunning the engine, fishtailing as police approach.

Link lowers the window, and Pax walks over. "I'll handle the authorities and let Marge know what happened."

Link nods.

"Meet you back at home."

"Tessa lost her keys."

"Roger that."

With a nod, Link smoothly accelerates, leaving the lot before law enforcement arrives.

"Oh God," I whisper, slumping back against the leather seat. "Oh God, oh God." My whole body is trembling now that the adrenaline has worn off, and I'm left hollow and wrung out. Tears threaten to spill, but I furiously blink them back. I haven't shed a single tear since this whole thing started, even when I boarded a bus and found my way to a shelter, and I refuse to now.

"Breathe," Link orders, his eyes never leaving the road as he expertly navigates through sparse traffic.

His matter-of-fact tone snaps me out of my panic. I force myself to inhale, focusing on the rise and fall of my chest. As my pulse steadies, a new fear takes hold. Why were they in the parking lot?

My head snaps up, and I blink. He'd called me Tessa.

How does he know my real name?

"You're safe," he says softly, as if he's read my mind.

Safe.

Am I? Or have I just traded one danger for another? "Thanks for the rescue, but you can take me home now."

"You're not going back to your place."

"Don't be ridiculous, Mr. Merritt." Despite the fact the car is moving, I reach for the door handle. All I need is a stoplight...

"Doors won't open unless I put the car in Park."

Frustrated, I squeeze my eyes shut. Does he miss anything? "Just go ahead and drop me back at my car. I'll be fine."

Gripping the steering wheel expertly, he shakes his head. "You're going home with me. *With us.*"

Fear turns my stomach inside out. I've escaped Axel's men only to land in the clutches of Vulture.

In the rearview mirror, our gazes meet. "You can relax. If I meant you harm, I would have simply left you to those thugs."

His cryptic answer sends a fresh wave of fear through me.

At a stoplight, I try to escape, testing his words. But the door won't open.

He shoots me a knowing smile.

When he takes off again, the city lights blur past us, and I hug myself tightly, trying to hold myself together. I'm hurtling into the unknown, trapped between the devil I know and two men who might very well prove far more dangerous.

A part of me wants to leap from the car, to run and never look back. But where would I go? Axel found me once. That means his resources are deeper than I ever imagined.

And despite my fear of Link and Paxton, a tiny voice in

the back of my mind whispers that they might be my only hope.

As we turn into a neighborhood with tall, brick fences shielding mansions, my anxiety spikes. After a couple of turns, Link steers the car through a gate that seems to open automatically for him. I watch in the side mirror as it slides shut behind us with a soft mechanical whir, sealing me in.

Link parks near a massive mansion. "Let's go."

I've been anxious to get out of the car, but now the back seat feels like a sanctuary.

He opens my door and offers his hand. I ignore it. "Where are we?"

"Home."

His place—with its meticulously manicured lawns, a pool, and swaying palm trees—is a stark contrast to the dingy apartment complex where I live.

We enter through an imposing back door. The interior of the ultramodern two-story home is every bit as imposing as the exterior.

Link shrugs off his suitcoat. "Have a seat," he says, gesturing to the island with its line of bar stools.

Because it might offer me some distance from him, I slide onto one, setting my purse on the chair next to me. He drapes his jacket over the back.

"Something to drink?" he offers. "Water? Tea? A glass of wine to calm your nerves?"

"I'm fine. I won't be here that long."

Link studies me for a moment. Then he heads to the refrigerator and returns with a bottle of water. After twisting off the cap, he places the beverage in front of me.

Reluctantly I drag it toward me. The coolness against my palm is grounding, and I take a small sip, grateful for the distraction.

We've only been here for a few minutes when a motorcycle roars, the sound growing closer. Light fills the driveway.

Moments later, the back door swings open with a soft creak. Pax strides in and pulls the door closed behind him, then types a series of numbers on the nearby keypad.

He shrugs out of his motorcycle jacket and carelessly tosses it on top of Link's suitcoat.

The sight of the ruthless bodyguard makes my breath catch in my throat.

He continues past me to stand next to Link. They're two massive, implacable male powerhouses, and being at their mercy makes me shiver.

As I look at Pax, I notice the small cut above his right eyebrow. Another, angrier gash slices across his cheekbone. "My God." I jump off my seat. "You're hurt. Let me—"

"It's nothing." He waves a hand dismissively, and something glints in his free hand.

My keys.

He sets them near me with a soft clink. "Thought you might want these back."

"Thank you." A wave of relief washes over me, followed quickly by a renewed sense of guilt. He'd thought to take care of that, even though he was hurt—because they wanted to protect me.

But why?

I'm nobody to them—a cocktail waitress. I shouldn't matter.

But then Marge's words echo in my mind, fragments of conversations we've had over the past weeks.

Pax isn't just a bodyguard. Though I've searched, I haven't learned anything about him since that first night. That leaves most of his past shrouded in mystery and danger.

I play with my keys, and both men fix their gazes on me.

"It's time for the truth, Tessa" Pax says, his voice low and firm, cutting through the silence.

His shocking green eyes unnerve me. Pax isn't looking at me. He's seeing through my constructed walls and half-truths.

My mouth dries, and I struggle against the urge to fidget under their scrutiny.

He leans forward. His voice is cold when he lashes out with, "All of it."

CHAPTER FIVE

Tessa

I clutch my keys tightly, the metal biting into my palm. The pain grounds me, reminding me that this is real. I'm with two men who might have saved me tonight but are scary beyond words. The way Pax dealt with all of those men…

"Thanks for everything you've done." I bring up my chin. "But I need to go."

Link's eyebrow arches. "Go where, exactly?"

"Home."

Pax crosses his muscled arms. "It's not safe. Those guys were able to find you at work. No doubt they know where you live."

A chill runs down my spine. He's right, of course. The realization makes my knees wobble.

Reality closes in on me.

For the first time in my life, I don't know what to do.

"Start talking," Pax says.

I swallow hard. Part of me wants to lie, to protect myself in the only way I know.

But they risked their lives for me.

"As you've already figured out, my name's Tessa." I pause to pick up my water. Stalling. Slowly I take a tiny sip. "My brother…" I stop. Then I tip my chin. I've done nothing wrong, and I have nothing to be ashamed of. "He is selling me to settle his debts."

Link's eyes narrow, but he doesn't show any other sign of surprise.

"To the highest bidder. Who apparently is a man named Emiliano Sartori." I shudder involuntarily at the thought of him and his leering gaze…the way he looks at me as if he owns me and wants to break me.

What I don't tell them is that I'm still innocent. That particular detail is too personal to share.

"You have no other family?"

"My parents are dead," I reply, the familiar ache of loss smacking me in the stomach. "Car accident two years ago."

Neither man seems surprised.

"No extended family? Aunts? Uncles?"

"No."

"Friends?"

No one is capable of protecting me from Axel. I shake my head.

"What do you know about your brother's…business?" Link asks, his voice carefully neutral.

"Not much." Since my hands are shaking, I slide my water back onto the island. Then I wrap my arms around myself, not as if that will actually protect me. "After our parents died, Axel…changed. He took over my dad's accounting firm. Then the gambling started." Unless it had been going on for a long time and I didn't know. "He won some, and it made him…" I think back. "Obsessive. Then he started to lose." I sigh. "He kept telling me he was going to win big, the next time." The losses kept piling up. Sure he had some good days, just enough to keep him hooked.

Pax's jaw tightens.

"I tried to get him to stop..."

"And the debt?" Link prompts.

How much does he know? "My brother has kept me in the dark. But I overheard things. Phone calls, conversations when he thought I wasn't around. He owes money to some dangerous people." *A lot of money.*

"And that's where you come in," Pax says, his voice low and angry.

"Yes." Anger sears me. "A couple of months ago, I found an email he was writing. He said he had an *asset* that could clear his debts." *Me.*

The silence thunders.

Both men's eyes are cold. Calculating. Dark. "I ran," I continue, my voice barely above a whisper.

"Look, Tessa..." Link plows a hand into his hair.

I tilt my head. Though I don't really know him, I've never seen him looking anything less than totally in control.

"He owes money to the mob."

The *mob?* Beneath me, the room tilts, and I grasp the edge of the island to steady myself. Frantically I shake my head. *"No..."* I grab my purse and shove my keys inside. "I have to go." *Run. Again.*

Link shakes his head. "You'll stay here while we figure out a more permanent solution."

"I can't."

"We have resources," Pax says.

Though his voice is steady and firm, it doesn't reassure me.

Shaking my head, I rush toward the back door.

"Think it through," Link urges.

Frantically I turn the knob, but the door is locked. Of course it is. I watched Pax type in a code.

"You have nowhere to go," he adds.

Maybe the shelter for now? While I figure out my next move. "One of you can drop me at my car."

"You're willing to bet it's not being watched?" Link asks.

Hating that he's right again, I change tactics. After all, the last months have taught me to be resourceful. "I'll call a ride." *If the service will pick me up without a credit card being on file.* "Or you could take me to the bus station."

"No." Link snaps his response. "You're staying, Tessa, fucking like it or not."

Mutinously, furiously, I glare at Link. "You don't get to tell me what to do."

"Want to try me, little dove?"

Tension charges the air, crackling like lightning.

"Look…" Pax raises his hand. "It's the middle of the night." His tone is measured and calm. The voice of reason. "There's not likely to be any buses running. You don't want to sit there alone." He waits for a beat. "You never know what could happen."

Like he intended, my mind supplies a million scenarios.

What if Link and Pax hadn't been there to save me earlier?

Defeated, I allow my shoulders to sink against the door.

"Stay tonight," Pax says, even though Link scowls at him. "You can make a plan in the morning, when you're rested."

"I…"

"One night," he repeats.

What choice do I really have?

"You'll have your own room," Pax goes on. "With a lock on the door."

Link remains quiet, his jaw tight.

Much as I hate to admit it, Pax's suggestion makes sense, and I should be grateful. Instead I feel trapped.

Suddenly the fight drains out of me, and I'm more exhausted than I ever remember being.

Even though I can't form the words, I nod.

"You'll stay?" Pax arches an eyebrow.

I clear my throat. "Yes."

Relief flashes across both their faces, but Link hides the emotion quicker.

"I need to let my roommate know."

"Roommate?" Pax asks, and the men exchange glances.

Once I find my phone, I text Natalie.

She doesn't respond, which isn't a surprise. When she's cleaning the office building, she has to keep her phone in a locker.

Still, we have promised to keep each other updated if our plans ever change.

"We'll show you around, so you're more comfortable," Pax says.

My cellphone battery is almost dead, and of course my charger is in the car. So I turn off the device and drop it into my purse, leaving it on the back of a chair where I can easily grab it on my way out the door in the morning.

"Shall we?" Pax invites.

Link's body language is stiff as he leads the way deeper into the house.

The main floor living room is luxurious with its leather sofas and chairs and gleaming hardwood. A state-of-the-art home theater system takes up one wall, while floor-to-ceiling windows overlook the backyard.

Another time, I might appreciate how elegant his home is.

"The gym and my office are down that hallway." Link points. "So is my office."

We climb the sweeping staircase to the second floor, and

Link indicates a door at the far end of the hallway. "That's my room."

"Where does Pax live?"

For a fraction of a moment, Link hesitates.

The two men exchange glances.

Finally Link answers, "He has the guest house out back."

Which is obviously something I didn't notice earlier.

Just how big is Link's estate?

Halfway down the hall, he stops. "This is yours." Link pushes open the door. "The bathroom's through there." He tips his head to the side.

"Let us know if you need anything else," Pax adds.

I won't. "Thank you." Without waiting for them to say anything else, I close the door. Then I lock it.

I remain in place until I hear them move away.

Then I really exhale for the first time in hours.

Now that I'm alone, my heart rate slowly coming down, I take in my surroundings.

The suite I've been assigned is enormous. A king-size bed dominates the space, and it's piled high with pillows and a plush comforter that looks sinfully soft. A sitting area with a small sofa and coffee table occupies one corner, while a writing desk sits beneath a large window.

Once, on a family vacation, I'd had a room like this. But that was before—

I shake my head to cut off the thought. No matter what, I won't feel sorry for myself.

Resolved, I head into the bathroom. There's a walk-in shower and an oval-shaped soaking tub. Of course there are double sinks, along with lots of fluffy white towels.

This space isn't just comfortable, it's wonderful.

"I'm only here one night," I remind myself. Promise myself.

After undressing, I take a long, hot shower, needing to

wash away the stench of the bar and the feel of the attacker's hands on me.

When I finally emerge, I notice a robe hanging from a hook.

Link has thought of everything.

Once I'm snuggled in it, my hair wrapped in a towel, I pad back into the main room.

Not wanting to sleep naked, just in case, I keep the robe on and crawl beneath the covers.

Sleep comes in bits and pieces, and my dreams are plagued by shadowy figures and Axel's cold laugh.

I wake with a start.

Sunlight is streaming through the windows.

Desperate to throw off the dreams, I rise onto my elbows and blink the world into focus.

Slowly I remember where I am, and memories rush back. Axel's thugs. Link and Pax rescuing me.

Looking around, I notice a duffel bag on the floor.

Not just any bag, but mine, with a broken zipper and a tear in one corner.

Its presence chills me.

My door has a lock, but clearly that didn't stop at least one of the men from entering while I slept.

Did they watch me?

Shaking, I toss back the covers to cross the room.

Unnerved, I crouch to open the bag. It's stuffed with my belongings. Jeans, T-shirts, toiletries. Bras and underwear are tucked into one corner.

They were in the bedroom at my apartment.

The realization sends a chill through me. Did Natalie let them in? Or did they break in?

How dare they?

I bring my chin up. Anger replaces all other emotions.

No one gets to make decisions for me.

I need to leave, and fast.

Once I'm dressed, I crack open the door.

Seeing no one around, I hurry down the stairs and quietly slip into the kitchen.

Freedom is steps away, so close that my heart begins to gallop.

I snatch up my purse from the back of the barstool, and when I reach the back door, I grab the doorknob, hope surging through me—

"Going somewhere, Tessa?"

Link's cold voice freezes me to the spot.

But I can't miss my chance.

Determinedly I turn it.

"You don't want to do that." Pax's warning is soft, but firm.

Despite my sudden anxiety, I pull the door open.

Alarms shred the morning air.

"Authorities have been notified. Authorities have been notified."

On and on a mechanical voice goes, ricocheting off the walls.

Frantic, I swing to face them.

With cool, measured calm, Pax closes the distance between us. Then he reaches above me to shut the door before typing into the keypad.

This close, I'm helpless, trapped.

He angles his wrist, showcasing his pricey smart watch. Then he taps a button, says some nonsensical phrase, then adds, "All clear."

Moments later, the sudden silence almost deafens me.

I'm facing both men.

Link folds his arms across his chest, pulling his white dress shirt taut across his muscles.

Suddenly as frustrated as I am angry, I scowl at both of them. "Are you keeping me prisoner?"

CHAPTER SIX

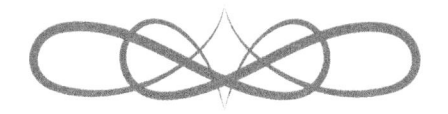

Tessa

"We prefer that you think of yourself as our guest," Link responds.

"Guest?" Hysteria bubbles up inside me. What the hell have I gotten myself into? These men, demanding and powerful, have me trapped.

Link's jaw is clenched, his eyes blazing.

Pax's expression is calmer, but his jaw is set too.

The way they fill the space of the kitchen, all broad shoulders and raw masculinity, makes me feel small, vulnerable.

Link stands near the kitchen island, his posture tense, while Pax finally steps back, giving me some much-needed space.

"Why don't you have a seat, Tessa," Pax says, his voice gentle but firm, letting me know this is an order, not an invitation.

His words jolt me from my spiraling thoughts.

Without their permission, I won't get far, and I need a minute to regain my composure.

"Let's talk about this," he encourages, walking to the coffee maker to dump lots of grounds into the basket.

I take my time, reluctant to move away from my escape route but realizing I have little choice.

My legs are wobbly as I make my way to one of the barstools at the island, and I perch on the edge of the seat.

Moments later, the rich aroma of the much-needed caffeine fills the air.

The normalcy seems surreal.

Then I scoff. There's nothing normal about sharing a kitchen with a billionaire and his bodyguard who have me locked in the house.

When Pax finally slides a mug in front of me, I trace the gold-colored logo on the front, and I see the name Hawkeye Security. The firm he works for?

My eyes widen when he pulls a carton of hazelnut creamer out of the fridge and places it in front of me. The flavor is my favorite. How does he know?

I shake my head.

He doesn't *know*. He was in my house—without my permission.

"Sugar?" he asks, reaching for a container.

"No. Thank you." The words come out automatically, more from habit than genuine gratitude. If it were up to me, I'd be miles away, maybe in another city, maybe New Orleans or Miami, trying to lose myself in the crowds.

Link's gaze burns into me as I wrap my hands around the beverage, glad to have something to occupy my shaking hands.

Between us, the silence stretches and grows, thick with unspoken tension.

When Link finally speaks, his voice is tight with barely contained frustration. "There are things you need to know before making any rash decisions, Tessa."

"Then why don't you damn well enlighten me?" *And let me get on with my life.*

Pax leans his hips against the counter, studying me above his drink, his shockingly jade-green eyes intense. "While you were sleeping, your phone rang."

"That's not possible," I insist. "I turned it off."

"Clearly not," Link fires back.

I sigh. Sometimes one of the buttons on the side of the secondhand device doesn't function the way it should, but I'm not about to admit that to them.

"It was Natalie," Pax continues, his voice not as harsh as Link's. "I answered."

Who the hell do these men think they are? "You had no right—"

Link interrupts me. "She called because the lock on your apartment door was broken."

The mug slips from my grasp, clattering against the island. Coffee splashes across the marble surface and drips onto the floor. "Oh my God."

Pax grabs a wad of paper towels and cleans up my mess. "I told her not to enter, but to get back in her car and drive somewhere public. A coffee shop, where there are a lot of people."

I dig in my purse for my phone.

Sure enough, it shows an incoming call from Natalie several hours ago.

"I met her there." Pax pours a second cup of coffee for me. "Then we went back to your apartment. After I made sure it was clear, I told her to come inside."

Not trusting myself to be steady with my mug, I leave the drink untouched.

"Your place was ransacked."

My world tilts again, and I grip the edge of the island to steady myself.

What if Natalie had been home? The full weight of what happened crashes over me.

Link's jaw is tight as he regards me. "She's okay."

Has he read my mind?

"We put her up at a hotel," Pax goes. "Under a false name. My associates handled notifying the authorities and dealing with your apartment management."

My head is pounding. I need the coffee to help clear the fog.

"Before we left, I had her pack some belongings and some for you."

So they didn't go through my things. *All my assumptions...*

"Everything that's been done has been to keep you safe and comfortable," Link says. "Everything."

Pax's words finally penetrate my haze, and I'm filled with gratitude for what he did. "Thank you for taking care of Natalie." My voice is hoarse with emotion. "I mean that."

"And what about you?" Link demands.

Overwhelmed, I force out a breath and attempt to gather my fractured thoughts. "I appreciate what both of you have done." More quietly, I add, "But I need the freedom to make my own choices."

Once more, Pax's calm voice cuts through the tension. "We know it's a lot to take in."

I can figure it out.

Have to figure it out.

First of all, I need to talk to Natalie so that we can make a plan to get out of Houston.

Guilt gnaws at me. Because of me, her life has been turned upside down.

"Look, Tessa..." Link drags a hand through his hair. "You already know your brother owes money to the mob."

"And you were promised to Sartori," Pax adds.

Despite myself, I shiver.

"This isn't just about Axel anymore," Link says, voice flat, cold. "Sartori wants what's due him."

Meaning...

"He's part of the Chicago crew, Tessa." He pauses. "The mob is after *you.*"

Link's unemotional words are like a slap, reminding me of the harsh reality of my situation. Defeated, I sink against the back of my stool.

As always, the voice of reason, Pax says, "We're trying to help you, Tessa, but you have to stop fighting us."

"And trust us," Link finishes.

"Trust you?" I laugh, a sharp, bitter sound. Link's been warning me about the mob, but there are rumors about him as well. "I've seen pictures of you with—"

"Tread carefully." His order is laced with threat.

The warning ricocheting in my mind, I back off. Instead, I finish with, "I've traded one nightmare for another."

Link and Pax look at one another.

"You don't really have a choice." Link's tone is cold, chilling me. His blue eyes are dark with a gathering storm. "I am not letting Sartori have you. Which means one thing. You are going to marry me."

CHAPTER SEVEN

Tessa

Marry you?

I shake my head to clear it. There's no way I could have heard him correctly.

"You need to think about it."

Link's suggestion is pure madness.

My mind reels as I try to grasp the implications of what he just said, but it's drowned out by the frantic thumping of my heart in my ears. "You can't mean that."

"I assure you, I've thought this through completely."

The earth beneath me shifts, and I'm standing on the edge of a cliff, teetering dangerously. My stomach churns, and I wrap my arms around myself, suddenly chilled despite the sunlight streaming into the room.

This isn't happening. *Can't* be happening.

I search his eyes for a hint of a joke, some sign that he's messing with me. But Link's expression is deadly serious. There's no humor in his eyes, no hint of a smile on his perfect lips.

The realization that he means this crashes a wave of panic over me.

I take a step back, needing space, needing air, but the fact I can't escape makes the walls close in around me. I'm being suffocated by the sheer absurdity of his proposal.

My thoughts scatter, and all I can think about is how wrong this is. How utterly impossible. I can't marry him. I barely know him, and what I do know terrifies me. He's the exact thing I'm running from. "No..." My voice trembles. "This is crazy."

I turn away from him, looking out the window, desperate to escape that insanity that's pressing down on me.

But there's no way out.

"Accept it."

I can feel his gaze on me, sharp and determined, and I swing back to face him.

Why me? The question burns in my mind, and before I can stop myself, I blurt out the question. "Why me?" I shake my head. "You can have any woman on the planet. In fact you've already had half of them. Why would you want to marry *me?*"

He takes a couple of steps toward me, coming closer but not threateningly so.

I tip my head back up to him, trying to find something, *anything*, in his expression to make sense of this.

His eyes—cold, searingly blue—are locked on me.

He takes yet another step in my direction.

Though he could reach out and touch me, he doesn't.

"This isn't about what I want, Tessa. It's about what you need."

His statement knifes down my spine. "No. I don't need marriage." To anyone. Especially him. Using logic, I state the obvious. "I don't belong in your world."

"You do," he counters, his voice flat, inviting no argument. "More than you know."

He reaches out then, and his fingers brush lightly against my arm. His touch rocks a shockwave of heat through me.

"You belong with me, Tessa. Now and forever." His voice is low and firm, leaving no room for argument.

For a flicker of a moment, there's a softness in his eyes, something that's not calculating.

I want to pull away, to reject everything he's saying, but I'm rooted to the spot, frozen by the certainty in his gaze and the sheer force of his powerful, masculine presence.

Link gently takes my shoulders, making it impossible to breathe. His grip is strong and sure but not painful.

I could escape if I wanted, but I don't try.

Slowly he leans toward me.

He won't try to kiss me. *Right?*

And if he does, I'll shove him away.

Right?

"You're mine, Tessa." His voice is a rough whisper. "Soon you'll accept that."

His possessive statement swamps me with emotions I don't know how to handle.

And then, with a sharp inhalation, he releases me and takes a step back.

Whatever gentleness I thought I saw earlier is gone, buried beneath his steel facade.

"I'm not marrying you," I repeat, not sure which one of us I'm trying to convince.

"You'll see that you don't have a choice." He pushes his hands into his pockets. "By tomorrow, you'll be suggesting it yourself."

No.

I want to scream, to argue, to tell him he's wrong.

But as I stand there, staring at the enigmatic man who's just claimed me, I wonder what's driving him. He can't possibly want to be tied to me any more than I want to be married to him.

Before I can fully process everything, Pax takes a step forward, breaking the tension that's crackling between Link and me.

"This isn't a decision you have to make right now." He frowns at Link to keep him silent. Then he glances back at me. His green eyes are softer than I've ever seen them. "You've been through a lot."

His suggestion gives me a sliver of hope—an escape, if only for a little while. The man is an oasis of calm in the storm that is Link Merritt.

Pax's watch beeps loudly, and he swipes the screen. "Torin and Mira," he says to Link.

Link nods tightly, and Pax taps his watch again.

"Who?" I ask with a frown.

"People we've been expecting," Link replies, as if that explains anything.

"Look," Pax says. "We'll take this one step at a time."

I nod.

Slowly a massive black SUV backs up the driveway and parks in front of Link's vehicle.

Two people emerge, a tall, broad-shouldered man in jeans and a dark shirt, and a woman with her dark hair pulled back in a sleek ponytail.

Pax disarms the security system and opens the door before either has a chance to knock.

The moment they're inside, Pax closes the door behind them and resets the alarm.

"Carter." Pax shakes hands with the man. "You broke away from Nevada."

"Need to stay sharp. And I enjoy fieldwork." As he speaks, his gaze flickers to the woman, a look so charged with unspoken intimacy that I wonder if there is more between them than just a professional partnership.

"Araceli." Pax smiles as he greets the woman.

"Torin Carter, Mira Araceli, meet Link Merritt and Tessa Tremaine. Link, Tessa, these are Torin Carter and Mira Araceli, two of Hawkeye's best agents."

"Ma'am." Torin nods respectfully, his stunning features set in a mask of professionalism.

Mira, on the other hand, offers a warm, reassuring smile, and I like her immediately. "It's a pleasure to meet you both."

"You're in good hands, ma'am," Mira says. "I promise."

Good hands? These agents are here because of me?

Then Link speaks to me. "I want you protected when you leave the house."

So I'm not a prisoner?

"No doubt you'll want to see your friend. Natalie."

"My..." This was his idea?

"She's waiting for you. Pax and the other agents will take you."

I'm momentarily speechless.

His lips quirk a little.

A smile? A truce? A little breathless, I manage, "Thank you."

Pax places a hand on my shoulder. "You ready to go?"

I nod.

Once more, Pax disables the alarm. Torin and Mira exit first, scanning the area. For threats?

Surely this is overkill.

In the doorway, I stop and look over my shoulder.

Link has remained in place, legs spread, arms folded, studying me.

Unsure what to make of him, I shake my head and then follow the agents.

Pax is right behind me.

Once Mira seals Pax and I in the back seat of the SUV, he suggests I let Natalie know we're on the way.

"Good idea." Immediately I send the text.

Torin drives with the same quiet efficiency that seems to define him. Mira sits beside him. Her head seems to be constantly moving as she looks ahead, then in the side-view mirror.

Less than a minute later, Natalie responds to my message.

Can't wait to see you. So many questions.

Then I drop my phone back into my purse and turn to Pax. "Where are we going?"

"Sterling Uptown."

"The...?" Can things get any more surreal? The Uptown is one of Houston's newest hotels and supposedly the most expensive ever built in the city. The place is reported to be opulent with amazing food and even a luxury car dealership in the lobby.

In my wildest dreams, I'd never be able to afford a single night there, and my rescuers have paid for a room there for someone they don't even know? "Are you kidding me?"

"Their security measures are renowned."

From what I've heard, getting a reservation at the Uptown takes a small miracle. "Surely there are other hotels in the city that have great security." Where a one-night stay doesn't cost more than my monthly rent.

"There are."

"So why this one?"

"For you."

"For...?" I blink.

"She matters to you." His words are stated simply, as if the explanation is self-explanatory.

Link and Pax put my friend up at the best place in the city as a favor to me?

I can't begin to think through what that means.

Finally we approach the hotel, but Torin bypasses the main entrance with its curved driveway, manicured lawn, beautiful fountain, and colorful awning.

"Where are we going?" I ask, turning to Pax with a frown.

"There's a second entrance for high-profile guests."

And we qualify?

Though I suppose nothing should surprise me anymore.

The turnoff is not marked, and it's clearly meant to be far away from the prying eyes of the public.

Torin brings the SUV to a smooth stop, and he and Mira swiftly exit the vehicle without waiting for a valet.

They move with precision as they scan the surroundings and open the back door on Pax's side.

This whole event feels a little like theater, but after how close I came to being abducted, I appreciate the caution.

"This vehicle stays here," Torin instructs the valet who approaches.

"The keys, sir?" the man asks.

"No." His tone leaving no room for argument.

"If you have an issue, take it up with your manager," Pax advises, slipping the man a twenty as he steps out of the vehicle.

"Of course, sir."

After Pax also takes in our surroundings, he extends a hand to help me out.

Though he closes his hand around mine reassuringly, he doesn't linger.

The back entrance looms ahead, a stark contrast to the bright, inviting facade that we drove past a couple of minutes ago.

Mira and Torin fall into step—one in front, one behind us—as we swiftly move through the back of the hotel.

As opposed to the pictures I've seen in *Scandalicious* of the lobby, the corridors here are narrow and utilitarian. But still, the floors are polished, reflecting the soft overhead lights.

Pax leads us to a service elevator and presses the call button.

None of the hotel staff has paid any attention to us. Maybe these kinds of arrivals are not as unusual as I imagine.

Finally the doors open with a soft chime, and we are whisked upward.

When we arrive, I feel as if I've stepped into another world.

The hallway is wide with beautiful carpeting. Elegant artwork is hanging everywhere, and ceilings are adorned with stunning light fixtures.

We come to a door with two men positioned on either side.

Pax and Link also arranged security for Nat?

After silently acknowledging the agents, he knocks and announces himself.

After what seems like an eternity, I hear the sound of the deadbolt turning.

The door opens slowly, and Natalie peeks through the small crack.

"Natalie." Relief floods me as the door swings open, and I see she looks okay—exhausted, but with her signature mismatched earrings glinting in the light.

"We'll be right outside," Pax says. "And—"

"Keep the door locked. Don't answer unless it's one of the agents or you," Natalie interrupts, shaking her head like she's heard the safety drill a hundred times.

Pax raises an eyebrow, evidently amused by her attitude. "Exactly."

Then he looks at me. Wishing I'd be that agreeable?

Not a chance.

With a tight nod, he pulls the door closed.

Once we're sealed in tight, we fall into each other's arms, and the worry and stress hit me hard, leaving me breathless.

"Oh my God, Nat. I'm so sorry. I'll never forgive myself for getting you involved in this."

"Don't start with that shit." Natalie pulls back, giving me her no-nonsense look. "From day one, you told me your brother was trouble."

But even I'd had no idea he was involved with the Mafia.

"I need all the deets."

Glancing around, I follow her deeper into the suite.

The living room area has floor-to-ceiling windows and a comfortable-looking couch, along with two chairs. And she even has a large vase filled with flowers.

Off to one side, a table is set with a silver pot. Coffee, I guess, since it's accompanied by several smaller pitchers and a sugar bowl. And she has an enormous tray filled with fruit and pastries and cheese, and even some brightly colored macarons.

"There's enough here for a small army," she says with a shrug. "All I wanted was a bagel and a cup of coffee."

With what I know of Pax and Link already, I'm not really surprised that they'd arrange for a feast.

I skip the offerings, except for a bottle of water.

My insides are still too jumbled for food.

I drop into a chair, and Natalie sits opposite.

She stares at me, her expression a mix of concern and confusion. "What the hell happened last night?"

CHAPTER EIGHT

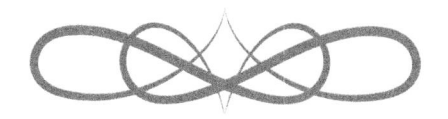

Tessa

Where to start?

I sigh as I drop into a chair. "It's a long story."

Natalie grabs her cup and sits across from me. "You look like you haven't slept."

"I haven't," I admit. "But neither have you."

"No." She shakes her head, her expression tightening as she glances toward the window, almost as if she's trying to find the right words. "When I came home after work and saw that there'd been a break-in, I was terrified. I didn't know if you were in there. Or if your brother had found you. So I called your cell phone." She shrugs. "Pax told me you were okay and that I needed to go somewhere safe."

Guilt stabs through me, making me shudder. "Nat…" A lifetime of apologies will never be enough.

"He wouldn't tell me much."

So it's up to me to fill in the details. "When I left the Rusty Nail, some of Axel's men tried to grab me."

"Link and Pax were at the bar?"

"No." I shake my head. "They showed up after I got off."

She grins. "I told you Link had a thing for you."

Though I shake my head, nothing else makes sense.

"Anyway…" There's no way to make this easier. "The guy Axel sold me to? Turns out he's a mobster."

"A…?" She scowls, as if she can't believe a word I'm saying. Then she shakes her head. "Wait a second. You can't be serious right now. The mob is something out of a Hollywood movie."

I don't respond. Until a few hours ago, I'd believed the same thing.

"You're dead ass serious?"

When I nod, she momentarily stares in disbelief.

"This is messed up. You know that, right?"

"It gets more unbelievable." A headache builds behind my eyes. "And Link proposed to me." If giving me an order could be called that.

"Proposed?" She blinks. "Like, actual marriage?"

I nod.

"And you think he really means it?"

"He seems to." I shift a little. "He says it's the only way to keep me safe."

Natalie finally takes a sip from her cup. Then she looks at me over the rim. Moments later, she draws her eyebrows together. "You know, it's not exactly romantic, but it's not the worst plan I've ever heard."

"Nat! Could you be serious right now?"

"I'm just saying, Tess. The guy's rich, powerful, and clearly wants to protect you. I'm not saying you should walk down the aisle tomorrow, but…think about it."

"Why would he suggest that?" He hadn't really answered my question, and Pax stepped in, changing the subject.

"I've seen the way he looks at you."

"Even if the idea made sense, I couldn't just marry someone I barely know. Especially…"

"Especially?" she prompts.

Before I can change my mind and remain silent, I rush on, "I saw pictures of him in *Scandalicious* with men reported to be mobsters."

"First of all, it's a gossip rag."

Even if it is better than most sites.

"And secondly, he's a gazillionaire. He obviously knows a lot of people. Even if he hangs out with those kind of people, it doesn't necessarily mean he's a gangster himself. Right?"

I hesitate. "I don't know. But I don't want to take that risk."

"Okay, fair enough." Natalie sighs, putting her mug down. "What are your other options? Running?"

"I've been thinking about that," I admit. "New Orleans?" The ride will only take a few hours by bus. "Maybe Miami." Perhaps even the opposite coast. Nat and I can lose ourselves in Los Angeles.

"Look." She sighs, as if trying to be reasonable. "You thought you'd be invisible in Houston. You were really careful. Few people even know your real name."

Her words hit hard, and my shoulders slump.

"They found you once. Do you really think you can hide from the mob forever?" Natalie studies me for a moment before switching gears. "I'm sorry to be so blunt."

I shiver.

"Look, Tess. I'm not trying to scare you, and you don't have to make any rash decisions. You've got time to figure this out."

Trying to steady myself, I uncap my water and take a drink.

A few moments later, she clears her throat. "There's something else I need to tell you."

"Oh?"

"I know my timing is terrible…"

"Go ahead and say it." My life can't get much worse.

"David asked me to move in with him."

"Really?"

She grins, her happiness obvious.

"Are you going to do it?"

"I think so."

My own drama momentarily forgotten, I put down my water and hurry across the room to give her a hug. "Nat! I'm happy for you."

"You're not upset?"

"Never!" After everything she's been through, she deserves someone like the hotshot lawyer who treats her well.

After a final hug, I return to my chair.

"I don't want to leave you hanging."

I shake my head. "You have to live your life for you." Besides, there's no way I can live in our apartment ever again.

"Now with everything…"

"It's safer if you are staying somewhere else," I finish.

"That's what David thinks too."

"Speaking of… Where is he?"

"On his way back from Dallas. He had business meetings up there, but I called him right after I talked to Pax last night. He said he'd head back right away. I told him to get some sleep first." Then she waves her hand, and all her bracelets jangle. "He didn't like hearing another man put me up at a hotel."

"Oh my God." I bet he didn't.

"That's why you have to marry Link." She flashes a grin. "So David doesn't have to be jealous."

"Best reason I've ever heard to walk down the aisle."

"Think about it," she says more seriously. "The protection you'd have as his wife."

But at what cost?

"You can't keep running."

I exhale. "I'll think about it." What choice do I have?

As Natalie and I say goodbye, I'm hit with devastating emotions. I'm happy for her and David, but I'm sad we're going in different directions.

At the door, she holds me tight. "You're stronger than you think." Then she's all Nat. "I want an invite to your wedding."

I shake my head. "You're impossible."

After a shared laugh, I unlock the door and peek out.

"Ready?" Pax asks.

I straighten my back. *Am I?*

Moments later, I nod.

Two agents remain at Natalie's door while Mira walks in front of me and Pax brings up the rear.

Torin is waiting in the SUV, and the engine is already running.

The doors are barely closed when he starts rolling.

As I settle in, Pax offers me a sleek, high-end smartphone. "For you."

The device is purple titanium, a work of art that is beyond gorgeous. From the ads I've seen online, the glass front is virtually indestructible, so it doesn't need a protective cover, making the user experience a sensual one. "A Bonds?"

"Nothing more reliable."

Or expensive. That single piece of masterful technology costs the same price as four months' rent in the apartment Natalie and I shared. Even when my parents were alive and money wasn't an issue, our family never considered buying anything that expensive. "Thank you, but I can't accept this."

"You will."

Why had I ever thought that he was less forceful and intimidating than his boss?

"Pax—"

"Take it up with Link."

I sigh. Even though I haven't agreed to marry the man, he's already running my life.

Reluctantly I accept the phone. The weight is less than I expect, and the combination of glass and titanium is irresistibly tempting.

Despite my resolve, I swipe my finger across the front, and vibrant colors leap to life.

A note comes across the screen.

Welcome to the Bonds family, Tessa. Enjoy your experience.

Beneath it is Julien Bonds's signature. "Is that standard on all Bonds devices?"

"No."

"No?" I turn to study him. "Don't tell me you know Julien Bonds?"

He shrugs. But instead of answering, he says, "Our numbers are programmed in, along with all the contacts from your old phone. All you have to do is press one for Link, two for me, three for Hawkeye Security. Or tap the screen twice and tell Holly what you need."

"Holly?"

"Your personal assistant."

The route we're taking doesn't seem to lead back to the house. Frowning, I turn to Pax. "Where are we going?"

"Link's office." His tone is flat, as if the answer should have been obvious.

The rest of the ride to the downtown high rise is quick, and the city seems to pass in a blur.

Flanked by Mira and Pax, we're whisked up forever to the fiftieth floor.

Another surreal experience.

The suite of offices is marked as Merritt Sovereign Capital.

The name is as pretentious as he is.

Mira opens the door and enters, and Pax nods at me to follow.

Inside, the sleek, modern decor speaks of power and wealth, making me feel even more out of place.

A woman sits behind a desk, her blonde hair styled in a sleek bob. She smiles at Pax.

"I'll let Mr. Merritt know you've arrived."

Moments later, after speaking into her headset, she stands and walks to the door. After knocking, she turns the handle, then steps aside.

Pax inclines his head in my direction. "After you."

To stop my hands from shaking, I ball them into fists.

Pax closes the door behind us with a decisive, echoing click.

Link is standing near the floor-to-ceiling windows, and he turns to face me.

As always, I'm unprepared for my reaction to him as his blue eyes lock onto mine, intense and unreadable.

"Have you made a decision?" he asks, his voice low and steady.

My heart races, and my tummy plummets.

The weight of the last twelve hours—Natalie's perspective, the fact I have nowhere to live, to run, and there's no hiding from the man who wants me—crashes onto my shoulders.

"Tessa?" he prompts.

"Yes," I whisper, then clear my throat and speak more firmly. "Yes, I'll marry you."

"Good."

Good? That's it?

"Have a seat." He indicates the small area off to one side.

There's a couch and two armchairs, along with a coffee table in the middle with bottled water. "There's something the three of us need to discuss before we move forward."

What more could there be?

At his nod, I perch on the edge of a sofa cushion.

Link sinks into one of the leather armchairs, facing me.

I don't have to wait long.

He leans back, steepling his hands in front of him.

Then he locks his attention on me. "Pax and I share everything."

Confused, I angle my head to one side. "What do you mean…everything?"

As if on cue, Pax moves from his position by the door to take a seat across from me, next to his boss.

His presence is commanding, and the way he fills the space is both reassuring and unnerving at the same time.

When Link goes on, his voice is steady, and each word is deliberate. "You'll be married to me. But you'll belong to both of us. Do you understand?"

CHAPTER NINE

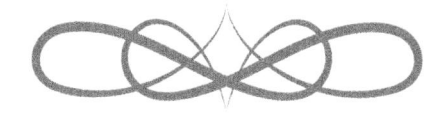

Tessa

Understand?

No.

Surely I misheard. "Both of you?" I repeat. "As in…" *I'll have two husbands?*

Neither say anything.

Reeling, I stand and pace to the window.

This can't be happening.

They remain silent until I turn to face them.

Pax speaks, his voice gentle but firm. His green eyes, usually so guarded, are open, honest. "We're a package deal, Tessa. Link and I…"

Trying to keep up, to process the loaded glance that the two of them share, I shake my head. My thoughts are a jumbled mess, and I struggle to form coherent questions.

Then I remember last night. Pax walked upstairs with us, and I asked where he lives. *"He has the guest house out back."* Link's answer had been evasive. He never said Pax stayed out there.

Blushing, I wonder how I could have been so naive. "So you two are love—"

"No," Pax interrupts, a hint of amusement coloring his tone. "We're not partners in that sense of the word. But we have a close relationship." He pauses. "Any woman we're involved with understands that."

My head spins, and a bead of sweat trickles down my spine.

"So…" I've barely wrapped my mind around marrying Link, and now *this*? "How does something like this even work?"

Link leans forward, and for a fraction of a second, his usual mask of control slips. "We'll both be there for you, always."

"For protection," Pax adds, his voice low and reassuring. "For support. Anything you need."

I swallow hard, my throat suddenly dry.

When I finally find my voice, it comes out as a whisper, despite my best intentions. "And…?" *How do I ask this?* "I'm sure you don't mean…intimately. Right?"

They exchange a look. Once more a form of silent communication passes between them.

Link nods, his expression serious. "I do mean intimately."

The room is suddenly too small, too warm.

Trying to sort all of this out, I wrap my arms around my middle. "This is…a lot to take in."

"It is." Pax's voice holds a note of understanding.

Both men remain where they are, giving me the distance I need.

"We're willing to take things at your pace," he goes on.

Then Link seems to lose his patience. Standing, he crosses the room.

He stops close enough that I can feel the heat radiating from his body.

Thankfully he doesn't try to touch me.

"We needed you to know the full picture before we proceed. No secrets, Tessa. That's crucial."

My mind races. This arrangement is unlike anything I've ever imagined for myself. Or for anyone else I've ever heard of.

It's shocking, unconventional, and yet… "I need time," I manage to say, my voice stronger than I feel. "To process all of this."

"We leave for Las Vegas tomorrow."

"Tomorrow?" My knees go weak. This has to be some bizarre dream.

Link's gaze is unwavering. "We'll be married the day after that."

Frantically I shake my head. "No."

Before he can respond, his phone buzzes.

With an annoyed sigh, he digs the device from an interior pocket in his suit coat and glances at the screen. "I need to take this. Excuse me for a moment."

He paces to the far end of the office.

As he talks in low, clipped tones, I'm struck by how he commands everything around him. King of all he surveys.

Including me.

Pax takes the opportunity to join me.

Though he's enormous and lethal, he intimidates me less than Link does. Maybe that's foolish.

He captures my shoulders and makes tiny circles on them.

His touch is electric, and I pull back from his powerful draw. It's either that or surrender completely.

To his credit, he doesn't try to touch me again.

When Link ends his call, he walks back to us.

I look from one to the other. And the idea of sleeping with both of them…

"Are you still willing to marry me?" Link asks. "Us?"

Do I really have a choice?

Unable to believe I'm agreeing to this, I close my eyes for a moment before nodding. "Yes."

As if he never doubted my answer, he announces, "In that case, we'll celebrate. With lunch."

My stomach flip-flops. How can I possibly eat when my entire world has just been turned upside down?

Before I can protest, Link places his fingers against the small of my back. Awareness of him crashes through me, and I shudder.

Pax moves ahead of us, speaking quietly into his watch, and he opens the door.

Link tells his admin to cancel the rest of his day.

"Of course, sir."

In the hallway, Mira detaches herself from the shadows where she's been standing guard.

The ride down and the walk across the lobby are silent, and when we step outside into the bright Houston sunshine, the heat is like a physical force.

At the curb, the SUV is waiting, Torin behind the wheel.

Mira holds the door for the three of us, and the moment she's securely in the passenger seat, Torin is rolling without wasting a single moment.

As we zip through the streets, I try to gather my scattered thoughts.

"Where are we going?" I ask, desperate for any distraction.

"Maestro's," he replies. His tone is casual, as if he's unaware that he's turned my entire life upside down. "Best steaks in town."

We pull up to a restaurant with a facade of gleaming glass and polished stone.

My parents had taken me to a place like this to celebrate my sixteenth birthday. In another lifetime.

I'm the last to leave the SUV, and Link offers his hand to assist me down onto the sidewalk.

His touch is firm, and he lingers for a few seconds.

Suddenly I'm feeling anything but safe.

Mira and Torin enter the restaurant ahead of us and survey the surroundings.

As if this is an everyday occurrence, the maître d' pays them no attention and instead greets Link. "Mr. Merritt, always a pleasure." He nods to Pax. "Sir."

"Gianluca." The men shake hands. "Please meet my future bride, Tessa. We're celebrating."

"Incantata. Welcome, welcome! We're delighted to have you."

"Our usual table, please."

"Of course, sir."

We're shown to a secluded table near the back of the dining room, partially hidden by an elegant partition. The decor is all dark wood and soft lighting.

As I take a seat in the chair that Link holds for me, I shift uncomfortably. The elegance of the place makes me hyperaware of my jeans and well-worn tennis shoes.

Unfortunately for me, I'm Cinderella. My fairy godmother showed up with two princes and a carriage. But there's not a single gown in sight.

As he always does, Pax selects the chair where he will have his back to the wall. And I notice Torin at a nearby table, all by himself.

Almost instantly, a server appears, a bottle of sparkling water already in hand. "Mr. Merritt, so good to see you again. Pellegrino for the table?"

"Thank you, yes."

As the water is poured, Gianluca arrives once more, along

with a bartender. They're carrying a tall, silver ice bucket and a bottle of champagne that he shows to Link.

"Compliments of the house, Mr. Merritt," Gianluca says. "If the vintage meets with your approval."

Link glances at me.

As if I have any idea. "I'll leave the decision to you."

"Thank you," he tells Gianluca.

He uncorks the bottle, and I catch a glimpse of the distinctive label that's shaped like a shield. It's everything I can do not to gasp. Even though I don't really drink, I recognize the brand.

A sample is offered to Link who lifts the glass, swirls it, then takes a sip. "Perfect. Thank you."

"Salute!" Gianluca says as he leaves the bartender to finish the service.

Once we're alone, Link picks up his glass as if to offer a toast, but I lean forward. "Link, this is all too much. I don't need…"

He silences me with a look, his blue eyes intense. "We're going to be married, Tessa."

As if that explains everything.

Maybe to Link, it does.

Undeterred, he lifts his glass and tips it in my direction, and then Pax's. "To new beginnings."

Pax raises his flute. "Hear, hear."

Both men look at me expectantly, waiting for me to follow suit.

My fingers are frozen in my lap.

I can't believe I'm engaged to the Vulture and an overwhelming bodyguard. How can I celebrate, knowing my future with them might be no better than the one I ran away from?

CHAPTER TEN

Link

Oh Tessa.
You need to stop fighting me.
This.
Us.

My stubborn wife-to-be and I are on the sidewalk in front of Rêve de Mode, one of the city's most exclusive boutiques.

Her chin is angled mutinously, and she's refusing to step inside.

The sun relentlessly beats down on us, and I worry because we're in public, exposed, despite the fact Mira is standing just behind Tessa.

Torin is parked illegally, parallel to the curb, and the back door to the vehicle still stands open. Pax is right there, ready to toss our future wife inside if we are forced to make a quick, strategic exit.

"You need clothes," I point out reasonably as I fight off my impatience with her and the situation. What the hell kind of woman doesn't want to go shopping on my credit card?

One with her kind of pride, evidently.

The fact she's so unlike anyone else I've been involved with is one of the reasons I want her. Yet right now, that's the most confounding thing about her.

"I have a drawer full of things at my apartment."

I bite back my temper. "You've agreed to be my wife, Tessa."

"I didn't agree to be spoiled and pampered."

Yes. You damn well did. "We'll be going out for meals, and you'll be expected to act as my hostess." And I'd noticed the way she'd tugged on the hem of her shirt, then glanced down, maybe to hide the way her cheeks flushed when we walked into Maestro's.

Now, though, her eyes flash with fire as she insists, "I'm sure we can find some place that resells designer brands, if a label matters to you."

I'm about to lose what little hold I still have over my patience. "You are not wearing discards."

A furious frown knits between her eyes. "If that's the way you see it, maybe we should rethink this whole arrangement since I'm not good enough for you, Mr. Merritt."

Confounding, annoying…

Pax clears his throat. "What Link means is that time is of the essence. We don't have time to run all over the city. In the future, you're welcome to shop anywhere you want."

The fuck-all she can. My wife will wear clothing that is beautiful and appropriate for her. I scowl at Pax.

But both of them ignore me completely.

"Once you're finished here, would you like to go to your apartment to pick up your necessities?" Pax offers.

The hell?

She looks at him. "Really? You'll take me?"

"I will."

Because his question deflected Tessa's attention and that suits me fine, I don't object.

"I would like that."

Once more, Pax is her hero, and I'm the villain. Irritated, I drum my fingers on the side of my leg.

Then she looks at me, and her half-smile fades as she pushes back strands of her hair. "I'll agree to get the bare necessities. We'll keep a tab, and I'll pay you back."

I open my mouth to object, but Pax shakes his head sharply and tells her, "I'm sure you can come to some sort of arrangement."

He's good at soothing her out of her arguments.

I shove aside the voice inside me that tells me I could learn a thing or two from him.

At my age, I have zero desire to change who I am.

Tessa needs to stop challenging me.

I win my battles. Always.

"Shall we?" I invite.

Mira opens the boutique's heavy glass door.

Tessa hesitates for a fraction of a second before stepping inside. I follow closely, as does Mira. The security agent takes her place near the door, nearby, but giving us privacy.

Pax and Torin remain outside.

The store's interior is beautiful, with racks of clothing artfully displayed, and a soft glow refracting from the crystal chandeliers.

"Link!" Amelia, the owner, joins us. "So wonderful to see you."

Tessa's spine stiffens slightly, and she frowns. Wondering about my history here?

"Amelia. Always a pleasure." Wanting any doubts Tessa is feeling to vanish, I gently place my fingertips at the base of her spine. "This is Tessa. My future bride."

Her breath catches.

"Congratulations!" Amelia's happiness for us is real. "You must be delighted."

When Tessa doesn't respond, I answer for both of us. "We are."

She continues to remain quiet. At least she hasn't contradicted me. I'll take that win.

"We're eloping," I explain to Amelia. "So she needs a wardrobe for Las Vegas. Anything you can think of. Skirts. Slacks. Leisure outfits. Handbag. Shoes."

Tessa's eyes widen, and she turns to me. "We agreed to a few essentials," she protests, her voice low but firm.

"It's nothing more," I insist, keeping my tone light. "And as Pax said, time is of the essence. We don't have time to go shopping anywhere else."

Amelia, ever the professional, pretends not to notice the tension. "We'll get started with some basics, shall we? Link, you're welcome to make yourself comfortable. Tessa, may I offer you a glass of champagne while we browse?"

"Thanks. But no." She's polite, but her shoulders are held back tight.

Instead of taking a seat, I walk over to one of the nearby racks and select a sleek black dress that will stretch to hug her the way I'd like to. Perfect for dinner in Vegas. "This is a good start," I suggest, holding it up.

"Excellent choice," Amelia says as she takes the hanger from me and then gives it to an employee with an instruction to get a fitting room started for Tessa.

My future bride tips her head to one side. "Don't you have somewhere else to be?"

"Not at all. As you heard, my schedule has been cleared for the afternoon." When she clenches her jaw, I grin. "I'm at your disposal."

"I think we can manage this without you."

Instead of arguing, I smile and take a page out of Pax's playbook. "Mmm," I respond noncommittally.

"Let's begin over here," Amelia says, directing Tessa's attention toward the back of the store.

I select an emerald-green silk blouse that I think will suit her, and I give that to the clerk, along with a couple of skirts.

A full twenty minutes later, Amelia whisks Tessa to her fitting room. I settle into one of the leather armchairs near a raised dais surrounded by mirrors where she can model the items.

"I'd like to see everything," I call out, steepling my fingers as I lean back to wait.

Maybe it's only my imagination, but I think I hear her stamp her foot from behind the closed door. I grin.

A few minutes later, she emerges in a sundress that leaves her arms and shoulders bare and ends just above her ankles. "Beautiful," I approve.

"I don't know." She wrinkles her nose as she studies herself from every angle. "We don't have a lot of summer left."

I shrug. "You will be glad you have it in the Las Vegas heat. And we'll have plenty of warm weather for you to wear it again."

"But..."

I wait.

"Surely I won't be going out all that often."

"Not even for coffee?"

She blinks, as if she hasn't considered all the potential changes to her life going forward.

"I usually wear leggings when I run errands."

"How about when you join me for lunch?" When she doesn't have a quick response, I tell Amelia, "We'll take it."

Tessa opens her mouth to argue, but she says nothing.

The next dress is more practical, shorter, suitable for

business, professional, and social gatherings. One of Amelia's picks, if I recall.

"Great choice," I tell her. Then I ask Amelia, "Do you also have it in other colors?"

"Royal blue," she says.

"I like this color," Tessa protests.

"So do I." I nod. "We want both."

"Both?" Tessa echoes.

"You've got good taste," I say simply. "The fit is flattering, and you like it. You should have it in every color."

She shakes her head. "You're impossible."

Turns out, I enjoy spoiling her.

A few minutes later, Tessa appears again, in a tailored blazer and slim-cut trousers, along with the green blouse I chose.

She takes my breath away.

In this suit, she's a force to be reckoned with.

I can't wait to have her by my side.

"A couple more shirts and sweaters will make this outfit more versatile," Amelia says. "Stay there for a moment."

"Link, really. We have more than enough now." With a concerned frown, she checks the price tag of the jacket.

"Wait and see what Amelia suggests. She might be able to pull together a number of different outfits with only a couple more pieces." This may be the first time someone has taken Tessa shopping with no budget in mind. But it's also the first time I've entered a shop with a woman who has glanced at the cost of something.

Amelia returns with several tops, another skirt, a second pair of trousers, and one more blazer. "You've got at least a dozen outfits here by mixing and matching," she says. "Add some accessories, shoes, and boots, and you can go from summer to winter."

I nod in agreement, but Tessa shakes her head. "There's no way I need this much stuff."

"If we don't take her advice, we'll need to come back next season." I keep my voice reasonable.

"Which is fine," Amelia agrees. "We're constantly getting in new stock. And we'll have a trunk show in October where we highlight our winter collection. We'll even have holiday dresses."

"No." Tessa's protest is immediate. "This is fine."

With a resigned sigh, she returns to try on more pieces.

I veto some because they are too loose on her, and a couple I request in a smaller size.

"You know," Amelia says, "I could use you as a model for the trunk show. You've got the look."

Tessa pales, and her eyes grow wide.

She's so accustomed to being in hiding that the thought must terrify her.

At some point, I hope she has the confidence to accept that kind of compliment.

"Now the evening wear," I prompt.

Amelia instructs one of her helpers to bring in several pairs of shoes.

Just then, another employee who has been ringing out a customer at the cash register comes over and speaks quietly to Amelia who gives us a quick apology. "I'll be right back, I promise."

A few minutes later, Tessa is still in the dressing room.

Curious, I stand and wander over to the door and knock. "Everything okay?"

She takes a long time to answer. When she does, there's reluctance in her tone. "I'm struggling with this zipper."

"Allow me," I offer.

"Uhm…is Amelia still busy?"

Even if she wasn't, I'd lie. "Yes."

For a few moments, there's no response.

She turns the knob and cracks the door open a fraction of an inch.

"Your modesty is safe with me." Another lie. This one is so blatant that it almost stuck in my throat.

There's nothing more I want than to corrupt her entirely.

"Fine." With that, she vanishes from view.

Realizing I won't get an invitation, I enter the small room.

She's standing in the middle of the space, her back to me.

Does she believe that I find the creamy expanse of her back any less tempting than the front of her?

I step closer, and my fingers brush her spine as I grasp the zipper.

The contact sends a visible shiver through her, and her breath catches. Slowly, deliberately, I lean in closer to ease the small tab up, savoring the moment.

I'm close, so close, inhaling her feminine scent.

Innocence, wrapped in vanilla, and layered with amber. Different from what I'm used to, but even more intoxicating. From the soap in her bathroom? If so, I'll have the housekeeper order a case of the stuff.

As I finish, my nose nearly brushes against her hair.

Instinct urges me to bury my face in the crook of her neck and breathe her in more deeply.

But I'm already too close to losing my control when it comes to her.

Having her beneath my roof, so near…

Determinedly I call on my restraint and instead twirl a tendril of her hair around my finger.

Our gazes meet in the mirror.

Her eyes are wide, her lips parted a little, and her chest rises and falls with her rapid breaths.

I'm struck by the image we make together, her delicate

frame dwarfed by my larger one, the contrast between us stark and appealing.

She can fight me all she wants, but she recognizes this spark between us. My Tessa is as attracted to me as I am to her.

"Will it be so bad?" I ask softly, my breath against the beautiful shell of her ear. "Being my bride?" Then I can't resist any longer. I gently kiss that vulnerable spot where her neck meets her shoulder. "Being *mine?*"

CHAPTER ELEVEN

Tessa

"Ready?" Pax asks, his voice gentle.

A few moments ago, Torin stopped the SUV near my apartment building.

I've dreaded arriving here since we dropped Link back off at his office.

But I want to get my things.

"Tessa?" he prompts.

Not trusting myself to speak, I nod.

Mira unfastens her safety belt and opens the rear door.

Pax exits before me and then offers his hand.

I'm not nearly as apprehensive with him as I am Link. Why, I'm not sure. He's every bit as threatening as his boss. Maybe more so.

He closes his hand around mine.

With Mira in front of me and Pax on my heel, we climb the stairs to the second-story unit.

As we approach the door, I see the first signs of the break-in.

The door frame is splintered, and some wood fragments litter the concrete.

My heart races as Pax pushes the door open.

The sight that greets me sucks the air from my lungs. This apartment had been a refuge, a space Natalie and I tried so hard to make into a home. Now it looks like something out of a war zone.

The couch is overturned, its cushions slashed open and its stuffing oozing out. The coffee table is shattered.

Without a word, Pax follows me inside and closes the door, with Mira keeping watch outside.

In the kitchen, drawers hang open, and all our silverware and utensils are strewn across the vinyl floor. Shards of broken dishes litter every surface.

The devastation is impossible to take in.

Numb, my legs wooden, I move into the bedroom.

The drawers to my small dresser are in pieces. Clothes that once hung in my closet have been ripped from hangers and are strewn about like confetti.

My bed has been destroyed, the mattress knifed apart like the couch. "Oh God." I collapse against the wall as tears sting my eyes.

This apartment wasn't much—a small place in a not-so-great area—but it was the place I started over. It was supposed to be my safe haven. "I thought I was prepared."

"You couldn't have been." His eyes are dark, ominous.

"This..." Knowing I need to be strong and wanting to get the hell out of here as quick as possible, I push away from the wall. "I've never had a break-in before." Nothing seems to be missing. "Is this usual?"

He doesn't answer right away.

"What aren't you saying?" I ask, dreading the answer but needing to know.

He hesitates, and he frowns. "Tessa…"

"You can't protect me from everything," I say, my voice stronger than I feel. "Please, just tell me."

"This is extreme." Pax sighs, running a hand through his hair. "They were looking for something specific. A clue to your whereabouts, most likely."

There's fury in this kind of destruction.

Was it my brother? One of the henchmen from last night? The man they sold me to?

I shudder, wrapping my arms around myself. Earlier I had protested the need for three bodyguards, arguing that it was overkill. Now, standing in the ruins of my life, it doesn't feel like nearly enough. Can anything truly protect me from this level of determination?

With shaking hands, I gather what few clothes I can salvage, but most of my belongings are beyond repair.

In the shared bathroom, my toiletries have been smashed, leaving nothing usable.

As I load my meager belongings into a garbage bag, I feel utterly violated.

"We should go," Pax says softly, his hand warm on my shoulder. "We'll stop and get you some essentials on the way back."

Unable to think, I tie the red drawstring and follow him to the front door.

Then I stop. "I need to clean up this place." Especially if I'm never coming back.

"I'll handle it."

"But…" I look around. Where would I even start?

"Hawkeye has experience with this kind of thing."

I hate that I'm okay with his suggestion.

I don't feel safe here, and I never want to come back again. "Thank you."

Pax takes the plastic sack from me and pulls the door closed behind us.

Sadness overcomes me.

Over the last couple of months, I'd started to let my guard down. I had a job I liked, a good friend, and the boy I loved babysitting.

Now, for a second time, I'm walking away from everything I know. And I need to let Serena know I can't take care of Miguel ever again.

"You okay?"

Since there's a lump lodged in my throat, I remain silent.

Within a minute, we're pulling out of the parking lot, and I don't look back.

Torin drives us to a nearby drugstore, and Mira shadows us inside, staying close and ever vigilant.

I shop for a few cosmetics and other necessities.

Pax pays.

I'm mentally keeping a tally of what I owe the men, but at this point, the amount they've spent is in the five figures.

Since I don't even know when I can return to work, the debt is enormous. I shove aside the awful, niggling voice that says maybe I'll never be able to have a job again.

On the drive back to Link's house—my new home, I suppose—Mira yawns.

Long day for them, and I have no idea if they even had the opportunity to eat. More guilt heaps on top of me.

"Coffee run?" Torin suggests to Mira.

"Please," she responds.

The thought of something warm, rich, soothing appeals to me. "Me too," I murmur, surprising myself by speaking up.

What's another seven dollars on top of what I already owe Link and Pax?

In the rearview mirror, Torin catches Pax's eyes. He nods his ascent.

Apparently grabbing coffee is a potential risk.

Mira orders a straight-forward beverage, lots of caffeine, no sugar. Maybe because she's working?

My mocha-and-caramel concoction is amazing, but after a couple of sips, I stare at the lid, and my mind reels, replaying the horror of the last twenty-four hours. Twenty-four? Maybe closer to twenty.

We arrive back at the house. Mira carries in the garbage bag filled with my belongings, and I carry the paper bag filled with things I bought at the drug store.

Link walks into the kitchen and stops near the counter. Though he's in dress slacks and a shirt, he's taken off his tie and suit coat.

He's more approachable, drop-dead gorgeous.

My heart rate soars.

Glass of wine in hand, he sweeps his gaze over me.

Maybe my exhausted mind is playing tricks on me, but I'm certain he lingers on that spot he kissed, and my skin seems to tingle all over again.

Nervously I slide my cup onto the counter and hang my purse from the back of one of the barstools.

A bottle of wine is open on the kitchen counter, two empty glasses next to it. After the day I've had, the sight of it is almost too tempting to resist.

"Anything else tonight?" Torin asks.

"Food," Pax says. He looks at everyone. "Pizza?"

Despite my filling lunch and the coffee with enough calories to fuel me for days, the idea of melty cheese and crispy pepperoni makes my mouth water.

Since I ran away from Chicago, I haven't been able to afford anything other than the paper-thin frozen variety from the grocery store.

Everyone nods enthusiastically, and Pax calls in an order and includes a pan of chocolate chip cookies as well.

A few minutes later, Mira and Torin head back out to pick up our dinner.

"Not allowing any deliveries onto the property," Pax explains.

Another reminder of how mad my life has become.

"Wine?" Link asks.

"Thank you." I tuck my leftover coffee into the refrigerator.

The red wine is rich and flavorful, and the effects seem to go straight to my head.

Pax and Link talk, and I perch on a barstool and listen. Already I have a favorite place to sit in the kitchen.

As Torin and Mira arrive back home, Pax opens a cabinet and removes several plates.

"Can I help?" I offer, needing to do something useful. The pampered princess role I've been thrust into is so unusual, and it doesn't suit me.

Pax shakes his head. "After we're back from Vegas, you can."

The reminder of our impending trip—our wedding—sends a jolt through me. The day after tomorrow, I'll be married to not one, but two men?

Mira and Torin pass on the invitation to eat with us and instead carry their own box out of the house.

Instead of getting back into the SUV, they continue walking past the pool to the guest house. "They're staying on the property?"

"Having them close by is essential," Pax says.

The aroma of melted cheese and spicy pepperoni fills the air as we settle around the kitchen island, pizza boxes spread before us. Despite the comfort food, tension hangs heavy in the room. I'm hyperaware of Link's presence beside me. His arm occasionally brushes mine as he reaches for another slice.

Suddenly, Pax's phone chirps. He glances at the screen, his brow furrowing. "Excuse me," he murmurs, moving away from us.

I don't even pretend to focus on my food. Instead I turn toward him and eavesdrop.

My heart stops when I hear him ask, "Marge?"

The slice of pizza slips from my fingers, landing with a soft plop on my plate. "Pax?"

But he pays me no attention. His expression is dark, unreadable, and his body is tight, poised for action.

After he ends the call, he immediately dials another number. This time, I leave my chair and walk over to him, desperate to hear more. Only one word reaches me clearly. *"Inamorata."*

My mind races. Inamorata? Isn't that Italian for…sweetheart? Beloved? What does that have to do with Marge?

"Need cleanup at the Rusty Nail," Pax says tersely into the phone.

Cleanup? A chill runs down my spine. In movies, *cleanup* usually means.…

No.

Refusing to think like that, I shake my head.

As Pax ends the call, I reach out, gripping his wrist. "What's going on? Is Marge okay?"

His eyes meet mine, and for a moment, I see a flicker of sympathy before the professional mask slips back into place. He nods once. "She's fine."

Relief floods through me, quickly followed by a new wave of dread. "Then…" *Someone else isn't?*

And why did she call Pax?

Is this something related to me?

Pax doesn't answer. Instead he turns to Link, his gaze hard. "You got this?"

Link nods, and a silent understanding seems to pass between them.

As Pax shrugs into his motorcycle jacket, my world tilts off its axis once again. He makes another call, this time to Torin, updating the couple on the situation.

Moments later, Mira and Torin arrive at the main house.

"I'll show you to the security room," Link says to the couple.

Security room?

Until now, I didn't know he had one.

Not that it should be a surprise. Link and Pax don't seem to leave anything to chance.

"I'll roll with you," Torin says to Pax.

His reply is clipped. "I'll be faster alone. On my bike."

"You don't know what's out there," Torin replies.

In the end, Pax agrees to go with Mira in the SUV while Torin stays with us.

"Call Inamorata for more backup," he tells Torin. Then he indicates his head toward the driveway. "Let's go."

Torin and Mira exchange glances, and a thousand unspoken words pass between them.

Judging by the concern in Torin's eyes, I wonder if there's something more than a professional partnership between the two.

Suddenly me and Link are alone with Torin, and once the sound of the vehicle fades into the distance, the house seems to echo with silence. A chill slides down my spine.

"Nothing we haven't dealt with a thousand times before," Torin reassures me with a half smile.

Mobsters? Abductions? *My virginity being sold?*

Not comforted, I rub my arms, trying to warm up.

Link shows Torin to the security room. Then, when he's back, he says, "Come here."

I'm so exhausted, overwrought, that I barely register what he says.

But then he crosses to me, wrapping me in a strong embrace and easing me against his broad chest.

The emotional dam I've built since the night I found out Axel's plans bursts. With gasping sobs, I finally cry.

Even though I'm soaking his crisp white shirt, he doesn't let me go.

His heart thumps steadily beneath my ear, a reassuring rhythm. One of his hands strokes my back in soothing circles while the other cradles the back of my head.

"Lean on me," he encourages, his breath warm against my hair.

I've spent a long time relying only on myself. And the idea of counting on someone else—especially someone like Link—is terrifying. And yet…

Despite my intentions, I melt against him, drawing strength from his solid presence.

I breathe in deeply, inhaling his scent—a mixture of confidence and pure masculine power. Though it shouldn't be, the combination is comforting.

As my tears subside, I slowly pull back, looking up at him. The way he studies me makes my breath catch. "I'm sorry," I whisper, suddenly embarrassed by my breakdown. "Your shirt…"

He shakes his head, cutting off my apology. "Not necessary." His voice is gruff but soft.

Slowly he brings up a hand to brush a strand of hair from my face.

His touch sends tingles across my skin, and I look up to meet his blue eyes. There's emotion in their depths that I've never seen before. *Admiration? Desire?*

Surely I'm imagining things.

"Don't apologize, Tessa. You're the strongest, most

resourceful woman I've ever met. What's happened in the last twenty-four hours would destroy a lesser person."

With his thumb, he traces my cheekbone, wiping away the last of my tears. My heart races as he leans in slightly, and his gaze drops to my lips.

Are you going to kiss me?
Will I let you?

CHAPTER TWELVE

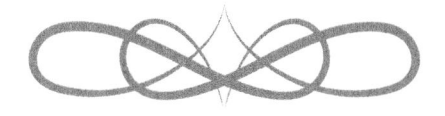

Las Vegas
Tessa

I'm living someone else's life. I have to be.

The thought echoes in my mind as I stand at the floor-to-ceiling windows of our palatial suite at the Bella Rosa resort, gazing out at the Las Vegas skyline.

The view is breathtaking, a sea of shimmering glass and steel stretching as far as the eye can see. In the far, far distance, the Stratosphere Tower pierces the sky like a giant needle. To the south, a golden facade glimmers in the afternoon sun. And everywhere in between, there are hotels and casinos.

But it's not just the view that has stunned me. It's the ridiculous amount of luxury and the fact I now carry a credit card with no limit.

The bell person has just finished unpacking our luggage—a task that took forever given the ridiculous amount of clothes Link insisted on buying me yesterday.

He hands the man a tip that makes him grin like a fool.

Evidently my future husband is a very generous man.

Finally we're alone—me, Link, and Pax. My fiancé and his...partner? Bodyguard? Co-husband?

I can't wrap my mind around our unusual arrangement.

"Are you ready to head down?" Link's voice breaks through my reverie.

He's standing near the door, impeccably dressed in a tailored suit. Will I ever get accustomed to the breathtaking sight of him?

I smooth down the front of a dress he selected for me.

Pax moves in closer, his presence reassuring despite the butterflies in my stomach. "You look beautiful, Tessa. Lorenzo's going to be impressed."

Lorenzo Carrington. The mysterious owner of this magnificent resort. The man Link and Pax seem eager for me to meet.

Mira and Torin are with us as we leave and head for the private elevator.

Just beyond the obvious, another world exists, one I hadn't known anything about two days ago.

Once we're inside the lift, Link presses his finger to a pad, and buttons light up. He selects a number, and the doors slide close behind us. The compartment moves so fast that I instinctively bend my knees to keep my balance.

"Should have warned you," Pax says, cupping my elbow and offering stability.

Especially in these heels. I'm teetering in them to begin with.

When the doors open, we step out into a quiet hallway I'm certain most guests never see.

Link leads us to another set of elevators, these even more exclusive than the last. He presses his thumb to a biometric scanner, and the doors slide open silently.

"Lorenzo's office is on one of the top floors," Link

explains as we enter. "He likes to keep an eye on his kingdom."

The ascent is breathtaking, both in speed and view. As we rocket upward, the Strip unfolds beneath us through the glass walls of the elevator. It's dizzying, exhilarating, and more than a little terrifying.

When we finally reach the top, I feel as if I'm still moving.

Once more, I'm grateful for Pax's support as we enter a reception area that could double as an art gallery. Even though I know next to nothing about paintings, I recognize one of the impressionist pieces hanging on the wall.

A sleek, modern desk dominates the center of the room, and a woman with the striking good looks of a model sits behind it. She smiles warmly as we approach. "Mr. Merritt, Mr. Carter, welcome back to the Bella Rosa." She smiles at me. "Ma'am. Mr. Carrington is expecting you all."

She presses a button, and a set of massive double doors swings open silently.

Lorenzo's office speaks of power and class. Floor-to-ceiling windows offer a stunning view of Las Vegas. In the distance, beyond the strip, lies the starkness of the desert.

"Welcome," Lorenzo says, standing to greet us.

He's every bit as striking as *Scandalicious* claimed. Tall, dark, and undeniably powerful, he exudes an aura of authority that makes Link seem tame in comparison.

"Link," Lorenzo greets warmly, coming around the desk to embrace him. They clap each other on the back like old friends. Then Lorenzo turns to Pax and shakes his hand firmly. "Good to see you."

Finally his gaze locks onto me, and I feel like he's seeing all my secrets. Despite myself, I clutch my purse tighter.

"You must be Tessa. Delighted to meet you."

Aware of how out of place I feel, I return the greeting.

"It's a pleasure to meet you, Mr. Carrington." Should I curtsey or something?

"Lorenzo, please," he insists, taking my hand. "We're delighted to have you here. I hope you're finding everything to your liking?"

"It's a little...much," I admit, then immediately wish I could take my words back.

Lorenzo laughs, putting me slightly more at ease.

"I hope that's in a good way. Please, have a seat. Can I offer you a drink? Champagne, perhaps?"

Before I can answer, a bar cart materializes, pushed by a silent, efficient server. Lorenzo pours four glasses of champagne that probably costs more than my old car, handing them out with practiced ease.

As we settle into a seating area with a view that makes me slightly dizzy, Lorenzo turns to Link. "I understand congratulations are in order."

"They are." Link takes my hand. "Thank you again for accommodating us on such short notice."

"Anything for you." With that, he lifts his glass, taking in the three of us. *"Che l'amore e la felicità vi accompagnino sempre."* Then he switches to English. "May love and happiness always be with you. Salute!"

I glance at Link. Love has nothing to do with this.

All of us raise our flutes.

After we've all had a taste, Lorenzo looks at Link. "How are things progressing with our mutual...interests?"

The conversation shifts then, into territory I can barely follow. They speak in a shorthand of names and places I don't recognize, interlaced with financial terms that make my head spin. Pax contributes occasionally, his deep voice a counterpoint to Link and Lorenzo's back-and-forth.

As the men talk, I sip my champagne and study them. There's a rugged edge to Lorenzo, a hint of danger beneath the polished exterior that reminds me of Link. These are men accustomed to getting what they want.

Even though I would give anything to be walking into the Rusty Nail for my shift right now, I'm swept up in their world.

After what feels like an eternity but is probably only another fifteen minutes, Lorenzo thanks us for stopping by. "I'm sure you have wedding details to attend to."

We're being dismissed. Politely, but firmly.

He stands, and we all follow suit. "Tessa, it was a pleasure to meet you. I look forward to seeing you both at the ceremony."

We make our way back to the elevator, Link's hand on the small of my back as always, his touch possessive.

In the privacy of the compartment, I look at Link. "I feel like I just had an audience with royalty."

Link inclines his head. "In a way, you did. Lorenzo is the crown prince of Vegas."

The rest of the ride to the floor where we catch the other elevators is quiet.

Once we're inside the next lift, Link turns to me. "We have an appointment with the wedding planner in ten minutes. Are you up for it, or do you need a moment?"

I almost say yes, but then I catch sight of the stranger reflected back at me in the mirrored wall of the elevator. Maybe it's the champagne and the clothes, but this version of Tessa is poised and elegant, and she almost looks like she belongs in this world.

If I pretend long enough, will I start to believe it?

"I'm ready," I respond.

Even though we're a few minutes early, we're shown into a conference room in the event planning suite and greeted warmly by a woman named Nora.

She's a whirlwind of efficiency, armed with a tablet and a

video of other weddings that they've hosted.

"The next part showcases the Bella Rosa's Sky Chapel. Mr. Carrington has reserved that for your ceremony."

Oh?

The videos show brides walking down an aisle. In each clip, the room is arranged slightly differently. The room appears casual in some, very formal with pedestals and arches in others.

"It's on the fiftieth floor, with panoramic views of the Strip. As you can see, the space can be transformed for an intimate ceremony or something more elaborate."

In the next sequence of shots, there is a floral arch in front of a bank of windows. Some shots have sunshine and puffy clouds as a backdrop. Others have a sky painted for sunset. The final one is a nightscape.

Even in my princess-for-a-day fantasies as a girl, I couldn't have imagined anything this beautiful. "This is breathtaking," I say, even though I didn't mean to speak the words aloud.

Link places his hand right above my knee, sending warmth through me. "I agree, little dove."

When the video ends, the planner pushes a button on her remote, and the room lights slowly blaze to life. "Did you get any ideas?"

"This will be a small gathering," Link says. "Around fifty people."

With a gasp I look at him. On what planet is that many guests a small wedding? *"Fifty?"* Who has he invited, and how can anyone get away on such ridiculously short notice?

He looks at Pax.

"Give or take," Pax answers for them both.

There could be more?

"Something simple is fine with me," I tell Nora.

"More formal than not," Link contradicts. "Everything in

the last segment of the video, the petals, the covered seats, all of it."

"What?" I blink. "Why?"

"It's your wedding day." He locks his gaze on me. "You should have something memorable."

I don't want anything like that. Standing in front of a justice of the peace, even a small chapel with a fake Elvis is fine with me. "Link—"

"Let's say fifty for the ceremony," he tells the woman. "Sixty for the reception."

Are you kidding me?

Avoiding my gaze, she types into her pad.

When she glances up, she looks at me. "Do you have music you'd like to walk down the aisle to?"

"No." All these questions are making my head swim.

"The wedding march?" she suggests.

I shake my head. This arrangement in no way resembles a real ceremony, and I can't imagine myself being traditional at this point.

"'A Thousand Years.'"

We both turn to look at Link. He's thought about this?

"Instrumental version, violin and piano only."

"Ah. Excellent choice," Nora approves.

Though I know the song and love it, I've never heard an instrumental version.

"Recessional?"

No wonder some brides take two years to plan their wedding.

This time, Pax speaks up. "How about 'Beautiful Day'?"

"By U2?" Link asks. "Done."

"Music for when your guests are arriving?"

"Soft jazz, no lyrics. Miles Davis. Chet Baker. That sort of thing."

After making her note, she adds. "And a specific song

you'd like to have playing as a signal it's time for you and Pax to join us?"

My two men exchange glances.

Then Pax looks at me. "'I've Got You Under My Skin.'"

Wondering what Nora thinks, I shift. But she's either unconcerned or oblivious to our dynamic. "Also instrumental?"

Link picks up the conversation. "Of course."

That settled, she moves on to her next, exhausting question. "What kind of flowers would you like?" she asks.

Everyone in the room looks at me. "None."

Link shakes his head. "You need a bouquet."

"And a selection to fill the vases next to the arch," she adds.

"Roses?" Link suggests.

Vehemently I shake my head. "No." They remind me of my parents' funeral. Arrangement after arrangement had been delivered to the house, to the funeral home. And Axel and I had some made for the church, with sashes over them reading Mom and Dad. If I never see another rose again, it's too soon.

"Perhaps we can leave that to your team?" Link suggests.

"Certainly, sir." Her glance takes in all of us. "Do you have specific colors in mind?"

When I shake my head, Link responds, "Black and white."

She makes a note.

How is he so calm and confident when my brain is on overload?

"Any specifics on music?"

Around me, the conversation continues.

Link and Pax decide on a DJ, agree to send him guidelines for music, arrange for a cocktail hour, agree to a multicourse plated dinner with wine pairings, and the time that each event begins.

"And will you need a cake? Our pastry chef is one of the best in the business."

When Link nods, she opens her pad to show us a number of options for design and decoration.

Between the three of us, we agree to a tall, multi-layered cake, some tiers round, others square. The frosting will be white, with black accents. And our flowers will be used for added decoration.

"How about a topper?"

Why does it need one? "How about flowers are fine with me."

"Our first initials," Link contradicts. "LTP. In black."

Though I hate to admit it, his idea is a good one.

And I am more than a little surprised that Link seems to have thought all of this through.

"Have you considered the flavors?"

"I'll select those," I insist. Maybe I should have some say in this.

The pair look at each other and shrug.

After accepting the pad from her, I scroll through the offerings.

"Choose as many as you'd like."

I opt for all my favorites. "Hazelnut for one. Dark chocolate. A salted caramel mocha." After sliding the device back to her, I add. "And one that is prosecco."

"Excellent choices."

Both men remain quiet.

Maybe I should be more decisive more often.

"Will you require a photographer? Videographer, perhaps? Social media manager?"

That's a thing?

"Got that handled," Link responds.

Shocked once more, I look at him.

"Perfect." She gives a crisp nod. "Is there anything else I can help with?"

"You've been wonderful." I reach for my purse.

"Tessa needs a wedding gown."

Before she can respond, I hold up my hand. "That won't be necessary. I have plenty of clothes." More than I can ever imagine wearing.

With an eyebrow raised, Link looks at me. "What are you thinking?"

"Going along with our colors"—*that he chose*—"I have that elegant, long black dress."

With passionate curse words, both men respond at the exact same time.

"And in case that wasn't clear…"

CHAPTER THIRTEEN

Tessa

"Fuck no."

"No chance," Link grits out.

Stunning me, the *fuck* came from Pax.

"You're not wearing black to our wedding." Link's voice is deadly calm.

I exhale. "The dress is beautiful. Elegant." He'd said so himself.

Eyes darkened with determination, Link turns to Nora. "Can you give us a recommendation?" he asks, as if I never opened my mouth.

"Is there a budget I would need to be considerate of?"

"*Yes.*"

"No." Link's authoritative voice overlays mine.

"Lumière Bridal Atelier. It's near the Shops at Crystals, if you're familiar? A private entrance."

"I am." He nods to Pax, who excuses himself, moving to the far end of the room, facing away from us.

She gives us the address and directions for ringing the bell. "They will stay up all night if needed for alterations. Eloise offers concierge services, meaning she'll have the gown delivered when it's ready and help your bride prepare. Shall I make an appointment for you?"

"We'll be there in..." Link glances at Pax.

"Twenty to thirty minutes," he replies, rejoining us.

Did I really think I could win many battles against Link? He's a force of nature.

"I'll need a tuxedo," Pax informs Nora.

Link frowns. "You didn't bring one?"

"Tried it on last night." He shrugs. "Jacket's a little tight in the shoulders."

"Ah."

"We have an excellent shop in-house," Nora replies. "Vestiture Luxe on the lobby level."

"Wait." The meeting is ending, and I'm swept up in their millions of decisions. "Don't you have a women's clothing place here also?" Surely I'm not the first woman who has come to Vegas needing a dress on short notice.

"We do." Nora nods. "One that's very high-end. I'm certain you could find something suitable."

Link turns to me. His eyes aren't just dark now. There's a glint in his eye that sends skitters down my spine.

Then he looks back at Nora. "Make the appointment." His tone is flat and allows for no argument.

"Of course, Mr. Merritt." Then she sweeps her gaze over all of us. "Before you leave, do you have an officiant?"

"Elvis is fine with me," I almost say.

"No," Link replies.

"We have one available for you, if you'd like."

"Someone who is amenable to... A rather *unconventional* arrangement."

"A...?" Her gaze takes all of us in.

Her eyes widen. Which answers my earlier question. She'd been oblivious to our relationship dynamics.

"The three of us will need to be included."

"Ahm…" She clears her throat. "You understand there are legalities—"

"We do," Link interrupts.

"I'm sure we can work something out." After typing into her pad, she nods. "Reverend Clara is available to meet with you in the morning. I'll…ah…explain the situation."

"See that you do."

"Will ten o'clock be suitable?"

Link looks at me, and I nod my ascent.

"That'll be fine."

"Followed by a rehearsal? Say ten thirty, just to give us a little time buffer?"

Again, he agrees.

"Both appointments will be at the Sky Chapel. Do you need a text or email reminder?"

"We'll be fine."

Pax types notes into his watch.

"Thank you." Link stands and offers his hand. "Darling?"

Darling? Is this an act for the planner?

If so, it's not needed.

Link and Pax thank the woman for her time, and she shakes hands with all of us.

She smiles at me. "I look forward to seeing you all in the morning."

When we leave the event planning area, Torin and Mira fall in step with us as usual.

Pax checks his watch. "We should have just enough time to make it."

And I'd rather go sit by the pool than go to another boutique.

But my protests don't mean much.

We leave the resort by the back entrance, the same way we arrived yesterday.

A sleek, black limousine is waiting for us, driven by the same Hawkeye team that picked us up from the airport.

Torin and Mira flank us as we make our way to the vehicle. And when we reach Lumière Bridal Atelier, Mira once again accompanies us inside.

The owner, Eloise St. Clair, greets us personally and welcomes us to her Parisian-inspired shop.

The store is larger than I expected, and an enormous chandelier dominates the space. Mirrors are everywhere, refracting the light in magical, dancing prisms.

Mannequins are stylishly dressed in every kind of gown imaginable, most in white or ivory.

There are racks with several different selections on each and mirrored glass cases with jewelry and headpieces and belts.

I feel as if I've stepped into fantasy land.

Of course, we're offered champagne.

In the last twenty-four hours, I've consumed more bubbly than I have in my entire life put together. "Thank you. No." If I drink any more, I'll need to sleep for a week.

"Are you gentlemen staying?" she asks my future husbands.

"We are." Link answers for both of them.

"Whiskey?" she offers. "Champagne? Beer?"

"Whiskey," the two reply simultaneously.

"Of course. Please make yourselves comfortable."

"We'll be waiting," Link says to me.

Eloise arranges for an assistant to show them to the far corner of the salon. Instead of the seating area being covered in a pinkish velvet fabric, chairs in that section are deep red and leather. A coffee table is stacked with magazines. But the area is still surrounded by mirrors, and there's a platform to stand on.

Moments later, another assistant wheels over an elegant cart with several crystal decanters and glasses on the top.

Makes sense. Alcohol loosens inhibitions along with wallets, no doubt.

"Now, dear, let's get you sorted out." Once we're alone, Eloise takes my hands.

This afternoon, there are only a few other people in the store, and it seems I have the owner's undivided attention.

"What kind of dress have you always imagined yourself wearing?"

Suddenly, unexpectedly, a lump lodges in my throat.

As a little girl, I remember talking to mom about my fairy-princess wedding, including a tiara.

Eloise waves over a clerk and requests water for me.

Though I want to instinctively protest that I don't need it, I'm grateful when the small, cold bottle is pressed into my hand. "Thank you."

After a few sips, I recover enough to blink away the tears that are stinging my eyes.

I've learned to compartmentalize my losses and focus on what I have to do.

Today shouldn't be any different.

"Would you like to browse? See if we can eliminate any styles." With that, she guides me around the showroom.

The boutique is a sea of silk, lace, and tulle, with gowns more elaborate than anything I've ever seen up close.

The more I see, the more confused I get. "I'm lost." Don't most brides have the chance to browse online or look at magazines, maybe even watch a few TV shows to see what they like?

"I suggest we try several different styles to see what you prefer."

Because I'm so confused, I seize on the suggestion. I'm more than happy to let the professionals do their job.

Before leaving me, she asks what size shoe I wear and if I have any preferences in styles. Pumps? Sandals?

Since I can't decide on that either, she says she'll bring back several for me to try on.

Finally I'm shown to a dressing room, and Eloise brings back several gowns along with a woman to help me dress.

Between yesterday and today, I have no modesty left.

First I try on a slinky sheath that makes me feel like a 1920s starlet. Link and Pax both shake their heads.

Though I always pictured myself in a ballgown, the one that I am laced into overpowers me.

"You look like you're drowning," Link observes when I step onto the platform in front of him.

"Like I'm…?"

"Drowning," he repeats himself. "A slow, painful, suffocating death."

"That's descriptive," Pax muses.

"Well, it feels like it, too." I can't help myself. I laugh. How long has it been since I did that? "I hate it."

"Thank God," Pax says. "I was trying to think of something polite to say."

Both men grin.

In that moment, there's an easy intimacy between the three of us that rocks me.

What if we'd met under different circumstances? And what if this was real?

Forcing myself back to reality, I pick up the hem and hurry back to the dressing room.

Next comes a daring backless number that also plunges in the front, making both Link and Pax's eyes darken with desire.

"As much as I love you in it, I will not have other men looking at you."

I start to ask if he's serious, but the expression in his eyes says he'll kill anyone who looks at me sideways.

"I have the perfect selection," Eloise tells me, sweeping into the dressing room with another gown.

She holds it up in front of me, and my breath vanishes at the sight of the crepe sheath with a stunning, square neckline. There's also a fantastic big bow right below the base of my spine.

"What do you think?"

"I love it." And I hope it's flattering so I can stop shopping.

She helps me, while her assistant arranges the back of the dress.

I've lost far too much weight to have any curves, but the gorgeous fabric flows over my body. But because the garment nips in at the waist, I have the illusion of a feminine shape.

"Let's try the sandals."

Both women help me balance while I slip into the beautiful silver heels with rhinestones on them.

Then Eloise steps back, but not before I see her nod and smile.

I study my reflection.

A small train adds a touch of drama, and as I turn, I catch sight of the exquisite detail on the back—a row of tiny buttons starting at the base of my spine and running down the length of the gown. But that beautiful bow adds a romantic flourish. Though the back is open, the dress still feels modest.

"Tout simplement magnifique." Eloise smiles. "Simply magnificent."

Emotion threatens to overwhelm me.

I wish my mom were here to see this, to help me choose,

to cry happy tears and fuss over every detail. I can almost hear her voice, telling me how beautiful I look. And Samantha, my best friend from what feels like a lifetime ago… She should be here too, gushing over the dress, planning my bachelorette party, and cracking jokes about my honeymoon.

But I won't be sharing this moment with anyone who matters, and life has turned my dreams into nightmares.

When I step out of the dressing room, the expressions on Link's and Pax's faces tell me everything I need to know.

"That's the one," Link says softly, his eyes never leaving me.

Pax nods in agreement. "You're even more gorgeous than ever, Tessa."

The dress is elegant without being too formal. It suits me —or at least, the version of me I'm slowly becoming.

As I continue to gaze at my reflection, a different feeling hits me.

Peace.

Eloise is standing to one side, slightly behind me. She's smiling. "Tessa, is this your gown?"

I blink back tears, but one clings to my eyelashes. *"Yes."*

Once we're back in the dressing room, Eloise brings a selection of veils for me to try. "So your gentlemen have some surprise for the wedding, no?"

Not that it should matter to me.

"Which one?"

I settle for one that will attach to the back of my hair.

"This dress was made for you, *ma chérie*."

Even I'm captivated by my image. The addition of the beautiful veil has made the outfit complete.

She asks her assistant to fetch the seamstress.

When she arrives, the two converse in French, and pins are stuck into the dress.

"What time is the wedding?" Eloise asks.

"Evening."

She nods.

A few moments later, the seamstress stands, studies me in the mirror, then nods in satisfaction and leaves.

"You are a beautiful Lumière bride," Eloise says, embracing me.

The dress is so beautiful that I don't want to take it off.

Five minutes later, I'm Cinderella again, and the princess becomes just another role I play.

In the showroom, Link and Pax have their arms full of lingerie.

Horrified, blushing, I hurry over to them. "What are you doing?"

"Thinking about the honeymoon." Link shrugs.

Pax nods.

Wearing a smile, an assistant joins us. "May I wrap these for you, gentlemen?"

Showing no signs of embarrassment, they hand them over.

But they're not done yet.

The pair return to the hangers and shelves that are filled with every kind of negligee imaginable.

My cheeks burn even hotter as they peruse the selections. White, black, red, purple. "I think you have enough."

Neither responds to me.

Pax lifts a hanger containing a short, clingy scrap of sheer black lace. "For tomorrow night."

I'm scandalized. That garment will cover nothing.

Less than nothing.

But Link nods. "Agree."

Then they both look at me, and my breath catches as I think about wearing it for them, the hungry looks of appreciation in their eyes as they slowly peel it off me.

"Pax is a connoisseur," Link assures me. "It's perfect."

Less than fifteen minutes later, we leave the boutique, bags in hand and with my head spinning.

Hours ago, I was a struggling waitress, scraping by and looking over my shoulder.

Now I'm planning my life with a billionaire and a bodyguard.

I have to be dreaming.

"There's one more thing we need to handle."

"Oh?"

"The justice center," Pax instructs our driver. He rattles off an address.

"Marriage license," Link tells me.

How did I not think of that?

Maybe because I'm on some sort of crazy carnival ride that never seems to end.

Once Link, Pax, and I are inside the Marriage License Bureau, I stop. "You're okay with this?" I ask Pax, waving my hand. "The whole thing, I mean." After all, I have no idea how a marriage between three people works.

"Link and I discussed it. And yes." He smiles, momentarily cracking his protective, badass veneer. "Thank you."

In his situation, I'm not sure how I'd feel.

Together Link and I figure out what we need to do to get the license.

All of a sudden, this has become too real.

After filling in my part of the digital application, I turn it over to Link.

Because I'm curious, I watch him fill in his name.

Lincoln Sovereign Merritt.

Sovereign?

So much for my assumption that the selection of his company name was an ego-driven, grandiose decision.

I was wrong about him. *Once again.*

"Shall we?" he asks as a clerk waves us over.

Link pulls out a credit card and pays the fee.

In less time than I imagined possible, we're issued an official license.

Document in hand, Link turns to me.

Then, with a wicked smile, he leans in close, stealing the air I need to breathe. "Too late to escape now, little dove."

CHAPTER FOURTEEN

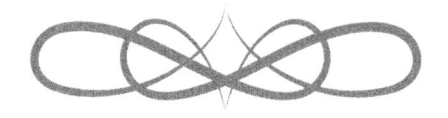

Tessa

"This is where I say goodnight."

Link's words hang in the air, heavy.

I frown.

We just had an amazing dinner, and I had no idea he wasn't planning on us spending the evening together.

He reaches past me to press the Down button on the elevator.

"Leave?" I ask.

"I have an appointment."

With who?

All through the meal at a table tucked away in a private alcove, both men were totally attentive.

A candle had flickered on our table, next to a small vase filled with tiny flowers. Soft jazz played in the background, and the nighttime view of the city took my breath away.

We'd dined European-style, and for the first time since this nightmare began, my tension slipped away.

Now, as we wait for the elevator, that bubble of normalcy bursts.

"I'll be back soon," Link promises, his voice low and reassuring.

He leans in, dropping a casual yet intimate kiss on the top of my head. The tender gesture sends a shiver down my spine.

His elevator arrives with a soft chime, and he enters the compartment, Torin a silent shadow behind him.

Link pulls out his phone, and a moment later, he vanishes from view.

"You knew he had plans?" I ask Pax.

"I did." He offers no explanation.

For a moment, I stand there, staring at the closed doors, a thousand questions swirling in my mind.

Pax presses the button to summon an elevator for us.

Its arrival interrupts my thoughts, and Pax gently guides me inside with his palm against the middle of my back. His touch is both grounding and electrifying.

We're not alone. Mira steps in, followed by a man I don't recognize. He's wearing a suit that screams *security,* and he positions himself in front of Pax and me, his stance mirroring Torin's earlier posture.

When we reach our floor, Mira and the unknown agent step out first, scanning the hallway in both directions before giving a subtle nod.

Mira takes up a position next to our door while the man continues toward the stairs.

Leaving nothing to chance?

As Pax presses his finger to the nearby pad, Mira nods. "Have a nice evening, ma'am."

"Tessa," I correct automatically, still uncomfortable with the formality. "Please, call me Tessa."

"Yes, ma'am," she replies, and I can't help but shake my head as I grin.

My new world is so foreign.

Pax and I step into the sanctuary of our suite.

When the lock engages, I exhale.

Suddenly I'm away from the outside world with its millions of complications.

Pax loosens his tie, and I kick off my stilettos.

"Nice dinner," he says.

"What was all that about?" I ask. "Link, I mean. Where is he going?"

Pax continues into the living room area and shrugs out of his suit coat.

The sight of the gun holstered at his side catches me off guard.

I gasp, but I shouldn't be surprised.

"Glass of wine?" Pax offers, his voice calm, as if he hasn't just revealed that he carries a deadly weapon.

I hesitate for a moment. "Will I need it?"

Pax looks at me, and his expression softens slightly. "Offering a nightcap, Tessa. Nothing more."

I nod. Despite the fact I had a glass with dinner, I'm still wound up.

While Pax busies himself with opening a bottle, I curl up in one of the plush armchairs, tucking my legs beneath me.

Pax returns with two glasses of white wine.

"Thank you."

He settles into the chair across from me, placing his own glass on the coffee table between us.

"So what's going on that I need to know about?"

Pax's eyebrow arches. "Need to know?" he repeats, his tone maddeningly neutral. "Nothing."

I resist the urge to roll my eyes. "Semantics," I counter. "If we're going to be married, don't I have the right to know what's going on with my husbands?"

Pax unbuttons the top button on his shirt. "Link is meeting with Lorenzo," he explains. "And Matteo Moretti."

A known mobster is in the hotel?

"After that, he's heading to the high-stakes poker room."

I wait for the shock to hit me, but it doesn't come. Instead, I feel a strange sense of resignation. "He doesn't shy away from risk, does he?" I muse, more to myself than to Pax.

A ghost of a smile touches Pax's lips. "He's more calculated than you might imagine."

"Does he do this often?" I press, hoping to understand this aspect of the man I'm about to marry.

"This?" Pax echoes, and I can't tell if he's being deliberately obtuse or genuinely seeking clarification.

"Gamble," I clarify. "Visit Vegas."

Pax takes a sip of his wine before answering. "Gamble? Isn't all life a gamble?"

Maybe to men like Pax and Link, it was.

A shiver runs through me as I remember the first night I met these two men. The story Link had told, so casually, about Pax shooting someone while balancing a tray of champagne.

"He's not like your brother, if that's what you're worried about. He doesn't take unnecessary risks, and he doesn't live his life on the turn of a card or the roll of the dice."

The memory surfaces unbidden, and I find myself asking, "Is it true? That story Link told that man in the bar? Or was it just meant to scare the hell out of him?"

Pax's expression turns serious, his green eyes locking onto mine with an intensity that steals my breath. "It was effective."

I nod.

"Given that, does it matter?"
I think about his question.
If it is true, do I want to know the answer?

CHAPTER FIFTEEN

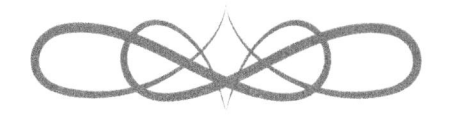

Tessa

The question echoes in my mind as I study Pax's face. His green eyes meet mine steadily, revealing nothing.

"You believe in the Machiavellian principle? That the ends justify the means?" I counter, leaning forward slightly.

Pax's expression remains impassive, but there's a slight tension in his shoulders.

"After the threat..." I rub the stem of my glass. "Did Link get his money?"

"The boss plays to win." Pax's tone is flat, his gaze unwavering.

That's probably as close to an answer as I'll ever get.

For a few minutes, I'm lost, staring into the depths of my wine, and questions I've had since I first looked the men up on *Scandalicious* return to me. Maybe it's the alcohol or the fact we're alone for once and that danger seems far away. But curiosity gets the better of me. "Is it true that he's a Titan?"

Pax's lips curl into a grin, the first real smile I've seen from him all evening. "The fictitious secret society?"

"Is it?" I challenge, raising an eyebrow.

He shrugs, the movement causing his shirt to stretch across his broad shoulders. "What do you think?"

I pause, considering my words carefully. "Seems fanciful." And yet so does this world that I'm now living in. "At one time, I believed my brother was misguided, maybe a little spoiled by our parents, but essentially a good human being. I never imagined he'd try to…" *What?* Prostitute me?

Shoving aside my upset, I go on. "I thought the Mafia was something that only existed in movies and history. And that I'd be able to stay hidden forever."

Pax leans forward, resting his elbows on his knees. His gaze never leaves mine.

"At this point, the idea of Titans doesn't seem any crazier than anything else. That influential, wealthy people would get together at an undisclosed location to discuss ideas, politics, try to solve world problems…"

He steeples his hands, quietly waiting for me to go on.

I shrug. "Other secret societies exist."

He waits.

"At exclusive colleges, for example." Warming to my topic, I study him carefully. "There's one that three former presidents belong to, along with two previous supreme court appointees."

As I score my point, he inclines his head to one side.

"So, if such an organization exists, I'd have no problem believing Link was a member." I look at Pax, studying the strong lines of his face. "Question is, are you?"

He says nothing, but I notice a slight twitch at the corner of his mouth.

"Is being a Titan a matter of birth?" I press, leaning forward.

"I'm sure, hypothetically, that couldn't hurt," Pax replies, his voice low and measured.

"Legacy. Like a lot of things."

"Yet if it were limited to that criteria, what would the point be?"

I nod slowly as things fall into place. "That's why people like Julien Bonds might have joined." After referencing the Genius of the Known Universe, I pause and gently swirl my stem. The wine catches the light, glinting like liquid gold.

"If such a group actually existed," he clarifies.

"Right." Since he hasn't told me I'm ridiculous or changed the subject, I'm more convinced than ever that at least one of my future husbands is a Titan.

Pax picks up his wine but doesn't take a sip.

I take his silence as an invitation to continue.

"At least tell me about Hawkeye."

"The man?"

"The myth, the legend," I add, grinning.

He laughs, the sound rich and warm. "Something like that."

All tension vanishes, and for that moment, I'm enjoying myself.

Since he hasn't shut down my questioning, I press forward. "I'm curious about the company itself. I mean, obviously you're adept at protective services. And I see online that the firm provides paramilitary operations."

"Yeah."

"And that many people who work there are former members of the military—especially special forces. And police. Even FBI, CIA. All the letters of the alphabet."

"You *have* been doing your research," Pax says, his tone a mixture of amusement and admiration.

"You were military." That's about the only thing I'm sure of.

I half expect him to dodge my statement. Instead he's straightforward.

"Army." He pauses, and I bite back my impatience and wait for him to go on. "Like my father before me."

"Oh?" Intrigued, I shift, and the soft fabric of my dress seems to whisper against my skin.

Pax's expression softens slightly as he continues. "We didn't have a lot. Mom died when I was young, so he did the best he could with an eight-year-old he didn't relate to. He left the military for me and joined the local police force." He pauses. "He was killed in the line of duty when I was seventeen."

"Oh God, Pax…" My heart aches for him, and I resist the urge to go to him.

"I was pissed at the entire fucking world. And…" He gives a wry smile. "The aunt who took me in gave me two choices. Join the military or be thrown out."

"Yikes," I murmur, my mind racing to imagine a young, angry Pax facing such a decision.

"She was more generous than I deserved."

I wonder if there's more to the story. "Special forces?" I persist.

"Yeah." He finally takes a drink. "Till I had enough, and Hawkeye recruited me. Recommended by a friend."

"Torin and Mira? Obviously you trust them?"

"With my life. They recently got married."

I suspected there was some type of relationship, but I hadn't guessed they were actually married. "I'm surprised the organization allows it."

"Company policy doesn't necessarily prohibit it."

Makes sense, I guess, since Pax is evidently more than just a protector to Link. "But that they get to go on assignments together?"

"They're both highly trained agents, and Torin teaches at the company's training center in Nevada. Fieldwork is an important component of instruction. They're not often assigned together, but Hawkeye doesn't want to risk losing either of them, so he ensures they have time together."

I have a million more questions, but suddenly I yawn.

"You've had a long couple of days," Pax says softly.

Is that all it's been?

"We have a lifetime to learn about each other."

Touched by the reassurance in his voice, I smile. "I guess that's true." I stand and pick up my glass. "Good night."

"Sleep well, sweetheart."

At the entrance to my room, I look over my shoulder.

He hasn't moved or taken his gaze off me.

My heart thumping a little from his endearment, I close the door.

For a few moments, still processing my time with Pax, I look out the window and sip my wine.

Finally, feeling drowsy, I try to undress. But my zipper is impossible to reach. No matter how hard I try, I can't manage it alone.

Giving up, I return to the living room. Pax has remained exactly where he was.

"Uhm…" I begin. Heat rushes to my cheeks. "I could use some help," I admit, gesturing to my back.

"Of course." After putting down his glass, he comes to stand behind me.

The warmth of his body sears me.

He grasps the zipper, and I hold my breath as he slowly lowers it. The brush of his knuckles against my spine sends rivers of awareness through me.

His fingers linger at the base of my spine, and I'm very much aware of every point where our bodies almost meet.

"Go to bed, Tessa," he murmurs against my ear, his breath warm on my skin. "While you still can."

Sensual warning is laced through his tone, and I'd be wise to heed it.

He moves his hands away, and I press my palms against the front of my dress to hold it in place.

The air crackles with tension, and intimacy hangs between us, like an invitation I don't dare accept.

After drawing a steadying breath, I turn to face him.

"Thank you." I order myself to turn, to run, but I stand there, riveted, as if held in place by an invisible force.

Gently he brushes a finger against my cheek.

"Fuck." Then he whispers, "Tessa…" He leans in closer, his breath mingling with mine in a shared heartbeat. And then he closes the gap between us, his lips meeting mine in a tender kiss.

Unable to resist, I melt into him, threading my fingers through his hair, holding on to this feeling of connection. The heat of his body seeps into mine, telling me I can trust him, erasing any doubts or fears I've had about how right this is.

His possession is not demanding or urgent; it's a gentle exploration, a silent promise of more to come. The taste of him is intoxicating, and I am drawn deeper into his embrace, losing myself in the moment.

His arms are strong, reassuring, and right now, there's nothing but the two of us, safety, and the moment.

He trails his fingers down my spine, igniting my nerve ending, leaving me dizzy, craving more.

With a moan, his erection hard against me, he deepens the kiss, and I start to lose myself.

I want...

He wrenches himself away, and I take a shaky step back, my breaths coming in little bursts.

Thank God one of us is capable of rational thought because I'd been so very close to giving into my need for him.

"Final warning, Tessa. I'm about done being a gentleman."

I shiver, and not from fear.

"Tessa…" My name is a growl and a warning.

Jarred back to reality, I clutch the front of my dress tighter and hurry away.

I reach my room. Then, before I can change my mind, I shut the door. I don't bother with the lock. Experience has already taught me that nothing will keep either of them out if they decide to enter.

I change into a sleep set Link bought me, either in Houston or earlier today at the bridal shop. The two-piece outfit—shorts and a top with spaghetti straps—is silky, and a delicate shade of peach.

I've told him not to spoil me, but I have to admit; these are the nicest pajamas I've ever owned.

Until I can find a job and get back on my feet, maybe I should just enjoy the moment.

The memory of Pax being so close won't go away, even when I slip beneath the cool covers and turn off the nightstand lamp.

The moment I close my eyes and roll onto my side, hoping to drift off, I'm suddenly wide awake.

I listen for sounds of movement, but I hear none.

An hour, maybe two later, I finally doze off with thoughts and images of Pax and Link teasing me, blurring the boundary between reality and fantasy.

I'm back in the living room of our suite, moonlight spilling through the open blinds, casting soft shadows across the room.

Pax is there, his shirtsleeves rolled back, and Link emerges from his bedroom wearing a dress shirt and a pair of pants. The air is supercharged with a sense of forbidden desire. My heart races with anticipation.

Link beckons.

Helpless to resist him or myself, I obey.

When I'm in front of him, he trails his fingers down my arm, igniting a response deep in me.

He doesn't ask permission as he reaches for the bottom of my sleep top.

Without being asked, I raise my arms, so he can sweep the garment up. Then he releases it, and it floats to the floor to pool there.

The air-conditioning whispers across my skin, making my nipples hard. At least I tell myself that's what's happening. Surely my reaction isn't just from the way the men are looking at me...with deep hunger.

I'm flooded with conflicting emotions, a thrilling mix of vulnerability and exhilaration curling in my belly.

They share a look that is charged with unspoken agreement. I feel exposed, yet strangely empowered and free.

"You're stunning, little dove." Link's voice is low, laced with a sexy huskiness.

"He's right." Pax comes closer. "You've never been more beautiful." He sweeps his gaze over my bare skin, looking at me the way he had earlier, leaving me yearning for more.

Slowly, with deliberate intent, Link reaches to cup my breast, his palm warm and firm.

I gasp, arching into his touch as electricity arcs through me.

Even as Link continues, circling my hardening nipple with his thumb, "Let go, little dove. Be mine."

How can I resist?

"Ask for it."

"Please," I whisper.

Link's hand is a dangerous promise, and his thumb brushes against my sensitive peak. I moan softly and slightly arch my back.

Pax cups my other breast, and he gently squeezes.

Each man's unique touch drives me mad.

Pax tightens his grip slightly, his fingers coaxing another soft moan from my lips. "Offer yourself to me."

Though I'm not sure what he's demanding, I rise onto my tiptoes.

I lean into him, silently begging for more of his touch. He rewards me by rolling my nipple between his fingers, sending a shockwave of pleasure through me.

Link, not to be outdone, dips his head to capture my other nipple in his mouth, his tongue swirling around the sensitive peak. I gasp, my hands instinctively going to their shoulders to steady myself as my knees weaken.

They support me, their strong arms wrapping around my waist, holding me up as they continue their sensual assault. I'm coming undone, trembling, lost…

I shake my head back and forth desperately.

Then all of a sudden, I'm somewhere else, disoriented, the room spinning, my heart racing.

Breathless, I blink the world back into focus, trying to reorient myself.

As reality seeps back in, I realize it was just a dream—nothing more. But it felt so real, so vivid.

The way they had looked at me, touched me… It had felt like more than just a figment of my imagination. It had felt like forever.

I drink in a deep, shaky breath, trying to steady my nerves.

I tell myself that it's just the stress of the past few days, the unceasing series of events that have devoured my life.

After pushing my hair back from my face, I climb out of bed. After slipping into a robe, I pick up my glass from earlier. Knowing I won't sleep, I make my way back to the living room.

A single lamp casts a warm glow across the space, and I wander over to the window.

Las Vegas is sprawled out below, twinkling lights against the night sky. I take a sip of wine, hoping it will help calm my jangled nerves.

My emotions are a tangled mess. The dream was... incredible.

I hardly recognize the version of myself in it. Would I really give myself over so completely to Link and Pax like that? The thought both thrills and unsettles me.

A soft sound breaks through my reverie.

Startled, I turn to find Link standing in the doorway to his room. Seeing him so near, right after my dream, jolts me.

He's wearing the same trousers from earlier. Though his tie is gone and the top few buttons on his shirt are open, he's still dressed for business. Does the man ever sleep? "Sorry if I woke you," I murmur.

"You didn't." He crosses the room to pour himself a drink. Then he comes to stand next to me.

I'm acutely aware of his proximity. The dream may have been a fantasy, but the real Link's effect on me is undeniable.

"Trouble sleeping?" he asks, his voice low and gravelly.

I nod.

"Want to talk about it?"

God no. "No."

At his slight frown, I soften my response. "Thank you, though." How would I even begin to tell him that my subconscious has conjured scenarios that excite and terrify me? That I want him and Pax terribly? As much as I want to *not* want them.

Link studies me.

The air between us hums with tension, like it had in my dreams. I take another sip of wine to distract myself from him.

"You don't have to be scared."

I freeze. How can he read me so easily? "I'm not." But my lie is a whisper, not a strong statement.

"You're a terrible liar, little dove." He reaches out, tucking a stray lock of hair behind my ear, just like he'd done in the dressing room of Rêve de Mode.

"I..."

Wordlessly he plucks the glass from my hand and places it on a nearby end table.

So like the dream, but this is oh-so real.

My world narrows, and it's just me and this compelling billionaire, standing in the soft glow of the Vegas night.

Link's hand cups my cheek, his touch gentle yet firm, grounding me.

"Little dove," he says, his voice a low rumble that resonates deep within me. "You're safe with me. With us."

If reality is anything like my fantasies, I'm definitely not safe with them. My reactions frighten me. "I barely know you." And what I do know isn't reassuring.

"Then ask me anything."

I take a deep breath, steadying myself. "Why are you doing this?" The question I've been holding back finally escapes. "Why marry me? Why go to such lengths to protect me?"

Link's hand drops away, and he takes a step back, giving me space. He turns away, moving toward the window, his gaze lost in the cityscape below. The silence stretches between us, and for a moment, I wonder if he's going to answer me at all.

"I have my reasons."

His response is guarded, as I expected.

"Some of them are...complicated."

I watch him, the play of light and shadow across his features, the tension in his shoulders. "Complicated how?"

"I told you once that I always win my battles. That's true."

He clasps his hands behind his back. "But in this world, the one I inhabit, victories often come with...strings attached. Alliances are formed; favors are owed."

He's speaking in riddles.

"Life is a game of chess, and every move has consequences."

Trying to follow his logic, I frown. "And marrying me... That's a move in your game?"

"More than that." Link turns to face me, his blue eyes like ice. "By making you my wife, I'm ensuring your safety. It's the most effective way to protect you."

"But why go to these lengths? Why not just...hide me away? Help me get a fresh start?"

"Because I want you to be mine." His gaze never wavers from mine. "That first night at the Rusty Nail... You were fierce, brave, and so damn beautiful."

But there's more. There has to be. He'd called me Tessa when he only knew me as Nikki. "You figured out who I was."

He doesn't attempt to deny it. "When I found out about the danger you were in, I knew I couldn't let anything happen to you."

A chill rocks through me as another terrible realization occurs to me. "You know Emiliano."

Once more, he remains silent.

"And you're taking me away from him."

"A bonus," he assures me. "Not my motivation."

How am I a pawn between them?

He closes the distance between us and gently curls his hands around my shoulders. "You're meant to be cherished. As my wife, you will be."

In the time we've known each other, is it possible, even a little bit, that this compelling man has developed feelings for me?

"And how does Pax fit into all of this?"

Link's expression softens slightly. "He's my closest confidant, my right hand. And he's committed to taking care of you as much as I am."

I think back to the kiss I shared with Pax, to the way he looked at me, touched me. There's a sensual connection between us, and I'd believe he cares for me, even if I have trouble believing that about Link.

Everything has happened so fast, but I can't deny the pull I feel toward both of them.

Before I can respond, he eases me toward him.

"This is real, little dove. And you know it."

Intentionally he leans forward to capture my lips, seeking entry.

Unable to deny him, I open my mouth.

This isn't the gentle, exploratory kiss from my dream. This is Link Sovereign Merritt staking his claim.

He fists my hair, holding me tight as he deepens the kiss.

I cling to him, gripping the fabric of his shirt, feeling his strength, his power.

I'm lost in the moment, in him.

Suddenly the main door to our suite opens. Then it closes with a sharp, starling click, making me pull back.

Pax stands there, arms folded, dressed in a suit. "Am I interrupting something?"

CHAPTER SIXTEEN

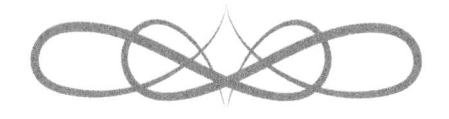

Tessa

Wide-eyed, as if I've been caught doing something I shouldn't, I meet his gaze.

Slowly Link releases me, sliding his hands from my hair to my shoulders, grounding me.

Then he turns to Pax. "Glad you're back. And no, you're not interrupting. Tessa had a bad dream, and we were enjoying a glass of wine."

"And thinking about the honeymoon?" Pax asks.

"Among other things," Link acknowledges.

My heart races, and I'm acutely aware of Pax's presence and the way his green eyes assess the situation, and me.

"Join us?" Link offers.

Join us?

"Wine?"

"Whiskey," Pax responds. But instead of waiting on Link, he crosses to the bar area and splashes the amber liquor into a glass.

Regarding me, Pax takes a slow sip, then sets the glass

down on the nearby table. He disappears into his room, returning moments later without his suit coat or shoulder holster.

His shirt sleeves are rolled back, revealing the strength of his forearms. Without his armor, he seems approachable, more human.

He joins Link and me at the window, and I drink in his scent—of lethal power and determination.

"Where were you?" Pax asks Link.

"Getting to know our future bride," Link replies, his eyes never leaving my face.

"Excellent idea," Pax agrees, voice a purr of approval.

I'm unsure what to do, how to navigate this foreign dynamic.

Link turns me to face Pax. Then he moves in behind me, his warmth radiating against me.

"You okay with me joining you?" Pax asks.

My voice seems stuck in my throat. "Yes."

"Tell me to stop at any time."

Whatever he—*they*—are offering, I desperately want.

I nod.

"Say it out loud," Link demands. "Give us the words."

Swallowing deeply, I meet Pax's eyes. "Yes," I whisper.

Approval flares in the depth of his gaze. Leaning down, Pax tugs on the knot holding my robe closed. Slowly the lapels part.

This is what I hunger for.

Pax's kiss is gentle at first, and I taste the smoky, rich undertones of his whiskey. His lips move against mine with a confidence that leaves me breathless, and I respond with an eagerness that surprises me.

His hands are firm but gentle as they frame my face, holding me in place as he deepens the kiss.

Behind me, Link's presence is solid and reassuring.

The contrast between the two men is stark—Pax's kiss is a bold statement, while Link's touch is a possessive promise.

Agonizingly he ends the kiss as Link begins to ease my robe from my shoulders.

The silk slides down my arms to pool at my feet.

I'm left standing in nothing but my sleep shorts and top, the cool air of the suite raising tiny bumps on my exposed skin.

Link skims his fingers across my shoulders, his touch lighting a trail of fire while Pax allows his gaze to travel my body, from bottom to top, appreciation clear in his eyes.

For the first time in forever, I feel desired, and more… safe.

"You are exquisite." Pax traces the V of my sleep shirt.

Instantly, just like in my dream, my nipples harden.

"So responsive."

Link wraps his arms around my waist and pulls me back against him.

His erection presses against me, making me gasp.

Holding my gaze captive, Pax captures the bottom of my shirt.

Suddenly I'm throbbing with need.

After pausing for only a second, he sweeps the silk up and off. Moments later, it floats downward, landing on my robe.

Instantly Link cups my breasts, brushing his thumbs over my sensitive nipples. I moan desperately as I arch into his touch.

Pax watches us, his eyes dark with desire.

Then, wordlessly, he drops to his knees before me.

Oh God.

This can*not* be real.

He places his hands on my waist. Then he hooks his fingers into the waistband of my shorts.

Lost, I tip my head back, surrendering to him. To them.

Even as Link continues to tease my nipples, Pax peels the fabric down my legs, leaving me completely exposed, vulnerable.

Then he presses a gentle kiss to my inner thigh, making me shake. I'm trapped in a vortex of sensation, my body aching for more.

"Tessa?" he asks, looking up at me.

"Please," I whisper, not entirely sure what I'm asking for, only knowing that I need something—something only they can give me.

Still massaging my breasts, Link presses his lips to the curve of my neck.

So, so wonderful.

Then he nips my sensitive skin.

With a groan, I tilt my head to the side, inadvertently giving him better access. I shouldn't want this, but I do.

Pax leans forward, and I automatically tense.

"Relax," Link whispers, continuing what he's doing, driving me wild.

With his fingers, Pax spreads my labia.

No man has ever touched me there.

Then he tastes my aching bundle of nerves.

Sensation rocks me, and I cry out.

Together, they explore my body, their hands and mouths mapping out every curve and hollow. I'm lost in a sea of pleasure, each touch, each kiss, pushing me higher and higher.

I don't know how to ask for what I want.

Yet my two men seem to know what that is even better than I do.

"We've got you," Link promises against my ear.

Pax circles my clit, each stroke deliberate and maddening as Link continues to pinch and roll my nipples. The slight sting of pain mixes with the pleasure Pax is so skillfully coaxing from my body. Together, they're driving me to the edge.

"Let go, Tessa." Link's voice is a seductive rumble.

At that instant, Pax increases the pressure, the rhythm, sending me spiraling. I cry out as an orgasm crashes into me, leaving me weak, my body vibrating.

As Link promised, they are both there for me.

He releases his grip to encircle my body, and Pax moves his hands to my hips, helping hold me steady.

As the aftershocks subside, I'm left shattered.

Gently Link turns me toward him, and he captures my lips in a searing, claiming kiss that steals what little breath I have left.

This time, it's Pax who moves in behind me, holding me captive between their two bodies.

"That was…" At a loss for words, I trail off.

"Just the beginning," Link finishes for me, his blue eyes filled with possession.

The dream had been stunning.

But reality is even more incredible.

"Think you can sleep now?" Link asks.

Staying awake would take more energy than I have.

Gently Pax scoops me from the floor and carries me toward my room.

He places me on the bed.

From where he's lounging against the door jamb, Link says, "Let us know if you need anything."

His words are suggestive, and my response is as well.

But I don't dare tell them what I really need…

"This time, little dove…" He pushes himself upright. "Dream about the honeymoon." After he pauses, "Because I'll be planning every single moment. Laying you bare to me…"

CHAPTER SEVENTEEN

Tessa

"And do you have rings?" Reverend Clara asks, looking between Link and me.

Rings?

What does it say that I never considered that we'd need them?

"We do," Link replies.

Blinking my surprise, I look at him. "We do?"

"For all of us." He looks at me. "I wouldn't have proposed without a ring."

"I hope it's just a plain gold band."

"Mm."

Which can mean anything from him. "Link, I mean it."

"Of course you do."

He strokes his thumb over the back of my hand in a soothing, reassuring touch that has me forgetting my own name.

Right now, Link, Pax, and I are seated in the Sky Chapel across from Clara, and Link has explained our unusual ceremony. And my men have reassured her that we all understand the actual legalities.

Because I had lots of dreams—all of them filled with memories of the night before with Link and Pax—I slept late. But when I joined the men, they had coffee waiting, and a full breakfast: fluffy eggs, bacon, sausage, waffles.

By the time we walked into the Sky Chapel to find preparations already underway for our ceremony, I was feeling awake and mostly human.

Though our chairs have not yet been covered in white fabric and wrapped with bows, there are already more than seventy seats that are decorated and waiting for our guests.

"And vows?"

Oh my God. I hadn't thought of that either.

"Will you have your own?" she asks. "Or we can make changes to traditional ones."

"I've written mine," Link says, stunning me once more.

Then he and Clara look at me. I have no idea what to say.

"Would you like me to send you some suggestions?" she offers.

"Please," I agree instantly.

"Feel free to make any changes, then send them to me before the ceremony starts."

I nod.

Just then, Nora enters, carrying her pad, wearing a black dress and sensible pumps.

After greetings are exchanged, she issues half a dozen orders.

"Mr. Merritt, Mr. Gallagher, you'll be in the room off to the side." She points. "Over there."

When they nod, she goes on, "At exactly seven, your song will begin playing. You'll enter and stand in front of the minister, facing the door. Tessa, that's when you and I will leave the bridal room. We'll have about two minutes, give or take.

She has memorized every detail, down to the second, it seems.

"I've arranged for the bridal room to be available at three o'clock."

Why so early? "Four hours before the ceremony?"

"Allowing time for hair and makeup."

"I—"

"I took the liberty of seeing to that," Link interrupts. "You're okay with that, darling?"

Left to my own devices, I really might have looked like the Cinderella before her fairy godmother showed up.

Nora finishes by adding that my gown and a woman from the shop will arrive an hour in advance. "Any specific foods or beverages you'd like to have in the room?"

"Chocolate. Everything on the menu."

She smiles. "Consider it done."

"Along with an assortment of other snacks," Link amends.

"Absolutely, Mr. Merritt. Any questions before we take our places?"

When no one speaks up, she nods. "Tessa, you can go out into the hallway."

"Absolutely not," Pax replies.

The woman blinks at his quick, ruthless response. Even I'm taken aback.

"Tessa can wait at the back of the room."

"Of course."

Cupping my elbow, Pax guides me to a spot near the door. "Don't go outside."

"Torin and Mira are here, though."

"But they're the only ones close."

How many people are needed for him to feel secure?

"Tell me you understand."

Even though he's overreacting, I nod.

"Thank you."

He's as demanding as Link, and yet totally different at the same time.

A few minutes later, I'm walking down the aisle toward them, and they look at me expectantly, even though it's just practice.

The reverend says, "At the end I'll pronounce you married. Would you like me to announce the reception?"

Nora responds. "It'll be in the Sky Ballroom."

"Perfect. At that point, I'll introduce you to the guests as Mr. and Mrs. Merritt, if that's okay?"

I haven't even considered whether to change my name or not.

"That's fine," Link replies, a possessive growl in his voice, as if daring anyone to contradict him.

If it's a battle I want to fight, I'll do it later.

"And then you can make your way back up the aisle."

"Will you be having a receiving line?" Nora asks.

"Yes."

Link seems to want every single piece of a traditional wedding ceremony. I'd be okay without any of them.

After we wrap up, Link tells me he's arranged for me to enjoy a spa day. "Facial, massage, manicure, pedicure."

"I've actually never had any of those."

"First of many."

Mira and Torin are off for several hours since they'll be providing security all night. And I'm introduced to two female agents who will be in the spa with me.

"Unobtrusively," Pax adds.

If that's possible.

I'm treated to an amazing, relaxing massage with hot stones, easing tension from my shoulders and neck.

Hours later, I've had a light lunch, my fingernails are buffed and shaped, and my toes are painted a pale shade of pink. The color is neutral enough to go with my shoes and wedding dress, but it will also complement the sundresses Link bought me.

Afterward I take my host's suggestion and head for the private pool. I'm the only one there, so I snag one of the cabanas and stretch out on a luxuriously padded chaise.

I'm wrapped in one of the spa's robes, eyes closed beneath the overhead fan. Because of it and the palm trees, the temperature feels perfect, relaxing.

"Champagne, ma'am?"

I open my eyes to see Link standing there, a glass of bubbly in hand.

Pushing myself up on my elbows, I look at him. "What are you doing here?"

"Making sure everything's okay."

"Perfect. Thank you for today." Otherwise I might have spent the entire afternoon worrying, pacing, a bundle of nerves.

He places the glass on a table next to me, alongside the glass of water that has cucumber floating in it. I have to admit, the bubbly sounds much more appealing.

As he turns to leave, he bends to drop a kiss on my lips.

In that instant, all the memories from last night flood back, leaving me breathless.

"Only a few hours until the world knows you're mine." Everything he says turns me inside out.

After he leaves, I leisurely sip my beverage, and I half doze until my phone chimes with the alarm I set.

I have just enough time to return to our suite to take a quick shower.

Pax insists on accompanying me to the bridal room.

There's a table off to the side that has an entire platter of croissant sandwiches cut into halves, a cheese and meat tray, and a tower filled with chocolate desserts.

As if that wasn't enough, there are bowls filled with wrapped, bite-size chocolates.

There's water, tea, a coffee service, and the ingredients for mimosas.

This hotel goes over the top on everything. Or is it just for certain people? A billionaire like Link Merritt who personally knows the owner?

Along with a private bathroom, the space has a plush sofa and several chairs, probably for ladies with their own entourage. I wish I had someone. Anyone.

"What number do you press for me?" Pax asks me.

Resisting the impulse to sigh, I say, "Two. One for Link. Three for Hawkeye."

"Or you can scream." He shrugs. "You'll get more attention than you know what to do with."

I grin. Then it fades quickly as I realize he's not kidding.

Like Link had, he drops a kiss on my lips.

They're both so commanding, self-assured.

"If you need anything, we're only moments away."

"I'll be fine."

He leaves, and I'm alone with Ariella—a Hawkeye agent—and the hair stylist. The makeup artist will evidently be here a little while later.

"Please," I tell them both, "eat and drink. Otherwise it will go to waste." Well, except for the bowl of chocolates.

Because the hair stylist wants to cause as little damage to her creation as possible, she has me change into a pale pink satiny robe that has the word Bride blazed across the back. Then she asks for a picture of my gown.

I appreciate how thoughtful she is, not just about what I want, but also the entire design.

Right as she's about to start, there's a soft knock.

Because I am not expecting anyone, I glance back at the Hawkeye agent.

"It's clear, ma'am," the woman assures me.

Does that mean that no random person can even get close?

"Surprise!" The door bursts open.

"Oh my God! Nat!" With a quick apology to the stylist, I jump out of the chair and rush to my friend, hugging her, laughing, demanding to know what she's doing here.

"Link made me keep this a secret."

Her being here fills me with comfort and joy, and I've never been more grateful to see anyone.

"He flew me and David in. Can you believe it?"

Tears sting my eyes.

All of a sudden, my day is brighter, and I know I'll get through the next few hours. "How long are you here for?"

"Two full days after this. And your man put us up here. So luxe."

"You look beautiful." And she does, in a figure-hugging dress and earrings that actually match.

"It's borrowed. A bit too small, but David isn't complaining." She giggles.

"It's fabulous on you."

"Thank you, darling," she says, breaking the final word into two pieces, making it sound like dah-ling.

Then she pours mimosas for us and the stylist.

Ariella, unsurprisingly, refuses. But I can't help but notice the way she eyes the brownies.

After replenishing the chocolate supply in front of me, Natalie chatters nonstop, about all kinds of different things, even pulling the hair stylist into the conversation. When she's finished, Nat is equally engaging with the makeup artist.

"Lawd, Tess, you have to try this," Natalie says, bringing over a decadent-looking chocolate truffle.

The rich, velvety sweetness melts on my tongue, and I close my eyes in bliss. "You're going to have to roll me down the aisle if I eat any more of these."

"Betting you will work off the calories later tonight," she says with a wicked grin.

"Nat!" I protest, but I can't help laughing. "You're terrible!"

Remorseless, she refills mimosas all around.

Right on time, a woman from the bridal store arrives with my gown, shoes, and veil.

I slip on the sandals, and then she and Natalie help me into the dress.

Finally the stylist moves back in to attach the veil to my updo.

And we have almost half an hour to spare.

"My God," Nat says. "You look like a princess. Truly, truly."

"That's sweet of you."

"Honesty."

She's so sincere I almost believe her.

"Thank you. And thank you for being here."

"I wouldn't have missed it."

Except for Natalie, everyone leaves. And the clock keeps moving forward.

Butterflies start to dance in my tummy.

There's a knock on the door, and Ariella opens it, admitting a woman with a camera.

With tons of confidence, she strides over to me. "I'm Marcella. You must be the future Mrs. Merritt."

Will I ever get used to thinking of myself in those terms?

"If you don't mind, I'd like to take a few photos."

"I'll get out of here," Natalie says.

"No, no." Marcella shakes her head. "These are your memories, Tessa. I'm sure you'd like a few snaps with your friend."

"I would."

She gets several candids of me and Nat. Then she reviews them before nodding. "Thanks. They're great."

"Now I'll get going." Natalie gives me a quick hug. "I wish you a lifetime of happiness."

"Thank you." I have no real idea what that means. Since that awful event in the parking lot, I've been focused only on the next moment.

"I need to get to my seat. I promised David I wouldn't leave him all alone."

"I'm looking forward to meeting him."

Marcella goes into work mode, posing me several different ways, standing, sitting, gazing into a mirror, sipping a mimosa.

Once more, she reviews her work. "These are what I was looking for." She smiles. "Link's a lucky man. See you in there."

I've barely exhaled when the door opens again, and Link barges in.

Dressed in a tailored tuxedo, he's glorious. Devilishly handsome and oh-so addicting.

"It's bad luck to see the bride before the wedding," I manage, even as my pulse races.

"I'll take my chances."

A minute ago, I was nervous, but now I'm swept up in him.

In several confident strides, he crosses to me, and he captures my shoulders.

"No fucking way was I waiting another minute to see you." With that, he sweeps his gaze over me.

His riveting blue eyes are filled with adoration.

Or maybe I'm making that up.

But right now, I don't care if I am.

"You're stunning," he murmurs, leaning in.

"Don't wreck my makeup," I warn. "I've spent four hours trying to look pretty for you."

"Little dove, to light up the world, you just have to be in a room."

Does he always know the right thing to say?

He looks back at the Hawkeye agent. "Leave us, please."

"Wait!"

She stops and looks back at me. "Ma'am?"

"Take some brownies."

"Some…?" She shakes her head. "I'm on duty."

"For a few minutes, you're not."

Link inclines his head. "Sounds like my future wife gave an order."

"But—"

"Take a brownie," I tell her again. "At least one."

She grins. "Thank you." Before leaving, she breaks a piece of one and pops it in her mouth.

Moments later, we're alone, and my pulse adds a few extra beats. "Link…"

"I figured you might be nervous."

More so than I ever imagined.

"So I brought a gift."

"No." I shake my head. "You've already done too much, and—"

"I insist." He releases me and reaches into a pocket inside his tuxedo jacket and pulls out a lacy white garter. "Wear it for me?"

His *gift* and question fluster me.

In typical Link fashion, he doesn't wait for an answer. Instead he lowers himself to one knee in front of me.

"What…?"

"Put your hands on my shoulders." With that, he lifts the front of my gown. Then he strokes up the inside of my thighs.

"Link!"

"Such pretty panties. I'll buy you dozens more like them," he says, as if I haven't protested.

Without warning, he dips inside the gusset and strokes my clit.

Desperately, I grab hold of his shoulders.

"Would you like an orgasm, little dove?"

Oh God. "No." *Yes.*

"No?" he asks. "Then why are you getting wet for me?"

I don't answer.

Can't answer.

"So silky." He continues his exquisite torment, sliding in and out, making me wetter with each slow stroke. Then he brushes over my clit with my own dampness.

"Oh..."

"Shall I stop?" He looks up at me.

"Link…"

He moves his hand away from my pussy, but he's still inside my underwear.

I whimper.

"Tell me what you want."

"More."

"You want me to bring you off?"

Embarrassed, I squeeze my eyes shut.

"Yes."

Once more, he brushes my clit, and I pitch forward. Desperately I hold onto him.

"Ask me for it, little dove. Beg me. Use your prettiest words."

I'm scandalized. Horrified.

And needy enough to do what he demands. "Please."

He parts my labia.

Gulping in a breath of air, I manage, "I…"

He makes a lazy, gentle circle on my clit. It's enough to drive me mad and not enough for anything else.

"Time is ticking."

As if I need to be reminded that the ceremony will start momentarily.

"Shall I stop?" But he slides inside again, reminding me what I'll be missing out on if I agree. "Little dove?"

"Keep going," I plead.

"You know what I want to hear."

Is the beast seriously going to make me beg?

Maddeningly he stops all his movements.

And I'm desperate enough that I may give into his terrible demand. "Please," I whisper again.

Confounding man does nothing.

I sigh. Then because I'm throbbing with desire, and I know I'll think of nothing else until we're back in our suite tonight, I repeat myself. "Please. Please, Link. I want you to make me come. I'm pleading with you. I want this."

Gently he touches me.

"I want you."

"Oh, little dove. How dangerous you'd be if you knew your power over me."

Focused on only me, he continues what he was doing, as if we have hours to spare.

Within seconds, though, I'm on the edge. "Link…"

"Tell me." His voice is guttural, demanding.

"I'm about to climax."

He leans in and moves the crotch of my panties to the side to lick me as he continues to finger-fuck me.

Stunned, I glance down to see the top of his head as he arouses me.

The eroticism of the moment, the licking, tasting… Everything is too much.

Weak, I bend my knees, opening myself more, begging now without words.

"That's it."

His breath is hot, and his tongue is pure pleasure. Suddenly a swirling inferno engulfs me.

"Come for me." He slides a second finger alongside the first.

That sensation, along with his mouth, are too much.

I tighten my grip on him. He's made me forget everything but him and this moment, and I'm all but fucking his face.

An orgasm ricochets through me, igniting all of my nerve endings.

He helps me to ride it before he gently eases from inside me. Then he places a whisper of a kiss on my lower belly.

Even that is enough to ripple aftershocks through my system.

"Pick up your foot."

Since I'm reeling from what we shared, it takes a moment for his words to filter through my haze.

When he taps my ankle, his instruction finally takes hold. He moves my foot onto his thigh.

I obey, and he slips the garter up my leg and settles it on my thigh. Then he nips the sensitive skin above it, making me yelp.

"Link!"

Apparently satisfied, he flips my dress back into place. Then I lower my foot.

He stands but thankfully keeps his hands on my waist until I stop swaying.

"Your panties are damp. You have two choices. Leave them that way or take them off and give them to me."

Speechless, I gape.

"Or I'll make the choice for you."

"I'll keep them on," I say quickly.

"That's unfortunate." My wicked husband-to-be grins.

His eyes intent with purpose, he leans in close, then closer, and he pulls me against him.

His kiss is demanding. He tastes of determination and my climax.

I've never experienced anything like this. It's hot. Erotic. Dirty.

He ruins my lipstick and leaves the room spinning.

"In case you still had any doubts that you belong to me," he murmurs.

Then he's gone, leaving me breathless and tingling all over.

With my hand shaking, I touch up my lipstick as best I can.

Before I'm quite ready, Nora arrives, her trusty pad in hand. Another woman who is carrying my bouquet accompanies her. Ariella re-enters the room right behind them.

As I smooth the front of my skirt, I blush. Does everyone know what I—what we—have been up to?

"Your gown is perfect on you," Nora enthuses.

"Eloise is amazing."

Nora waves away my words. "The bride makes the dress." When I start to protest, she goes on, "Why else would we need models?"

She adjusts my veil, then takes the flowers from the assistant and hands them to me.

The arrangement is gorgeous and bigger than I could have imagined, and I am grateful to have something to occupy my hands.

"Link and Pax"—Nora checks her watch—"will be entering the chapel in one minute."

Which means it's time for us to leave.

Taking a deep breath, I nod.

"You do look amazing, ma'am," Ariella says.

"Thank you for everything." *Especially for not saying anything when Link stormed in here.*

Right on time, we arrive at the Sky Chapel.

The grooms' arrival song ends, and there's a pause.

"This is your moment," Nora says.

The opening notes of "A Thousand Years" begin.

At the front of the room, facing me, stands Link, Pax, and Reverend Clara.

"Please stand for the bride," Clara says.

CHAPTER EIGHTEEN

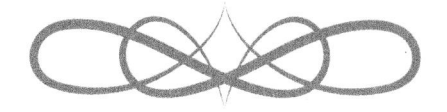

Tessa

For a moment, I am frozen in place.

And then I feel the heat of Link's gaze on me.

With two fingers, he beckons me and mouths the words, *"Come to us."*

He's both encouraging and commanding.

Drawing strength from him, I shove aside my sudden fears and doubts to take my first steps down the aisle toward him. *Them.*

Even though I thought the hotel staff had set up too many chairs, we have enough guests to fill the room.

Of course, I know almost none of the people who are looking at me.

As I near the front, I miss a step.

Marge is there, snapping pictures with her phone. She lowers the device to smile at me.

Link thought to invite her as well?

Instinctively I look to him, and my heart melts a little.

Even though Link has run roughshod over me, my almost

husband has done everything he possibly can to make the experience as wonderful as possible for me.

I continue on, seeing Natalie and David in the first row. On the other side is Lorenzo next to a beautiful woman. His wife, I guess.

Outside the plate-glass window, sunset has painted the sky a stunning mixture of pinks and purples.

As I near the devastatingly handsome men, the world fades away, and I no longer hear the music.

Instead of waiting for me, Pax strides toward me. In his tailored tuxedo jacket, he seems broader than ever.

"Tessa…" He smiles down at me. Then he offers his arm.

Grateful, I tuck mine inside of his.

When we reach Link, Pax surprises me by staying next to me instead of moving to stand in the traditional best-man position.

Both men are standing protectively by my side.

Link leans forward and brushes his lips against mine.

Reverend Clara laughs softly. "I'm afraid you've got the order of service wrong."

"No." Link shakes his head. "I've got it exactly right, Reverend."

Our guests laugh, and my tension shatters.

"You're welcome to be seated," Reverend Clara tells our guests.

Moments later, she begins the ceremony. "Thank you for joining us to celebrate the future and union of Tessa, Link, and Pax."

I'm stunned that they're bold in this pronouncement that we are a triad.

"They'd like to thank you for being here to witness and share in one of the greatest moments of their lives. Marriage is a bond based on trust, respect, and mutual support and the blending of lives into a shared path. As they embark on this journey together, we are gathered to offer them our encouragement and support."

After looking at all of us, she continues. "I will ask the three of you, as you stand before your friends and associates, to declare your commitment to one another. Your promises are a reflection of the life you will build together."

We form a semicircle.

"Link?" the reverend prompts.

"Tessa, I pledge my life to you. I stand here with you, at your side, because fate has woven our paths together. What began as a necessity has turned into something more. I vow to protect you. My strength is yours to rely on. I pledge my loyalty."

For a man who was rumored to have dated half the women in the world, his promise surprises me.

Realizing he's still speaking, I shake my head to bring myself back to the present.

"Together we are stronger, and today I promise to uphold our bond, no matter what may come."

The words aren't meant to be ominous, I'm sure, but a shiver goes through me.

Reverend Clara looks to Pax.

He takes my hand in his much bigger, stronger one. "We didn't begin this journey the way others do, but that makes it no less meaningful. I will stand as your protector and keep you safe in ways seen and unseen. My commitment is to your well-being and to the future we will create together. I will watch over you, fight for you, and be the calm in whatever storm we face. Today I pledge my life to you."

I'm breathless, lost in the vows these men have created.

It's my turn, and Pax offers a reassuring smile.

Link lifts his hand, palm up.

I slide mine against his.

Then Pax closes his hand on top. The three of us are bound together.

"Link, Pax, I never imagined I'd be here with you like this." My voice falters, and they both offer their support.

After a small exhalation, I manage to continue. "I promise to stand with you both. I will respect and honor you always."

"Do you have Tessa's ring?" the minister asks.

Pax pulls out a massive oval cut diamond ring from inside his jacket.

I gasp as he hands it over to Link.

I knew he wouldn't settle for a plain band, but this is over the top,

"The wedding ring is an unbroken circle with no beginning, no end," she goes on, "representing your eternal commitment to one another. Link, repeat after me..."

A few moments later, he takes my hand and looks me in the eye. "I give you this ring as a symbol of my commitment."

This stunning gem sparkles in the light as he slides it onto my finger. I can't help but stare at its magnificence.

It seems to weigh a ton, much like the obligations we've just made to each other.

Pax offers me a ring to slip on to Link's finger, and I follow the officiant's lead. "Link, I give you this ring as a symbol of my commitment to you."

Then Link gives me a band for Pax and I repeat my vow to him.

Reverend Clara smiles. "I now pronounce the three of you partners in life."

My world seems to tip off balance.

"You may now kiss the bride."

But Link has already moved in, and the buzzing in my head drowns out her words.

No way is he waiting for an invitation to claim what is his in the eyes of the law...

CHAPTER NINETEEN

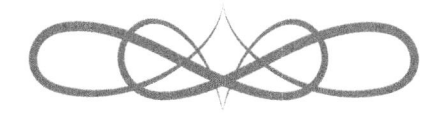

Tessa

"What are you doing?" I demand as Pax places his fingers against the small of my back and guides me away from the chapel's foyer.

"Taking you somewhere private."

"But—"

"We're starting the honeymoon early."

I gasp. "You can't do this."

"Who's going to stop me?"

"Pax!" There's no reasoning with him. "We have guests."

"All of whom have seen you, how beautiful you look. Not one of them would blame us for wanting a few minutes alone with you."

This is crazy, impossible. This gorgeous bodyguard is as determined and unswayable as Link is.

At the entrance to the bridal room, Ariella opens the door, looks inside, then nods at Pax and resumes her position.

Torin and Mira are still with Link, and I understand other agents have moved to the place where the cocktail hour is being hosted.

"No one but Merritt is allowed inside," he informs the agent.

"Yes, sir."

Moments later, we're sealed inside.

"Seriously," I say, pulling away from Pax and turning to face him. "We can't do this."

"Oh yes, we can." He grins wolfishly. "And will."

I shake my head. "You're impossible."

"Might as well relax for a few minutes until Link joins us."

Since I walked out of this room, I've been swept into a flurry of activity.

After the ceremony, Link had kissed me deeply—indecently so—as people cheered. In the background, I was hyperaware of Marcella snapping dozens of photos.

The moment we were in the foyer area, attendees started filing out, which didn't leave the three of us even a moment of alone time.

For at least half an hour, I honestly believed the receiving line would never end. I've never shaken so many hands in my life. I met people whose names I'll never remember, and others I know are important to Link or Pax.

One bright spot was hugging Marge and hearing her promise that she was staying for at least a little bit of the reception.

Then Natalie introduced me to David, who was lovely and seemed to give my friend plenty of attention.

I was happy to see Lorenzo and meet his wife, Zara. And of course, Hawkeye was there, along with the mysterious Inamorata.

Pax is right. A moment to relax in some peace and quiet might not be all bad.

But I know they have something in store for me, and that anticipation makes me tingle.

"Looks as if there's still an unopened bottle of champagne over here."

"It was for the mimosas. So it might not be up to your standards."

"I'm not as much of a wine snob as Link."

I fake gasp. "Don't tell me you even drink beer."

He lifts one shoulder and flashes a grin. "On occasion."

As always, around him I relax, though I should know better.

His movements silent and stealthy, Pax crosses to the side table, pulls the bottle from its now-melted ice bath, then removes the cork. He pours two glasses.

"You're serious about this?"

"Meaning exercising our conjugal rights?" he asks with a grin.

Heat rushes up my face.

Do they really intend to make love to me here, or do they plan to drive me mad once more?

"I'm sure we'll be missed."

"Link and Nora are directing everyone to the open bar. I promise you; no one is upset."

He offers me one of the flutes, which I gratefully accept.

A moment later, Link strolls in, all restrained masculine energy and devilish good looks.

In a quick move, he locks the door behind him.

Being in the Sky Chapel with them is one thing, but being in a small room and seeing the determined gleams in both of their eyes is another entirely.

"Where were you?" he asks.

"Getting ready for a toast." Pax pauses. "Before other things."

Needing to settle my sudden flush of nerves, I swallow a big drink.

Once he's poured himself a glass, he joins us. "To our future."

The three of us tap our glasses together, then take a sip.

Link lifts his upper lip. "We'll do this again later tonight with a decent vintage."

"I told Pax you wouldn't approve."

"It's the Bella Rosa, so it's tolerable."

To me, the champagne tastes divine, though I do admit it doesn't compare to the bottle he bought at Maestro's. Of course, this one probably costs less than half of the brand he prefers.

Pax regards me. "I understand Link put something on your leg before the ceremony."

The garter?

Pax plucks the glass from my hand. Then he places both of them back on the table before moving toward the mirror. "Come here, Tessa."

Nervous with excitement and anticipation, I move to the spot he indicates.

With a nod, he says, "Lift up your dress for me, Tessa."

His tone is so uncompromising that it never occurs to me not to follow his command.

"Higher," he instructs when I reach knee level. "I want it up over your hips."

Since it's a sheath, I have to wiggle in order to do what he says.

He stands in front of me, then lowers himself to his knees and trails his fingers up the outside of my legs, sending shivers down my spine as he helps raise the fabric higher.

Watching my own expression is unnerving.

Moments later, Link places his glass alongside ours.

I see him in the mirror, directly behind me, his expression unreadable.

Then he shocks me by kneeling behind me.

I have no idea what's going on, but Pax's warm breath tickles my thigh as he leans in closer, his lips just grazing the delicate lace.

With a tantalizing slowness, Pax uses his teeth to tease the garter down my leg. The act is electrifying, every touch sending a jolt of pleasure through me.

Link's hands are on my back, providing a reassuring touch.

As the tiny scrap of material finally falls around my ankle, I gasp.

Pax captures my foot and lifts it to slip off the lacy scrap.

Hunger in his eyes, he pockets it.

I've heard of a groom removing the bride's garter, but never like this.

"Now the panties," Link says.

What?

"You want me to take them off?" I ask, hating that I can't see his expression.

"No. Not at all. We're spoiling you."

They are planning to remove them?

Link hooks his fingers in the waistband of the fabric.

My knees weaken, forcing me to grab Pax's shoulders for stability.

Pax eases his hands up my thighs, his fingers dancing on my skin.

I can't believe this is happening. Excitement and desire whirl inside me, crashing into my nervousness to create a potent cocktail.

He looks up at me, his dark eyes laced with primal desire.

Both men hook their fingers inside the waistband of my silk panties and gently ease them over my hipbones.

They work together to slide them down my thighs, a torturous inch at a time.

Pax's touch lingers on me, as if he's memorizing every curve and dip.

The air is cool against my skin, and I'm vulnerable and exposed.

When the material is finally at my ankles, Pax taps my right foot.

Obediently I lift it. Once the material is free, I raise the other.

"I'll take those." Link's tone is firm.

He leans to the side a little, so that I can watch as he lifts the material to his nose. "That scent... Of you, your arousal..."

I'm scandalized.

"From earlier?" he asks. "Before the ceremony? Or from what Pax just did?"

"I..."

"Be honest, wife. Otherwise you might earn a spanking."

I dig my fingers into Pax's muscular shoulders. *A spanking?* Link can't be serious. Yet his features are set, and there's no hint of teasing in his voice.

Would he really do that?

Pax's hands, still on my thighs, begin to move upward again, his thumbs tracing circles on my inner thighs. I can't look away from the reflection of Link in the mirror, holding my panties, his gaze locked on mine.

"You might want to answer him, Tessa," Pax murmurs, his voice a low rumble as his fingers inch closer to my most intimate place.

"Both," I admit, my voice barely a whisper. "From before and from just now."

Link's eyes darken, and he nods, a small smile playing on his lips. "Such honesty. That's our good girl," he praises.

His outrageous words send pleasure through me.

Pax's fingers reach the apex of my thighs, and I gasp as he parts my folds, exposing me. I'm aching with need. He runs a finger along my slit, gathering my dampness, then brings it to his mouth, tasting me.

I whimper.

Pax wraps one arm around my waist to steady me while his other hand explores my pussy, spreading my wetness, circling my clit.

With each touch, pressure builds in my body.

Link stands and tucks my panties in his slacks' pocket.

He comes around to stand in front of me, next to Pax, who moves to the side but doesn't stop what he's doing.

"You're so wet for me, Tessa. For us," he murmurs, his voice like steel wrapped in silk. "Is this what you want? Both of us touching you, fucking you?"

I nod, my breath coming in short gasps. Pax's fingers are magical, dancing over my sensitive flesh, driving me wild. "Oh…"

Then he slides a finger inside me. In total pleasure, I whimper. "Yes," I plead, my hips moving in time with Pax's hand. Was it only earlier that I was speechless when Link demanded I beg? Now it seems so natural.

"Open your mouth," Link demands.

When I do, he sticks his finger inside. "Get it wet."

I swirl my tongue, doing as he says.

"That's it. Very nice, little dove."

Link eases his finger from my mouth and moves it between my legs. He can't mean to…

Even while Pax is pleasuring me, Link eases inside me too, impossibly stretching and filling me.

I'm surrounded by them, consumed by their touches, their scent, their heat.

Pax and Link thrust in and out, their rhythms steady and relentless.

It's all too much, and yet... Will I ever get enough of them?

I'm sucking in desperate gulps of air, my body coiling tighter with each stroke. "I've... I need..."

"Tell us," Link demands.

Words fail me.

"To come?" Pax suggests, his voice low and sexy.

"Please."

Link groans, a sensual, promising sound. "You're perfect."

Their movements, the way Pax presses harder against my clit... I thrust toward them, my orgasm building.

"Come for us, Tessa," Link whispers in my ear, his voice commanding. "Let us see you fall apart."

They move faster, their fingers fucking me, their strokes more insistent.

A wave of pleasure threatens to crash over me.

"That's it." Link's voice is a deep growl.

I'm lost.

With a scream, I come, my body convulsing as the pleasure crests over me.

Link props a palm beneath my head to support it, and he claims my mouth.

They slow slightly, drawing out my orgasm.

Finally I'm worn out, sated, and my body goes weak, but Link is there to catch me, just like he's always been. Somehow both of his arms are around me, and he holds me up.

Pax gently pulls out. With his gaze capturing mine, he tastes me.

They're both so sexy and bold, and I can't imagine making love with any other man.

"That was just the beginning, wife," Link promises. "To

give you a hint of what will happen as soon as we can get you away from the reception."

A wild part of me that I don't recognize wonders if we can skip attending.

"Ready to face our guests?"

CHAPTER TWENTY

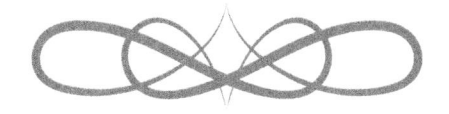

Tessa

"Ladies and gentlemen!"

Holding hands, my husbands and I have just entered the cocktail party, and we pause inside the wide-open double doors.

I'm stunned to see internet billionaire sensation Jaxon Mills on a small stage, acting as our emcee and at least double the number of people who attended the ceremony.

"Smile," Link coaches.

"Please welcome Link Merritt, Pax Gallagher, and their beautiful bride, Tessa Merritt!"

On either side of me, my husbands raise my hands, and our guests turn to cheer and clap.

For someone who has tried to hide for so long, being seen like this is still surreal.

From in front of us, Marcella repeatedly snaps the shutter on her camera, just like she had when we emerged from the bridal room a few minutes ago.

My hair is a mess, with curls framing my cheeks and

several cascading down my back. It must be obvious what the three of us were up to while people were waiting.

But I don't have a moment to think about that.

Finally they allow me to lower my arms.

"Show time," Link says.

"We'll stay with you," Pax promises.

Good thing. I'm not sure I could navigate this without them.

The reception line should have helped me remember who people are, but I'm drowning in a sea of names and faces.

Maybe that shouldn't surprise me. After what my husbands just did to me, I can barely recall who I am.

The first people we make our way toward are Lorenzo and Zara.

Obviously Link is strategic with the way we're greeting people.

As we approach, Lorenzo raises his champagne flute in greeting. Zara is sipping what appears to be soda water with lime. Which makes sense as I recall Link asking how their baby daughter is doing.

Zara hugs me. "You've got your hands full with this pair."

Link shrugs in agreement.

Lorenzo shakes hands with my men, then acknowledges me.

"Thank you for coming," Link says beside me, his voice warm with genuine affection. "Zara, we're delighted you could get away."

"We're so happy to have shared your celebration," Zara says. "Forgive us if we don't stay much longer."

"Gabriella's waiting for us at home. This is one of Zara's first outings."

With a laugh, she looks at her husband. "You should see this one with her," she says, nudging Lorenzo playfully. He responds by sliding his arm around her waist and easing her closer. "Gabriella has her daddy wrapped around her little finger. It's adorable."

Lorenzo doesn't even try to deny it.

This formidable man lights up at the mere mention of his daughter.

"What can I say? I'm powerless against her beautiful eyes. Reminds me of my *principessa*." He smiles at Zara. Then he returns his attention to us. "Your guests are waiting."

"I hope to spend more time with you in the future," I tell Zara, and I mean it. She's warm and inviting.

"If you are in Las Vegas long enough, I'd love to have you come and meet Gabriella."

I look to Link. "I'd like that."

Gently Link's hand returns to my back, and he guides me toward three men who are standing in a circle.

As we approach the trio, their conversation halts. They part to allow us space to join them, and their attention turns to us.

Even though I technically met all of them immediately after the ceremony, I really don't know who they are. Maybe because of that—or maybe because of the fog still shrouding me—I can't recall names.

They shake hands with my husbands and offer their congratulations before Link once more places his hand on my back, a comforting presence as I face these powerful figures.

Then he more formally introduces me.

"Altair Montgomery," Link says.

Even in the warm glow of the reception lighting, there's something powerfully otherworldly about him and the depth of his gaze. His handshake is firm but cool.

"Charmed, Mrs. Merritt," he says, his voice smooth as silk and compelling as any I've ever heard. His eyes are dark, fathomless. "Your ceremony was delightful."

"Thank you. But I can't take credit. Link planned most of it."

"Indeed?" Altair asks.

"Altair owns the Retreat." After a short pause, Link goes on. "A BDSM club in downtown Houston."

Unable to respond, I blink.

BDSM?

My mind spins back to Link's pseudothreat to spank me. I'd told myself he must have been kidding.

But what if he wasn't?

No doubt he's attended in the past.

But will he want to go in the future? With me?

Butterflies—nerves unlike any I've ever experienced—dance through me.

Next I'm reintroduced to Dorian Vale. His billion-dollar smile is disarming, but there's a calculated gleam in his eyes that speaks of ambition beyond mere wealth.

"Tessa, it's a pleasure to spend more than fifteen seconds with you." In contrast to Altair, his handshake is warm but very firm, radiating power. "I see why you enchanted the notorious Lincoln."

He releases me, the gemstones in his ring flash, and I take a second look.

If I'm not mistaken, the design on the front is an owl, and the stones for its eyes are emeralds. According to *Scandalicious,* that's the symbol of the Zeta Society whose members are known as Titans.

A coincidence?

"Your husband is the only man I know who is more cutthroat than Vale," Altair tells me.

Dorian flashes a lethal smile, a predator's warning poorly disguised as charm.

Link introduces Brennan West, who I am sure did not come through the receiving line.

The man exudes an air of barely leashed danger. A jagged scar runs from his left temple to his jaw. But it's his eyes that truly unsettle me—steel gray and penetrating, as if he can see right through me to every secret I've ever kept.

Though he's not at all like the man my brother tried to sell me to, he terrifies me just the same.

"Mrs. Merritt," he says, his voice a low growl that sends goose bumps racing across my skin. When he takes my hand, I have to resist the urge to pull away. His grip is neither too tight nor lingering, but I'm glad when he releases me.

"Brennan's been instrumental in some of our more...delicate business matters," Pax explains.

Pax is menacing enough. I can't imagine a situation where they'd need to call on someone even more cutthroat.

I force a smile. "It's nice to meet you, Mr. West."

"Brennan," he corrects. "I don't stand on formality."

"I'm glad you joined us," Altair says. "I'm trying to convince Vale to run for governor or the senate."

It takes no imagination to picture Dorian in such a position of power. He wears authority as easily as his impeccably tailored suit.

"That'll cost tens of millions of dollars," Pax muses.

Altair nods. "He can self-fund."

"Always an advantage," Link adds, his tone neutral but his eyes sharp.

"There are many of us poised to contribute," Altair states.

These men, this inner circle, wield influence far beyond what I'd imagined. How can it be possible this kind of conversation is happening at my wedding reception?

"There are...issues in my past."

"That's what fixers are for," Altair counters, and my gaze is drawn back to Brennan, who has responded with a nod.

I wonder just how many secrets this man has buried.

A server passes, and Link asks if I would like a drink.

I nod, grateful for something to occupy my hands.

"I'm happy to set up a meeting with Everett Parker," Link offers. "Worth at least considering. Let him vet you."

Dorian doesn't respond.

Into the silence, Altair says, "I'll be hosting an event at the end of October. I'll send an invite." Altair's gaze slides back to me. "Be sure to bring your wife."

The way he says it—a command, not a request—makes me once more acutely aware of the world I've married into.

I look at Link.

Will he comply with Altair's wishes?

CHAPTER TWENTY-ONE

Tessa

I can't shake the feeling that I've just been granted a glimpse behind a very dangerous curtain.

Link's touch is as reassuring as it is possessive. He and Pax have offered their protection, but also I'm now part of this world of shadows and secrets.

I take another sip of champagne, steeling myself for whatever comes next. One thing is certain: life with Link and Pax will never be boring.

"If you'll excuse us, gentlemen," Link says.

As we move away, I let out a breath I didn't realize I'd been holding.

"You did wonderfully." Link strokes my spine, but I don't relax. "Little dove?" he asks.

"Are you…?"

He considers me.

"I mean…"

I'm flustered, blushing, but he waits.

"Will you want to attend his club?"

"Absolutely."

My legs don't want to support me.

"We'll do everything to ensure your comfort. But you will be with us on our next visit."

His expression is implacable, his words flat, a proclamation that doesn't allow for arguing.

I look to Pax, and he doesn't contradict Link.

Why didn't I know this before we were married? Before it was too late?

What seems like an hour later, Nora checks in with us to let us know it's time to be seated for dinner. Since my feet have started to hurt and a smile seems to be frozen in place, I'm grateful.

"Have Jax make the announcement."

Once everyone has found their chairs, the three of us enter the ballroom.

In addition to another two people, a judge is seated at our table, near me.

As he picks up his water glass, gemstones in his ring dance in the candlelight. The exact same ring Dorian was wearing.

Any doubt I had that the Titans were real vanishes. Whether Pax will admit the truth or not, evidence is hiding in plain sight.

Dinner is a ridiculous affair, multiple courses with wine pairings. Thankfully it passes in a blur.

In a way, being with these gazillionaires isn't a lot different than being a cocktail waitress who's hustling for tips...except here, no one grabs my ass.

Then I remember what happened right after the ceremony.

Well, no one except my husbands.

Realizing the judge is talking to me, I force my wayward thoughts back to the conversation.

Smile, I remind myself, just like I did at work. Be attentive, make people feel good.

Shouldn't be that difficult.

Effortlessly we move to the next room for the reception.

Link must have rented out the entire floor of this tower.

Once we're there, a DJ is already spinning tunes, and a few people are dancing.

"We have a few obligations," he says, leaning close. "First dance. A toast from Pax, and one from me. Saying hello to late arrivals."

I nod.

"After the cake is cut, we're leaving. And you'll be ours in all ways."

His expression is so laden with meaning that I instantly become damp.

We spend half an hour mingling, and I notice Marge, Nat, and David standing at a high-top table, cocktails in front of them.

The DJ spins a ballad, and David leads Natalie onto the dance floor, leaving Marge by herself.

"Will you excuse me?" I ask.

Pax frowns.

"I want to talk with Marge. Alone." Something I haven't had a chance to do yet.

He looks to Link before nodding. "Five minutes."

Pax turns away and speaks into his watch.

As I walk toward Marge, Mira and Torin—dressed impeccably so no one would guess they're security—move to a nearby table.

I sigh. But since I'm finally going to have a few minutes alone with my friend, I decide to keep my mouth shut.

When I near her, she puts down her whiskey and gives me a big hug. "Miss you at the bar, sugar."

Recently the Rusty Nail was my life. Yet at the same time,

it seems like forever since I walked through the door for the last time.

"You look happy."

Do I? "Because you're here! How did you find out?" I'm embarrassed that I didn't ask Link to invite her.

"Pax showed up with a ticket, hotel reservations, and transportation to and from the airport both ways." She shrugs. "Man won't take no for an answer."

I look up and unerringly find my husbands. Pax is watching us.

"He's assigned a security detail to the place." She shrugs. "Not that I need it."

"Which…" I lean toward her. "What happened that night? I was so scared something happened to you."

"Took care of the bastard."

"Took care of…?" She can't mean what I think she does.

"No one threatens or hurts the people I love and gets away with it."

I blink.

"Pax handled the cleanup."

Oh God. I remember the story about her sawed-off shotgun. And I have no doubts. Marge means exactly what I was afraid of.

"That's all you're getting from me." She shrugs. "If you want to hear more, ask Pax."

I nod.

When the song ends, Natalie and David return, cutting off conversation, which is fine because Link and Pax join us.

"Sorry to sweep her away from you," Link says. "Maybe we can get together when we're all in Houston."

After promising we'll make arrangements later, Link moves me toward more new people, including Matteo Moretti. He's accompanied by bodyguards, but he's polite, though his dark eyes miss nothing.

THEIRS TO CORRUPT

The man is unsettling as hell.

I can't imagine how it was possible to get this many high-profile people in the same room.

And every minute, more guests seem to be arriving.

"Ready for our first dance as a married trio?" Link finally asks.

The DJ asks for the floor to be cleared and announces that we'll be out there alone for a while.

Link takes my hand and leads me to the middle, beneath a spotlight. Pax is off to one side, Marcella and her camera next to him.

The opening notes of "Something" by the Beatles begin to play.

He pulls me close, and beneath my ear is the reassuring pounding of his heart.

His body is warm and strong, and the song achingly romantic.

If only this was a wedding we both wanted.

Softly he croons the lyrics, only for me.

Surprised by the resonance of voice, I look up at him as we sway to the ballad.

Our guests, even the room fades away, and for a moment, it feels like we're the only two people in the world.

"I chose this song on purpose."

Halfway through the song, Link turns me over to Pax.

Link places a soft kiss on my forehead before stepping back.

My other husband pulls me close, one hand on the small of my back, the other holding mine. His touch is different from Link's—equally firm, but with its own unique energy.

"You look radiant," Pax murmurs as we move together. "We're two very lucky men."

Lighting begins to change, with the room becoming

brighter and the spotlight fading as the DJ invites others to join us.

When the song winds down, Pax spins me gently, right into Link's arms.

As the final note plays, the three of us have our hands entwined.

Both of my men kiss me gently.

In this moment, I'm happy, maybe happier than I recall being since my parents passed.

It can't last, though. Life has taught me that joy is fleeting. For now, I shove aside my sudden feeling of doubt.

Another ballad follows. Then the DJ segues into "Twist and Shout."

While we make our way to the edge of the dance floor, many others take our place. There are smiles and laughter all around the room, and some people appear deep in conversation.

"You know how to throw a party," I tell Link, impressed and doubly glad that he handled all the preparations for the event.

"With more to come."

"Surely not always this many people?" And on this scale.

"Not always," he agrees.

Which means that some might be.

Link is a consummate host, ensuring that everyone feels welcome. And Pax excuses himself to go and talk to Hawkeye and Inamorata.

Time rushes in a blur before the DJ announces it's time for the toast.

Once more, we're in the spotlight.

Pax joins us, and Link helps me up onto the stage, no easy feat with the way the dress hugs my body.

There's a small table near us with three glasses of champagne.

Servers make their way through the room, refilling glasses and offering flutes to people who don't have them.

Wondering what the men will say and self-conscious at being in the spotlight once more, I ball my hands at my sides.

Noticing, Pax slides an arm around my shoulders.

I honestly didn't know it was possible for anyone to notice such tiny details about me.

Totally comfortable, Link accepts the microphone from the DJ and once more thanks our guests for sharing our special day and promising that the open bar will remain available until one a.m.

"Not that we'll still be here by then," he adds, flashing a devilish smile that makes my tummy turn a somersault.

Catcalls and cheers greet his comment.

"Generally the best man proposes a toast," Link continues. "As you've might have noticed, there's not much about our wedding that's been traditional."

"Hear, hear!" someone calls out while others laugh.

When our guests have quieted, Link picks up a glass and looks at me and Pax. "Pax, you've been at my side—"

The overhead lights suddenly flicker. The soft background music vanishes, replaced by an explosion of sound that rocks the atmosphere.

Then music that sounds like the opening of a Hollywood blockbuster shakes the room.

"Jesus," Link says.

A booming voice echoes through the room.

"Stop this! Stop this immensely!"

Pax swears under his breath and checks his watch. "Bonds."

"Goddamn it," Link mutters, slamming down his drink.

Julien Bonds? My eyes widen.

The double doors burst open, and Julien Bonds strides in, followed by an entourage and a film crew.

I blink at the spectacle.

He's wearing a suit, but his accessories are outrageous.

His bow tie is a garish yellow, not tied correctly, and it clashes horrifically with his neon orange sneakers.

Without slowing down, Julien marches across the room and leaps onto the stage.

When he lands, his shoes light up with silver wedding bells that race around the bottoms.

"This is an absolute travesty!" After saying hello to me and telling me I could have done much better in the marriage department, he yanks the microphone from Link's hand.

"You're absolutely right that a toast is performed by the most magnificent man. Clearly"—he pauses for dramatic effect—"that man is me."

With stunned confusion, I look back and forth between Link and Pax.

Link's eyes flash with annoyance.

Everyone around us is grinning, laughing, snapping pictures.

"Ladies, boys, and lovebirds." He gestures dramatically toward us. "We are gathered here today to celebrate a union as rare as a dodo bird in a petting zoo."

Oh my God. I can't help but laugh.

"Link and Pax... Congratulations on finding someone who will endure your brilliance and bullshit, of which there's many." Then he looks at me. "Tessa, you now have a future filled with herding guppies."

"Jesus," Link says again.

Julien, wedding bells still racing around the bottom of his tennis shoes, snatches away Link's champagne glass. Then he angles it toward each of us. "May the days be filled with happiness, and your nights make us jealous. Happily never after!"

He takes a long drink, hands back the flute, then jumps off the stage as everyone begins to applaud.

"Were you expecting that?" I ask Link.

"With Bonds, only the unexpected is expected."

Off to one side, the Genius of the Known Universe holds court.

After Julien's unexpected toast, the reception settles back into a more conventional rhythm.

Guests mingle, laughing and chatting, while the DJ plays a mix of upbeat songs and romantic ballads.

Even though I shouldn't, I steal glances at the entrance, anticipating the arrival of the cake. Each time the doors open, my heart races a little.

Finally the hotel staff gathers near a side door.

On cue, the DJ lowers the music.

The breathtaking cake is wheeled in.

I'd only imagined what it might look like, and this is beyond my wildest dreams. Multiple tiers, beautiful flowers, and our initials monogrammed in what appears to be chocolate and covered with black, sparkly paint. The T is in the middle, and it's flanked by an L and a P on either side, smaller, and all entwined with circles that resemble wedding bands.

"Ladies and gentlemen," the DJ calls out, "It's time for the newlyweds to cut the cake!"

Link presses his hand against my back, his touch sending ripples of electricity through me. Leaning close, he smiles. "Only minutes now, Tessa. Then you're ours…"

CHAPTER TWENTY-TWO

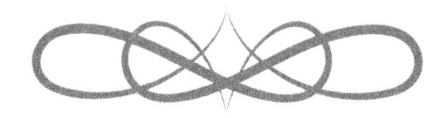

Tessa

"What are you doing?"

There's a determined gleam in Link's dark eyes as he leans toward me.

We've just exited the elevator on our floor, and he's captured my hand to pull me to a stop.

"Carrying our bride across the threshold."

In a lightning quick move that makes me dizzy, he sweeps me from my feet.

"Have you lost your mind?" I squeal and laugh as he cradles me against him. Instinctively I wrap my arms around his neck. "You're going to hurt your back."

"Not a chance."

His strides are as long as ever as he walks toward our suite.

The two Hawkeye agents who are on guard move farther apart to allow Pax access to the keypad on the wall.

With a soft beep, the lock disengages and he opens the door.

Once we're inside, Link kicks it closed behind us.

The suite is dimly lit, casting everything in a warm, intimate glow. Link doesn't pause in the living area. Instead he continues straight toward his bedroom.

Pax follows.

Near the window, Link gently lowers me to my feet, and I gasp when his thick, hard erection brushes against my stomach.

I barely have time to steady myself before he peruses me, from the top of my now-disheveled hair to the hem of my wedding gown.

"We've waited long enough." Link's voice is low, filled with promise.

In a mix of anticipation and nervous excitement, my heart soars.

Cupping my face between his palms, Link gently strokes my cheeks with his thumbs. Then he brings me toward him.

His beautiful lips are soft yet firm.

I melt against him, allowing my eyes to drift closed as his tongue explores my mouth with a gentle dominance that makes me dizzy.

Pax moves in closer, his body heat radiating against my back.

After sweeping my hair to one side, he exposes my neck and presses his lips to the sensitive skin there.

I gasp into Link's mouth as Pax gently nips my flesh.

Link pulls away slightly, his breath ragged. "You taste like forever, little dove." He takes a step back to shrug out of his tuxedo jacket and carelessly toss it onto a nearby chair.

Pax follows suit, his jacket joining Link's.

I watch as Link begins to unbutton his shirt, revealing a glimpse of his toned chest.

My gaze snags on his cuff links that glint in the soft light. I blink, focusing on the intricate design.

Owls.

With emerald eyes.

My breath catches, and I look up at him.

Link really is a Titan.

Then he seeks to distract me, capturing my mouth once more and tangling his hands in my hair to tilt my head back so he can deepen the kiss.

There's just us and the moment.

I moan softly, and Pax is behind me again, gliding his strong palms over my hips and up to my shoulders. Gently he massages me.

When they finally release me, I'm relaxed and tense at the same time.

Link tosses his cuff links onto the nearby table. Then he loosens his bowtie and tosses it aside.

Pax's lands on top, at an odd angle.

Before I've recovered, their hands are everywhere, exploring and teasing as they slowly work my dress up my legs. Both men trace patterns with their fingertips, leaving me without a single rational thought.

I sway as Pax caresses the back of my thighs, inching the dress higher while Link's hands slide up my sides, lifting the fabric over my hips. "We're going to pleasure you until you can't take anymore."

I shudder with anticipation as they continue, the cool air kissing my exposed skin.

They continue until Link traces the lace edge of my bra, sending jolts of awareness through me.

Pax clamps my waist and circles my hipbones with his thumbs.

I'm swimming in sensation as his length presses against my back.

Link's mouth moves to my neck, sucking and nipping as

he finally pulls the dress up and over my head, leaving me standing between them in just my bra.

Pax takes the gown from him and drapes it over the back of a nearby chair.

Link takes a step back, his gaze roving over my body as if he's trying to memorize my shape. "Exquisite." His voice is gruff. "Absolutely breathtaking."

Pax echoes his sentiment with a low growl of approval, sliding his hands up my back to unclasp my bra.

Link's eyes are feral, filled with hunger and appreciation.

I force myself to resist the instinct to hide. After all, Link was very clear that he'll be exercising his conjugal rights—as he'd called them.

My bra floats to the floor, and I stand naked before them, my heart pounding with a mix of excitement and nerves.

"Hands behind your back, little dove," Link instructs gently.

But there's no doubting the command in his tone.

I shudder.

Still, I comply.

"Don't move until one of us says." His expression is unreadable as he reaches out to cup my breasts.

He uses his two fingers to circle my nipples. They pebble in response to his touch.

"You like that." Satisfaction laces his words.

Once again, Pax captures my hips, and he pulls me back against him.

Because my hands are trapped between us, my palms are curled around his cock.

"That's it. A little harder, Tessa."

Link drops to his knees in front of me and kisses my stomach. Then he trails kisses lower, making me shake.

I need to grab hold of him for support, but I'm helpless, trapped.

"Stroke me," Pax demands.

How is it possible for me to obey when Link is driving me mad?

"That wasn't a request, sweetheart," he says against my ear.

I'm accustomed to Link's demands, but now Pax too?

Together they're terrible.

He moves one hand lower to cup one of my ass cheeks. Then he digs his fingers into my flesh.

Lost, I begin to slide my hands up and down, and he thickens against me.

"Good girl," he whispers.

My senses are swirling. I never imagined I'd hear those words, and now I crave them.

Link taps the inside of my right thigh. "Spread your legs."

This is brazen. Tonight they're demanding I become an active participant, rather than someone who gets to relax and enjoy as they explore.

"You'll hide nothing from us," Pax tells me gruffly. "Whatever we want. Whenever we want it."

I don't respond quickly enough, and Link pinches the spot he'd lightly tapped. Stunned, gasping, I obey.

Pax chuckles, the sound slightly triumphant, and it rocks my world. "There's the easy way and the hard way. Whichever one you get is entirely up to you."

"Understand?" Link asks.

I nod.

"Give us the words." To reinforce his demand, he squeezes my flesh again.

"Yes!"

"Yes, what?"

Is this really happening?

And why am I so, so wet?

"Yes," I repeat. "I understand."

Pax releases his grip, then slides his hands up to cradle my breasts. As Link tastes me, he circles my nipples and squeezes them. "Don't forget about my cock, Tessa."

Crying out a little, I concentrate on doing as I'm instructed.

I lean back against Pax's shoulder as Link explores every inch of me, licking and sucking until I'm a writhing mess. Pax is kissing the side of my neck and tormenting my breasts.

An orgasm looms, just out of reach.

With his tongue, Link traces the folds of my intimate flesh, making me tremble.

He holds apart my labia and finds the sensitive nub of my clit, circling it, applying just enough pressure to make me thrust against his mouth.

"That's it," Pax murmurs. "Fuck his mouth. Give us everything." He tightens his grip on my breasts, and he pinches and rolls my nipples even harder, sending sharp jolts of pleasure straight to the place Link is tormenting.

"I could devour you all night." Link's voice vibrates against my sensitive flesh.

Consumed, I tighten my grip on Pax and move faster, keeping time with the way Link is flicking his tongue over me.

Then Link slides two fingers inside me, stretching them out. He makes love to me with his hand and his mouth.

"Let go for us," Pax whispers against my ear.

Their combined efforts push me closer and closer to the edge.

In this moment there's nothing but us, the sounds of my ragged breathing, and their murmurs of encouragement.

My body coils tighter with each of Link's strokes and every pinch of Pax's fingers.

As I'm about to tumble over the edge, Link pulls back slightly to look up at me. "Let us see you fall apart."

With a final, deliberate stroke of his tongue, he sends me spiraling into ecstasy. Lost, helpless, my body convulsing, I cry out.

Pax wraps his arms around my waist, supporting me as I ride out the intense orgasm.

Long seconds later, Link stands up and claims my mouth. I taste myself on him. The act is erotic and intimate, and another ripple traces through me.

Without being aware of it, I stopped stroking Pax.

But my back is still pressed to him, and he's holding me upright.

"Let's get you to bed," Link says.

As Pax releases me, Link takes my hand and guides me to the edge of the mattress. Then he scoops me up and lifts me onto it.

I scoot back and sit up, propped against the headboard.

Pax undresses, revealing his powerful, muscular body, nicked with scars, including one on the outside of his thigh. A reminder of his military service?

Link follows, shedding the rest of his clothes, until he stands before me, naked and aroused.

My heart pounding with anticipation, I drink in the sight of them.

Their masculine bodies are so different—Link with lean, toned muscles, and Pax with his broad, rippling physique. And their enormous erections leave no doubt they desire me.

Link takes a step closer to me, allowing his gaze to trail over my naked body. The hunger in his eyes is predatory. "You're ours now, Tessa." His voice is possessive. "Completely. Utterly."

Pax closes the distance and stands beside him, his eyes dark. "We'll take care of you, sweetheart."

"You're a virgin." Link's words are a statement, not a question.

I grab a pillow and hold it against me.

How does he know?

Is it that obvious? Or something else…? "I…" *Have no idea what to say.*

"We'll be gentle." He sits next to me and tucks a stray lock of hair behind my ear.

Link's fingers linger on my cheek, his touch gentle yet possessive. "We want you to be comfortable, little dove. I'm assuming you're not on birth control?"

Oh God. What does it say that I never really thought about it?

That I'm swept up in them? "I… Uh. No. I'm not on birth control."

"Would you like us to use protection?" His voice is low, intimate.

Since this is all so new, I'm not ready for kids immediately. I appreciate the fact he cares enough to ask. "Yes."

Link nods.

I meet his gaze, searching for any sign he's disappointed in my answer. But all that's there is approval.

"We'll take care of everything."

Pax goes into the bathroom and returns with a small box.

My eyes widen.

Never missing anything, Link asks, "Problem, little dove?"

CHAPTER TWENTY-THREE

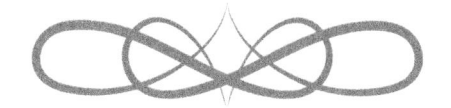

Tessa

"That's a lot." And the size is extra-large.

The men exchange glances, and they both grin. "Always believe in being prepared," Pax replies, dropping the box on the nightstand. Then he adds a small bottle next to it.

Their amusement restores my equilibrium and chases away my nerves.

Link plucks the pillow from my arms and pulls me into his lap, his skin hot against mine.

He trails his fingertips over my chest and breasts, reacquainting himself with every curve and line.

Relaxed, I surrender to him as he traces a path from my collarbone to my navel, his touch light and teasing. "We're going to find all the places that make you gasp, that make you moan, that make you scream with pleasure."

"Until you're begging us to stop," Pax adds.

They've already proven that they can make me do exactly that.

Link moves me so that I'm lying on my back.

Pax strides to the far side of the bed and joins us on my other side.

Link continues his lazy, sensual exploration, moving down to the apex of my thighs. Then he strokes lightly. Without words, he coaxes me to spread my legs and release any anxiousness.

His motions deliberate, he reaches for a condom and sheaths himself.

But instead of instantly moving over me, he licks me again, bringing me back to full, writhing arousal.

Only then does he position himself between my legs, his eyes holding my gaze prisoner.

"I've got you."

His heat, his hardness presses against me.

I suck in a breath, balling my fists as I tense.

Then Pax is there, dampening a finger and pressing it against my clit. "You're so perfect for us, Tessa."

Willing it to be over, I close my eyes.

Pax continues to tease me, and instinctively I lift my hips. Gently Link presses forward. "So fucking tight...

I wince at the slight burn as he begins to enter me. Even though they played with me, sliding in their fingers, nothing compares to his massive, thick cock and the feeling of being stretched and filled.

Nervous, I open my eyes, but Link has already pulled back, and the pressure is gone.

He strokes in again, not as far, then pulls out and repeats the motion, this time as deep as earlier, but no farther. He finds a rhythm that is slow and reassures me, but moments later, there's a slight pain.

When I gasp, Pax captures my chin and kisses me, swallowing my small cry.

Link pauses, giving my body time to adjust.

Pax continues to work his magic on my clit, and he deepens his kiss.

"That's it, little dove," Link encourages, his voice strained with restraint. "You feel incredible. So tight, so perfect."

He begins to stroke again until he fills me completely.

The initial pain ebbs, replaced by a growing pleasure.

Pax ends our kiss, and he moves his hand from between my legs to cup one of my breasts and tease my already-sensitive nipple.

"You're doing so well," Pax promises.

With one last surge, Link's hips are against mine, and he pauses, fully seated inside me.

His jaw is clenched, but the tenderness in his eyes makes my heart flutter.

The expression is one I've never seen before.

"Mine."

Claimed.

"Ours."

Link makes love to me, slowly at first, then with increasing rhythm.

Driving me to distraction, Pax's hands and mouth are everywhere, caressing, kissing, heightening my reactions.

A climax builds again, and my body coils tighter with each of my husband's thrusts.

Link's breath comes in ragged gasps, his body tensing as he struggles to maintain control. "You feel too good, Tessa," he groans, his pace quickening. "I can't… I won't last much longer."

Once more, Pax slides his hand down between Link and me. Maddeningly he circles my clit in time with Link's thrusts. The added stimulation is too much. Desperately I clutch Link's shoulders as my hips buck against him.

"Come with me, little dove." Link's husky voice is strained. "Let go, baby. Let me feel you come."

His command is the permission I need.

God. Oh God. Pleasure crashes over me.

"Fuck." Link thrusts deep one last time, his body rigid as he takes his own release. "Goddamn, little dove."

Pax slows his motions, drawing out the last shudders of my orgasm. He presses a soft kiss to my temple. "So beautiful, Tessa. So perfect."

Link and I look at each other, and I ache to soothe the lines that are grooved next to his eyes.

He holds my gaze before dropping a kiss on my mouth.

From earlier, he still tastes like me.

Gently he pulls out, his breaths ragged.

Pax curls against me, his cock hard as it presses against my buttock. He drapes an arm over me, warming my body that is a little damp from exertion.

Link leaves us momentarily to dispose of the condom.

Then he returns, and I'm deliciously trapped between the men I've promised my life to.

Both stroke my skin, smoothing the return from my high back down to reality.

I lie between them, sated.

The room is filled with the soft sounds of our breathing, the scent of lovemaking in the air. In this moment, I'm content.

Link props himself up on one elbow, looking down at me, eyebrows drawn together. "How are you feeling?"

"Amazing." I smile back, a warm glow spreading through me. "That was…incredible."

Pax rests his hand possessively on my hip. "That was just the beginning, sweetheart. We have all night, and we intend to use every minute. Starting now. Are you ready to be mine, Tessa?"

His question turns me inside out. I know Pax will

demand everything from me. And yet, isn't that exactly what I want?

"You're not too sore?"

"No," I whisper, turning to face him. His green eyes blaze with possessive intent.

Pax's gaze holds me in place as he trails his fingers down my ribs. He's not as gentle as Link. Instead Pax's touch is firmer, more insistent, as if he's barely able to contain his hunger, and he ignites sparks on my skin.

Link shifts, propping himself up on my other side.

In that instant, Pax captures my lips in a fierce kiss. His tongue seeks, then claims.

As Pax's possession makes me reel, Link traces the curve of my spine before placing a gentle kiss to the sensitive spot behind my ear. "Let us know when you're ready, little dove."

Pax slides his hand down to cup me, and he presses against my clit with precise, deliberate movements. Gasping, I shamelessly grind against his hand.

As he ends the kiss, Link guides me onto my back so he can knead and caress my breasts, rolling my nipples between thumbs and forefingers until they're hard, aching points.

The dual sensations, Pax's relentless torment of my pussy and Link's teasing touch, drive me to the brink of madness. They have me panting, writhing, begging for more.

Right as I'm on the verge of coming, Pax pulls away.

I sigh my frustration.

"A little patience," Link counsels.

Patience? I scowl. Easy for him to say.

Keeping his gaze on me, Pax reaches for a condom.

Teasing me, prolonging my agony, he takes his sweet time rolling the latex down his thick, hard cock.

Then he lies on his back. "You're going to ride me, gorgeous."

I inhale, but before I can form any kind of protest, he

grips my waist, lifting me effortlessly and positioning me on top, straddling him.

His heat and hardness press into me, making me hyper-aware of how large and dangerous he is.

"You're going to take me, Tessa, but first, I want to be sure you're ready."

"I am," I promise.

"You're not wet enough. And I don't want to hurt you."

"Come here," Link tells me, sitting up and repositioning me until I'm facing the headboard, my knees on either side of Pax's head.

They can't mean…

"Sit on my face, gorgeous," Pax commands, his voice rough with need.

Scandalized, I freeze.

When I don't move, Link captures my shoulders and gently but firmly pushes me down. "Do as you're told, little dove." His tone is harshly uncompromising.

Pax reaches up to grasp my hips, fingertips digging into my bones, and he guides me down until I'm seated on his face.

I can't believe this is happening.

Desperately I grab hold of the headboard, hoping to gain leverage to lift myself up. But Link holds me in place.

"Stay where you are."

Before I can protest, he cups my breasts and gently abrades the tips with his thumbnails, making me forget what I was going to say.

Pax delves between my folds, exploring and teasing me with his mouth.

In under a minute, I forget how nervous this has made me, and instead I shake from the pleasure rocking me.

He licks and sucks, making sure I'm aroused, my pussy drenched.

My body tightens as an orgasm builds.

Forgetting everything but the moment, I tip my head back.

Just as I'm about to come, Pax clamps his hands on my hips and lifts me off his face.

Aching for release, I whimper. *"No!"*

The two men, both terrible, move me once more, leaving me positioned over Pax's throbbing cock.

"Now you're ready."

More than.

"Take me, Tessa. All of me." He fists his cock, and he encourages me to go at my own pace, but there's an impatient hunger in his eyes that tells me he won't wait forever.

I lower myself a little, and he positions himself at my entrance. I'm already so wet, but as I begin to take him inside, I inhale sharply at the sheer size of him. He's bigger than Link, and my body struggles to adjust to his invasion.

"Easy." Link strokes my back.

Pax clenches his jaw, restraint visible in the tense lines of his body. Yet even he doesn't rush me.

After releasing a deep breath, I take him in inch by inch, my body stretching to accommodate him.

Being so full is incredible, and I ache from the deep satisfaction of being claimed so completely.

"That's it."

Once I'm fully seated, my pussy against his groin, he tightens his hands on my hips. "You're in control. Ride me, Tessa."

The idea that I might ever be in control of either of these men is absurd, but I begin to move, rising a little, then lowering myself again.

He groans.

Link's hands are everywhere: my back, my breasts, my ass. His touch adds fuel to the fire, making me lose control.

Suddenly Pax takes over, urging me to go faster, harder. He meets each of my downward strokes with a thrust of his own, his hips slamming against mine, and I get hotter by the moment.

Surrendering, I lean back against Link as Pax controls my movements, using my body for his pleasure and mine.

"Do you know how fucking sexy you are, little dove?" Link demands.

Pax's gaze is locked onto mine. "You're more than just sexy You're a goddamn temptress."

His words thrill me, and I grind down on him, accepting him even deeper. The mixture of pleasure and pain makes me cry out.

Pax groans.

The realization that I can affect him like that fills me with a sense of feminine power unlike anything I've ever experienced.

He thrusts again, and I rock faster, driven by his demands and my own needs.

Link reaches between us to circle my clit, keeping time with our lovemaking.

The added stimulation is... "Too much," I manage, but already a climax is unfurling again. This time it's more insistent because of the way they've denied me.

I go tense.

Pax is slick with sweat, his muscles rigid as he fights to maintain control. "Not yet, sweetheart. You don't come until I say so."

Is he serious?

In frustration, I force out a breath.

Link shrugs, a diabolical, nonsympathetic motion. "He's in charge now. I'm sure he'll make it worth the wait."

Pax's movements become more forceful, and his fingertips have to be leaving tiny marks on my skin.

Each stroke sends shockwaves through me, and I can barely breathe, barely think.

Link circles my clit even faster.

I can't hold out any longer. "Please." My voice is a jagged whisper. "Please, Pax. I need to come."

There's dark triumph in his eyes. "Do it. Come for me, Tessa. All over my cock."

With his permission, I shudder, and my climax crashes over me. I'm squeezing him internally as I toss back my head, shaking, crying out both of their names.

"Fucking hot." Link's voice is a purr of approval.

Thank God Link eases his hand away from me, but Pax continues on, drawing out my climax until I'm shuddering.

Remaining upright takes all my energy.

"Fuck." Pax's body tenses. *"Tessa..."*

With a final, powerful thrust, he ejaculates, his body rigid, his cock pulsing inside me. *"Fu-uck..."*

I collapse against Pax's chest, and his heart thunders beneath my cheek.

I'm completely exhausted, and I shudder from the little ripples of aftershocks.

Link is there, scooping back my hair. "We're proud of you."

Pax feathers a finger across my cheek, his touch surprisingly tender after the energy of our joining. "I know I'm not easy, but you were fucking perfect."

I offer a small smile, and I manage to lift my head a little so I can look at him.

His green eyes are softer now, fierce hunger replaced by a warmth. Gently I kiss him. "That was amazing."

I glance over at Link. He's hard. Ready.

Another reminder that our night is far from over?

"How about a glass of wine, little dove? We'll show some mercy."

"Oh?"

"Temporarily. The honeymoon is just beginning, and we want to be sure you're not too sore for what's going to come next."

Every time I feel like I can relax, they ratchet up my tension.

Across the room, a phone rings.

At this time of night?

Link excuses himself, leaving the bed, then grabbing a robe before heading into the living room for some privacy.

"Do you two ever stop working?"

Pax grins. "From time to time. But I've got an idea to keep you busy until he comes back…"

CHAPTER TWENTY-FOUR

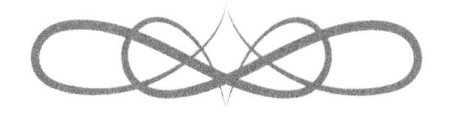

Link

Almost silently, the bedroom door clicks closed.

I glance over my shoulder. With his normal stealth, Pax heads my direction, wearing slacks and his dress shirt, though it's unbuttoned. His gun is nearby. Always prepared.

The soft glow of the lamps casts long shadows across the room. Outside, the faint hum of Las Vegas nightlife seeps through the windows. The air is thick with the lingering scents of champagne, Tessa's sweetness, and the unmistakable musk of us claiming our virgin bride.

I'd known she was going to be amazing. But I'd had no idea...

"Tessa asleep?" I ask quietly.

"Yeah. Told her I'd run her a bath after rubbing her shoulders." He grins. "She was out within less than a minute."

I'm not surprised. Her life has been turned upside down, not just by her brother, but by us.

He crosses to the small bar area and pours two whiskeys. Then he carries one to me. "Great ceremony, boss."

Served the higher good, making it effective. *Ends justify the means.* "Lorenzo's staff made it easy."

"No details left to chance."

Never. The way I like it.

"She's fucking spectacular."

Nodding agreement, I accept the glass.

I recall every moment of our day.

Though I'd seen her in the form-fitting gown before we were married, watching her walk down the aisle had almost been my undoing. She was dressed so perfectly, carrying her flowers, her gaze fastened on me, as if drawing strength and determination from me.

I'd never thought much about getting married, even though the best of the best around me had fallen into matrimonial bliss. Lorenzo Carrington. Rafe Sterling. Nico Moretti. I always figured it would happen when the time was right.

Then I saw Tessa, and I'd immediately been obsessed by her sweet innocence and beauty.

I had to have her.

After Pax discovered who she was, there was no way I could let her go.

And now that we're married, my life seems more complete, which surprises me. I never knew something was missing. But now…

Knowing she's close and will be that way for the rest of her life soothes the savage beast inside me.

"She did great tonight. The reception."

Pax's words interrupt my musings. "She'll be a great hostess." Smiling at the sharks, unrattled by anyone. Including me and Pax. Though she heard me tell the tale of Pax shooting someone, she'd promised to spend the rest of her life with us.

She's more fearless than I could have imagined.

Back here, in our suite, she'd responded to us so completely, with utter trust.

Fucking hell.

Over the years, Pax and I have shared dozens of women. *Dozens?* Maybe fifty or more.

None of them were as honest or perfect as our new wife.

"We're lucky men," Pax says.

Tessa is more than I deserve. "Indeed we are."

He lifts his glass in a silent acknowledgement, and I do the same.

We both take sips, then move to the seating area and drop into chairs.

"Marcella?" Pax guesses about my phone call.

I nod. "Everything's in place."

Within twenty-four hours, hopefully considerably less, Emiliano Sartori and Axel Tremaine will know Tessa is my wife, under our protection.

I harbor no illusions.

This is war. But I declared it on my terms.

I'm drawing them to me, and I will put them down once and for all, like the cockroaches they are.

As I contemplate what's to come, I feel a surge of fierce protectiveness. Tessa may have entered this arrangement out of necessity, but I'll be damned if I let anyone harm her. She's ours now: to protect, to cherish, to honor. The depth of my emotions surprises me, but I push them aside.

"Talked to Hawkeye and Inamorata. Everything's ready on our end," Pax says.

As if I had any doubt.

Pax is methodical, leaves nothing to chance, going over plans time and again. And then once more, just to be sure.

He has operatives on Sartori's crew and eyes on Axel. "Marcella gave the exclusive to *Scandalicious*."

"Good move," Pax approves.

"But she dropped a couple of photos to other magazines and influencers." Whatever the fuck they are.

"Unauthorized leaks." Pax grins

But not too many because then it would be obvious.

"Here's to winning it all," Pax proposes, lifting his glass.

"All of it." I lean toward him, and we clink our glasses together.

I'm not cocky enough to believe we've already won.

But round one sure as fuck went to us.

As I sip my whiskey, my thoughts drift back to Tessa. She's now an integral part of my world, and I'll move heaven and earth to keep her here and safe.

"Shall we?" Pax asks, putting down his glass and grinning. "Wouldn't want our wife to wake up and wonder where we are."

Tessa

"Oh my God, you're famous!"

I laugh as Natalie yanks open the door to her room. "Famous?" I ask. "Not in the least."

She hugs me tight and pulls me inside.

After shutting the door, she locks it, with Torin and Mira in the hallway.

I look around, and I'm so impressed.

Link didn't just get my friends a regular room. They're in a stunning suite.

"I still can't believe I'm here," she says.

And I'm so glad she is.

"Something to drink?" she offers. "I mean this is crazy. There was a bottle of champagne waiting for us when we got here, and all these divine treats." She waves her arm wide, showing off chocolates of all kinds. "There's no way we're going to be able to eat them all."

"Take them home with you."

"Then I'll eat them!"

I laugh, understanding. They're decadent and so loaded with calories.

"Breakfast arrived this morning without us ordering it, so we have coffee and tea and orange juice."

Since there's also a bucket of melting ice filled with water bottles, I help myself to one of them. Then I eye the truffles.

"Do it," Natalie encourages.

"You're terrible."

She shrugs. "Well, I won't feel as bad about the number I've already eaten if you help me out."

"That's some sort of messed-up friend logic." But it works on me, and I grab one of the treats. "Are they all the same?"

She shook her head. "And that sucks. I had one that was amaretto, and I've eaten another three while I was hoping to find another one like it."

Laughing, I take a small bite, sighing when the velvety creaminess melts in my mouth.

"That better not be amaretto," she warns.

"It's orange. Like orange liqueur."

"Oh God, no," she wails. "Now I need one of those." Scowling, she reaches for another of the slightly round confections.

As I watch, she sinks her teeth in. Then she moans.

"Amaretto?"

"I think it's Irish cream." After sampling it again, she nods. "It is!"

"And?"

"Better than the amaretto."

"Wow." But I can't imagine any of these not being amazing.

"You have to take the rest back to your room. I mean it."

"No chance." I see what she meant earlier. Having these around and not devouring every single one would be an unfair test of restraint.

She wraps the remainder of her chocolate in a napkin and drops onto the couch.

Since I plan to finish mine, I don't bother grabbing a small dessert plate. Then I sit in an armchair near her, but I turn to look out the window.

Though the floor she's on is not as high as where I'm staying with Link and Pax, her view is no less stunning.

I find it interesting that we're in Vegas, a city that never sleeps, with neon everywhere, yet the view is peaceful, even soothing.

I'm not sure I would ever get tired of looking at the city from all its different angles.

Once I finish my truffle, I place my water bottle on the coffee table. Then I brush my hands together and focus on Natalie. "Is David still at the fitness center?"

"Yes. And I can't complain. That's how he keeps his bod so hot."

Together we laugh.

Not too long ago, she'd sent me a message saying she'd be alone for at least an hour and that she'd love to spend a few minutes with me.

Though I wouldn't have ordinarily wanted to leave my husbands—especially since it's our honeymoon and last night was extraordinary, and I am eager for an encore—they were both occupied.

Link had another mysterious meeting outside the suite, and Pax was scheduled to meet up with Hawkeye and Inamorata before they headed for the airport.

Still, before leaving, I had to check in with Pax. He'd left orders with Mira and Torin.

When I agreed to have them accompany me, he relented. As long as I promised to come straight back.

"So how does it feel to be famous?"

I frown at her second use of the word. "Stop being ridiculous." Even though I married a billionaire and his bodyguard, I'm still the same woman I was last week. "No one knows who I am."

She shakes her head. "Not true. This morning I got a breaking-news email from *Scandalicious.*"

"*Scandalicious?*" I repeat. "You don't even read it."

"It's your fault. You got me hooked on it." Snatching up her phone from the coffee table, she shrugs. "So, anyway. You're in the magazine."

"Me?" I blink. "What are you talking about?"

Natalie opens her phone and shows me the screen. "Your wedding is on the front page. And you were featured in the breaking news email."

Praying she's joking, I frantically dig in my purse for my phone.

"Holy shit!" Her eyes are wide. "When did you get a Bonds device?"

"I was frustrated when I missed your call that night we had the break-in."

"So your men got you the most expensive thing on the planet?"

Embarrassment crawls through me. Having anything fancy is still strange and awkward to me, and I'm not sure I'll ever get used to it.

Focusing, I scroll to the *Scandalicious* app and open it.

EXCLUSIVE! BILLIONAIRE'S SECRET WEDDING SHOCKS SOCIETY! the headline screams.

There's a picture of Link kissing me before the ceremony started.

My heart sinks.

It's one thing to look at stars and celebrities, but another to see my picture there.

Suddenly I remember Marcella was everywhere yesterday, snapping picture after picture. And Link arranged for her to be there.

"You were an absolutely gorgeous bride."

Barely registering her words, I swipe to the next picture.

Link is slipping the ring onto my finger.

I'm so stunned that I can barely think.

The next is of me with disheveled hair leaving the bridal room.

I'm horrified.

There are at least two dozen snapshots. Almost all of them include me. Some include me and Link. Others have Pax in them as well.

There are plenty that show our reception, and everyone is identified by name.

Rafe and Hope Sterling. Lorenzo and Zara Carrington. Matteo Moretti.

I lower my phone.

Not long ago, I had judged Link for having a picture with a mobster.

And now here I am.

The magazine used to be my favorite. After this I'm not sure I'll ever want to look at it again.

"Can I get your autograph?" Natalie asks as I drop my phone into my purse.

Thankfully, as I know, there will be another breaking story in twenty minutes, and that will knock us much deeper in the feed.

At least I hope so. Pray so.

But plenty of people have already seen the scoop. With the way word spreads, no doubt the whole world knows about our relationship.

"You look totally radiant in all of them. I don't know how you did it. My smile would have frozen to my face halfway through the evening."

"And you think mine didn't?" Even though my insides are reeling, I keep my words light.

"I'm so happy for you and the way your life has worked out. It couldn't be more perfect."

I uncap my water bottle and take a sip, trying to steady my thoughts.

At one time, I believed in happiness, but that's when my parents were alive and I was heading to college with my whole life ahead of me.

"Feel free to invite me to every one of your parties."

"You're on the guest list." As if I have any say over that.

"Almost everyone stayed until the very end of the reception," she tells me. "Quite a party. We danced forever."

Since it will do me no good to agonize over the fact I've just had my face plastered all over the internet, I shove aside my embarrassment to focus on what Natalie is saying. "David seems really nice."

"He's wonderful." She picks up her truffle and takes another nibble. "And he kept me up half the night after we got back."

My men had done the same, and the memory is enough to make it feel as if someone has turned on the heater.

"Guessing your evening was pretty awesome too."

I tighten my grip on the water bottle.

"So you went from being a virgin to taking two guys in the same night?"

"Yeah…" I search for words and can't seem to find them. Then suddenly I can't help myself. "They're so different."

Her eyebrows are drawn together in great concentration. "I can't imagine."

"But you are trying to do exactly that, aren't you?" I tease.

"Guilty." She gives a delicious little shiver. "Who can blame me? I mean you've got yourself two delicious husbands."

She's right about that, but I don't give her any further details.

A minute or so later, when she seems to realize she's getting nothing else out of me, she changes the conversation. "I take it you haven't heard from your brother or Emiliano?"

I shake my head. "No." Which makes me wonder what Link and Pax have done to make that happen.

"Maybe Link was right," she muses. "All it took was marrying him."

I hope he was right. Knowing that awful situation is behind me will make my future so much brighter.

"I know I've said this before, but you are truly one of the best people I know. You really do deserve to be happy."

"You are the better person," I correct her. "You took in a total stranger, even though it was risky for you."

"How else would I have found my best friend?"

She always knows the right thing to say. "I'm lucky I have you."

Voices outside the room capture our attention, and I turn to look at the door.

Moments later, there's a beep, which signals someone has touched the keypad on the wall.

"I bet that's David." Natalie leaps up, but before opening the door, she looks through the peephole. "I'm still under orders from Pax."

"Aren't we all?" He's so bossy that sometimes I feel as if I should salute him.

Moments later, she lets David in.

As soon as the safety device is engaged, he drops a kiss on her forehead.

"Sorry I'm sweaty, baby."

She grins at him. "I don't care."

"No?"

"Nuh-huh." She links her arms around his waist.

"Let me take a shower. Then we'll hit the pool."

With a towel around his neck, David stops and says hello to me. "Great party last night. We can't thank you and your husbands enough."

"They were happy to do it."

"Because you matter to them," Natalie adds.

David continues to the bedroom, and Natalie walks me to the door. "Not trying to rush you off, but…"

"There's a naked man waiting for you." I grin.

"Well, that!" She laughs. "And we want to enjoy every moment we have left of the vacation."

"I don't blame you."

I reach for the door, but her voice stops me. "You know, you really are lucky to have them."

She's right. I can't imagine where I would be if they hadn't stepped in that night at the Rusty Nail.

But as I leave the room and Torin falls in step next to me, I remember back to David walking into the room and my friend's reaction.

They are clearly crazy about each other.

As we wait for the elevator to arrive, I'm lost in thought.

Even Mira and Torin appear to read each other's thoughts.

The vows in my wedding to Link and Pax were carefully worded. We talked about loyalty and respect and pledging to stand together. But none of us mentioned love.

And isn't that supposedly the most important ingredient to a successful relationship?

Obviously I'm foolish to even think about such a thing.

Link and Pax are both committed to keeping me safe.

But there's a cost.

And now, pictures of our ceremony and reception are all over social media.

He hired the photographer and gave her access to every moment.

A few minutes later, we arrive back at the suite.

As always, Mira and Torin nod as I go inside.

Link is sitting on the couch, his arm spread across the back. He's breathtaking in a snowy white shirt with the top few buttons undone and his sleeves rolled back.

"I've been waiting for you."

I fully intended to ask him about the pictures and *Scandalicious*, but he crooks his finger, beckoning me to him.

My thoughts scatter.

He spreads his legs and points to the floor in front of him. "Come here, little dove."

I am lost, helpless to resist him.

CHAPTER TWENTY-FIVE

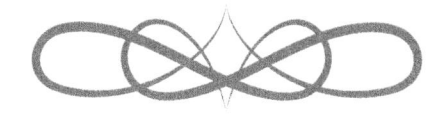

Tessa

I don't know why it never occurs to disobey, but it doesn't.

After placing my purse on a table inside the door, I kick off my shoes and walk across the room to him.

"I missed you."

My pulse becomes erratic as I start a sensual slide into becoming his, and slowly I lower myself to the floor.

I glance up to meet his unreadable eyes. "Pax knew where I was."

He nods. "I wasn't asking for an explanation."

In relief, I exhale. Just because he saved me doesn't mean he gets all my freedom.

"I've been thinking about you all morning."

I tear my gaze from his eyes to the front of his slacks, and I try to hide my grin. If appearances can be trusted, he has most definitely been thinking about me.

"I want to fuck you, little dove."

My insides turn molten.

"Undress me." The words aren't a request; they're a cold, hard demand.

I shove away my moment of hesitation. We're married. Of course he will expect this kind of attention.

After removing his shoes and socks, I kneel up a little to release his belt buckle.

"That's it. You're doing great."

His approval gives me courage.

I slide the leather from its loops and drop the belt on the couch next to him. Then I release the button at his waist. As I reach for the tab of his zipper, he captures my wrist.

"Stroke me first."

Swallowing my nerves, I nod.

I grasp him and gently move up and down his length, feeling the way his cock leaps and hardens.

"That's it." His voice is a low, rumbly purr of approval.

Emboldened by his pleasure, I close my hand slightly and squeeze harder.

"Fuck, little dove."

He brushes my hand aside and finishes removing his pants.

Impatient, Mr. Merritt?

But that he's been with so many women and wants me this badly is thrilling.

Suddenly as impatient as him, I release the buttons on his shirt, fumbling a little. Then I shove the material over his shoulders.

Unable to resist temptation, I trail my hand down his chest, lingering on his tight abs. Being this close, touching him, inhaling his pure, masculine spicy scent, has already made me wet.

"Not too sore from last night?"

Maybe a little, but I'm not confessing that to him. "Not at all."

"Then we need to try harder to wear you out."

I look up, and he's grinning. Having Link tease me is unusual, but I like it.

He stands.

His erect cock is right in front of me, a tiny drop glistening on the tip. Without being asked, without being coached, I do what comes naturally and lick it away. The salty tanginess on my tongue sends a fresh wave of arousal through me.

"Jesus."

Emboldened, I suck his cockhead into my mouth and swirl my tongue around it. He buries his hand into my hair, holding me tight as I try to take more and more of his length.

Finally my eyes water, and I choke a little. Pulling back, I look up at him.

Link's eyes are glazed, and that fills me with a feeling of power.

"You're so damn hot." He offers me his hand.

Instead of accepting, I lean forward to taste him again.

"That's enough."

With a small sigh, I slide my palm against his.

He draws me to him, his hard core pressing into my softness. Then he digs his fingers into my buttocks, making me moan. "I…"

"Soon," he promises as he releases me. "Now go into the bedroom."

Curious to know what he has in mind, I cross to the bedroom to find Pax already there, completely naked, his enormous cock jutting toward me.

"We thought we'd try something new this morning," Pax says.

I barely hear him over my thundering heart.

Link joins us in the room, continuing on to stand next to Pax.

Do these two plan everything they're going to do to me?

As I watch, he pulls out two condoms from the box. Then once more, he crooks his finger.

"Put one on each of us."

Pax nods at the floor, and I understand his intent. Without hesitation, I sink to my knees, my heart pounding with a mix of anticipation and nervousness.

I accept the first packet, and my fingers shake as I tear it open.

I start with Pax, his cock so thick and hard that it's a challenge to roll the condom down his length. He groans as I touch him, his eyes never leaving mine.

Then I turn to Link. He's watching me with a heated gaze, his cock twitching as if impatient for my touch. I open the second packet and smooth the condom over him, feeling the pulsing veins beneath my fingers.

Being on my knees in front of them shoots goose bumps down my arms.

"Good girl," Link praises, his voice low and husky. He offers me his hand, helping me to my feet.

Pax moves to the bed, lying down, his erection jutting up demandingly toward me. "Come here, sweetheart."

Once I've straddled him, Link lies next to us.

"Lean forward," Pax instructs, his hands gripping my hips to guide me.

When I do, he positions himself at my entrance, rubbing the head of his cock against my wetness before slowly pushing inside.

Like last night, I gasp at the fullness, the feeling of being stretched around him.

Pax begins to move beneath me, his thrusts slow and deep.

He draws me down to his chest, capturing my mouth in a searing kiss. Then he trails his hands over my body, lighting fires on my skin as he cups my breasts, rolling my nipples between his fingers.

I gasp, and heat builds in me.

Link slides his hand onto my belly, then moves lower, finding my clit and teasing it until I'm writhing against him.

Just when I'm on the edge, Pax grasps my hips and lifts me off him.

"What?" I ask, dazed.

"My turn," Link says.

"Your—"

My words are cut off when Link moves me onto his lap, my back to his chest. He lifts me slightly. "Take my cock. Handle it. Put it in you."

His demands are so sexy that my head spins.

He raises an eyebrow. "Do it."

I turn my head a little and reach behind me to grab hold of him.

A little nervous because I'm accustomed to them taking charge, I hold his dick steady and move myself onto his cockhead.

"Good." His tone is filled with approval. "That's it."

Feeling ridiculously awkward, I lower myself. Then I lift up a little.

"Fuck me, little dove."

Instead of waiting for me, he circles my wrist and pulls my hand aside to enter me with a single, powerful thrust, filling me completely.

I cry out, from pleasure, not pain.

He holds my waist firm, anchoring me against him.

I lift myself a little, moving with urgent, intense strokes, each one pushing me higher, closer to a climax.

My thoughts blur. Everything inside me begins to tighten, and he lifts me up.

I cry out my protest. My clit is throbbing. I want this. *Need* it.

"You'll come when we say, little dove."

"You're awful."

"Terrible," he agrees.

I'm shaking, and my pussy has never been wetter.

"Pax is waiting."

They're passing me back and forth between them?

Reeling, my mind barely able to string two thoughts together, I accept his hand as he helps me move into position. I'm shaking as I take him inside me once more.

Link kneels behind me and reaches around to cup my breasts and tease my nipples into hard peaks. He trails kisses down my neck.

I moan helplessly as every part of me responds to their dual touch, their dual possession.

Pax thrusts, building a steady rhythm.

Once more, his strokes push me closer to the edge. "Please," I beg. I'm desperate, coming undone, and I have no idea how long they intend to keep this torment going.

Link eases one hand lower to play with my clit, circling it, teasing it, driving me wild.

They've turned me into a panting, moaning mess.

Pax holds me tight, and his thrusts become more urgent, more demanding, each keeping me on the edge.

Tension coils in me. And still, Link is relentless.

"Please," I beg again, my voice a ragged whisper. "I need… I need to come."

"Yes." Pax's gaze locks onto mine, his eyes filled with a fierce intensity. "Come with me."

I shatter, wave after wave of pleasure crashing through me. My internal muscles clamp down on him. Moments later, he groans, calling my name, finding his own release, pulsing deep inside me.

Link's touch is lighter now. "You're beautiful when you come, little dove."

Pax trails his fingers up my sides to cup my breasts. "Gorgeous," he agrees, his thumbs brushing over my nipples, drawing out a gasp from deep within me.

I lean forward, resting my forehead on Pax's chest, trying to catch my breath.

"That was…" I struggle to find the right words. "Incredible."

Link chuckles, lying down beside us, his hand tracing lazy patterns on my back. "We're glad you approve."

Pax slips out of me, then rolls us so that I'm underneath him. He presses a soft kiss on my lips before moving away.

Link brushes back my hair as Pax walks into the bathroom, his cock still impossibly big.

"Marrying you may be the best decision I ever made," Link says.

His confession stuns me, and I have no idea what to say in return.

I'm saved from responding when Pax returns with a warm washcloth. I sigh as he gently soothes between my legs. After last night and what we've just shared, I'm a little tender, even if I wouldn't admit that to either of them.

"We're not quite finished," Link says, positioning himself between my legs.

They're insatiable, but I want this more than I could have imagined possible.

His eyes are filled with hunger, and he devours my mouth in a deep, possessive kiss.

He strokes into me, allowing me to feel every inch of his hardness.

This position seems more intimate. I love the passion the three of us have been sharing, but this is more than a fuck, as he'd called it earlier.

It feels like making love.

Or maybe I'm making up things that I want to be true.

Propping his weight away from me, he moves, taking his time, allowing me to savor their actions.

As I respond, becoming wetter, arching my back, he thrusts harder, deeper, each motion a mark of his possession.

"That's it. Give yourself to me. Everything you've got."

Pax strokes my spine. His touch is comforting, and it keeps the three of us grounded as lovers.

My body instinctively syncs with my husband's.

Deep inside, my climax builds

"You belong to us."

As if he owns me, he sends me over the edge, crying out his name.

Moments later, he groans, and he comes, his body shuddering. Then, for a moment, he holds me tight, and I drink in desperate gulps of air.

I'm shattered.

"You okay?" Pax asks.

"I'm not sure." It's the honest truth. I tingle, and I ache a little.

"She may need a breather." Pax shrugs

"You have time for a bath, if you'd like," Link says.

Not wanting our connection to end, I trace his jawbone.

"An hour long enough for you to get ready?" he asks.

"Ready?" I ask, frowning. "For what?"

"We're going to lunch, maybe take in a few sights."

"Maybe a cupcake from the ATM at the Royal Sterling?" Pax suggests.

Are they serious?

"We're on our honeymoon, and we're in Las Vegas," Link says. "Tonight after dinner and the cabaret show, we're scheduled for a helicopter tour of the Strip."

"Dress comfortably," Pax tells me. "You've got a long day—"

"*And night*," Link interrupts.

Pax nods. "*And night* ahead of you."

Am I going to survive my husbands and their never-ending demands?

CHAPTER TWENTY-SIX

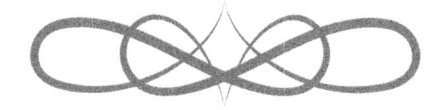

Tessa

The warm water cascades over us, steam filling the air as I stand beneath the expansive showerhead with Pax and Link.

I'm not sure I've ever been more exhausted.

Under the ever-watchful eye of some Hawkeye agents, we had an amazing lunch on the Strip, walked forever, then stopped in at the Royal Sterling for a coffee and salted-caramel bourbon cupcake topped with flaked sea salt and thin dark-chocolate shards.

I'd suggested we install an ATM that dispenses goodies at Link's house. He hadn't been very agreeable, even though Mira agreed my idea was a good one.

Afterward, an SUV had picked us up and zipped us back to the Bella Rosa where we changed clothing, then headed for the steak house. Then after the riveting burlesque show at the Royal Sterling, featuring the amazing the Sensational Miss Scarlet, we'd been dropped off for that helicopter tour.

I've never been so terrified and exhilarated all at the same time.

Then we came back to the hotel suite, and Link drew me to the bathroom.

Now Pax takes the shower wand from its holder, adjusting the setting until it's pulsating gently. He looks at me, a wicked grin spreading across his face as he kneels in front of me.

"No," I whisper, as horrified as I am excited. He can't mean…

"Oh yes," Pax confirms. "Spread your legs."

A little nervous, I take my time doing as he says.

Link stands behind me, and he reaches around me to part my labia, opening me up completely to Pax. I gasp at the sudden exposure, but the sound is quickly replaced by a moan as Pax directs the warm, pulsating water between my legs.

"How sore are you from the last twenty-four hours?" Link asks.

Water pulses against my clit, making words impossible.

"Little dove?"

"A little," I manage. After all, Link is enormous. And Pax is a demanding lover. "Not too bad."

"This'll help," Pax assures me.

Will it?

Getting turned on and needy?

Link stands behind me and holds my waist to keep me steady as Pax continues to tease me.

Then Link moves one hand between my legs to spread me wider for Pax.

Together the two of them are diabolical.

"Give in," Link encourages.

With a sigh, I rest the back of my head against Link's chest while Pax explores every part of me.

He takes his time, standing upright when he moves the

spray over my anus. The tingling and my response shocks me.

"A very concentrated place of nerve endings," Link tells me.

I can't believe that I don't want him to instantly move on.

After he rocks me to another climax, Pax hangs up the shower wand.

"How's that?" he asks.

The warm water soothed, but I'm on fire for them. "I may want to take more showers with you two," I surprise myself by admitting.

"Fuck. Little dove..."

They take their time, soaping me, their strong hands gliding over my skin. Then they rinse me off again.

But Pax is cursory with the spray between my thighs, rinsing but not bringing me pleasure.

Before I'm ready, Pax steps out of the shower. Instead of drying off, he holds a large, inviting, plush towel open for me.

Water droplets cling to his skin, seeming to highlight the well-defined muscles of his chest and arms. His cock is more than half hard, and I meet his eyes.

He tips his head to one side. "Our night is still young."

He's breathtakingly sexy, as protective as he is demanding. I can't believe we'll be spending forever together. "So the shower was self-serving?" Another first, joking with him. Right now, it's as natural as it is fun. Maybe I've put the danger behind me, at least for now.

"Of course not. All about you, Tessa."

"Mmm-hmm."

He wraps the towel around me, cocooning me in warmth.

Link steps out right behind me and grabs a towel of his own to hang around his waist.

A lock of his hair has fallen across his forehead, and I can't resist the temptation to brush it back.

He's so lean and classically handsome with his chiseled cheekbones. But there's a ruthless power about him that terrifies and lures me in all at the same time.

Once I'm dry, he offers me a robe, and I slip into it. Link drops his towel on the floor and leads me back into the living room.

He's comfortable being naked. Will I ever get used to it?

I swallow deeply when he sits on the couch, then pulls me onto his lap so that I'm straddling him.

His growing erection presses against me, and instinctively I grind against him.

"That's it." He moans from deep in his chest.

"Take off your robe," Pax says.

I loosen the knot, then shrug. He captures the fluffy terry cloth material, tosses it over the back of the couch, then caresses my back, sliding down to cup my ass. He leans down, his breath warm against my nape.

After squeezing one of my buttocks, he lands a light slap on my ass.

I gasp, looking over my shoulder.

He's standing right there, so close, naked and powerful, studying me.

"Too much?" he asks, caressing the spot he just spanked, soothing the sting.

I shake my head. "It didn't hurt. Just... I didn't expect it." Shockingly, though, I'm even more turned on, and I move against Link's hard dick.

"Again?"

"I..."

Link captures my chin. "We'll go slow, Tessa. You can stop us at any time. Just say the word."

"BDSM?" I manage, the letters almost lodging in my throat.

"A taste," Pax says. "Nothing more tonight."

"You two…"

Link quirks an eyebrow in a manner that should indicate interest but is a little intimidating.

"I mean…"

When I falter, Link picks up the conversation. "Open, honest discussion about everything matters."

I grew up sheltered, and I'm out of my depth. My parents never argued, at least not in front of me. In our house, things were whispered quietly, not exposed to the daylight.

"Ask your question," Pax encourages.

He hasn't stopped rubbing my rear.

"Trust us," he adds. "You've been able to so far."

Since he's right, I try. "You do this—that—the kinky stuff with other women?"

"Did," Link says. "Past tense. You are the only woman in our lives from this day forward."

"Since that moment at the Rusty Nail," Pax amends. "Link was obsessed."

I meet his gaze, and he doesn't deny his bodyguard's words.

Instead he tells me, "If you don't want this to be part of our relationship, we'll do without."

Yesterday, I was a virgin. And now I'm talking about kinky things I know next to nothing about. "But… Doesn't it hurt?"

"Did that spanking hurt?" Pax asks.

"Well…" I've already admitted it didn't. "No."

"The way we've squeezed your nipples?"

I shake my head. In fact, it was delicious.

"Some things can be painful." As I expect, Link is plain-spoken. "But only to enhance pleasure."

Skeptical, I wrinkle my nose.

"Consent," Link reasserts. "You can always say no."

"Most typically, you'll have a safe word," Pax explains. "You're welcome to choose whatever you want, something you won't say accidentally. To keep it simple, a lot of people choose red for stop immediately and yellow to slow down or maybe a time out if needed to talk about the situation or an emotional need. Things along those lines."

Since I'm unsure how to respond, I remain silent.

Pax goes on. "That said, we will be watching you at all times. You'll be our complete focus. We'll read your reactions, maybe before you're even aware of them."

Since no one has ever paid me that kind of attention, my skepticism deepens.

"In turn, you'll be aware of us on a level you've never experienced with anyone else."

"All of this sounds fantastical. Impossible."

"Does it?" Link asks.

I remember the lovemaking we've already shared and the way they've taken such good care of me.

"Always your choice," he goes on.

I take a shallow breath to steady my nerves. Then I nod.

"We need to hear your consent."

"Yes." My voice is so shaky. "I'm willing to try."

"Safe words?" Pax prompts.

"I'll go with red and yellow." Easy enough to remember. I hope.

"In that case..." Pax lands another slap on my ass, this time on the other cheek.

This one stings a little more, but that ache vanishes when he massages it away.

"Ride my cock," Link commands.

I frown. He's not inside me.

Reaching to hold apart my buttocks, he leans toward me.

When he speaks, his words are soft but undeniably sexy. "Do I need to repeat myself? You might not like the consequences."

My insides liquify.

Obediently I do as he wants. The friction of his bare, hard dick against my slightly swollen pussy makes me moan.

Link moves me, simulating lovemaking.

Pax alternates between spanking and caressing, each slap sending a small jolt of pain through me, each caress soothing the burn.

I'm lost.

Every part of me responds to them. I grind myself against Link, and my breaths become ragged, desperate gasps.

Pax becomes even more overwhelming, adding tiny pinches to my skin, then my nipples.

They're holding me apart, and sensations assail me from everywhere, all at the same time.

I lose track of where I am, what's happening.

All that matters is the swirling light around me and the way my body is on fire, needing release.

Pax squeezes my nipple harder than before, and I tip my head back.

He trails a fingertip down the column of my throat, then across my shoulder and down my spine.

Lazily he continues on, dipping between my ass cheeks.

I freeze.

"Did I say you can stop riding me?" Link's voice is harsh in a way that spurs me on.

"No!" Immediately I begin to move again.

Not knowing what to expect next is undoing me.

The men are in tune with each other, as if they can communicate without words.

Link holds my buttocks farther apart, and I suddenly know what Pax intends.

He circles the tight ring of muscle, applying a slight pressure that makes me gasp. "Relax, sweetheart," he murmurs, his voice soothing. "We won't do anything you're not ready for."

I take a deep breath, forcing myself to relax as Pax squirts some liquid onto his finger, then crouches behind me to gently probe my rear.

Oh God.

With his free hand, he cups my shoulder.

I'm trapped between these powerful, relentless men. The dual nature of their possession is mind boggling.

Pax begins to press into me. "Bear down."

I'm not sure I can do that.

"It'll be easier."

He's against a tight ring of muscle, and I clench involuntarily.

Sharply he gives me a spank, making me cry out and relax all at once, and he breaches past the barrier.

The initial discomfort vanishes, and he massages my rear.

I'm so full, and a strange pleasure unlike anything I've ever experienced washes through me.

Link moves me faster, and I'm griding against him in rhythm with Pax's movements.

I'm intoxicated... *"Oh!"*

"That's it, little dove."

I arch my back a little so my breasts are against Link's chest, my nipples abrading his chest.

Desire builds with each movement.

I feel Link and Pax everywhere, and their touch swallows me whole.

"Let go." Pax's words are a low growl against my ear.

His words push me over the edge.

I cry out. Then I collapse as waves of pleasure crash over me.

Link holds me tight, supporting me as I ride out the orgasm.

Gently Pax withdraws his finger, and he presses a kiss against the side of my neck as I come down from my climactic high.

Then he's gone, and Link captures my mouth.

Finally reality returns as Link ends the kiss and Pax presses a warm, damp cloth against my rear.

Beneath me, Link's cock is still hard as granite.

If this has anything to do with BDSM, I'm intrigued.

"Soon you'll be taking both of us at the same time."

"You mean..." I can't form the words.

"I can't wait to fuck your ass," Pax says.

Link adds, "While I fill your pussy."

Frantically I shake my head. I'm not just flabbergasted by their confidence. There's absolutely no way both my husbands will fit inside me at the same time. Regardless, I'm pretty sure I don't want to test the theory...

CHAPTER TWENTY-SEVEN

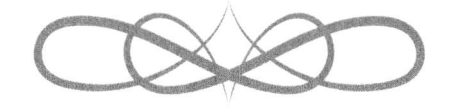

Tessa

"How about a nightcap?" Link suggests.

I'm tired, but I'm still a little wound up. So much has happened today, and the sex we just shared was so amazing that I'm not quite ready to go to sleep. "Sounds good," I respond as I snuggle back into my robe.

"Champagne, wine, something else?" Pax offers

"Surprise me."

"Whiskey, boss?"

Link nods.

Pax walks into the bedroom, and when he returns, he's wearing slacks and nothing else. There's an easy intimacy between us now that I find unusual but nice.

I honestly don't remember the last time I was this happy.

While Pax is at the bar area, Link goes into the bedroom, and I curl up on the couch.

Pax is methodical as he pours the alcohol. Then he drops ice into another glass, opens a bottle, then the refrigerator.

Link strides back into the living room wearing a pair of

black lounge pants. And obviously no underwear. For a moment, I can't help but stare.

When he catches me, he grins.

Blushing, I lower my head and look away.

Without a word, he goes and gets the glasses from the bar area. Then Pax carries a drink to me.

"What is it?"

"Chocolate liqueur and cream."

With cocoa powder on the top and some shaved chocolate.

"The alcohol may make you drowsy, and the milk should help you stay asleep."

Thoughtful. "Sounds good. Thank you," I say as I accept the cocktail.

"We need to be sure you get your rest."

"I see." Grinning, I swirl the ingredients together. "Who are you most concerned about? Me or yourselves?"

"Yes," Link replies, making me laugh.

The men drop into armchairs that are near each other. Both of them look like they are kings on their respective thrones.

A week ago, I couldn't have imagined that I'd be so comfortable with them that I'd look forward to spending this kind of time together.

"What do you think?" Pax asks, leaning forward to pick up his whiskey.

I take a small sample. "Delicious." My new favorite thing. "Feel free to make me one anytime. Every evening, for example." I smile. Already I'm feeling spoiled, and I wouldn't be honest if I didn't admit I like it as much as I enjoy our lovemaking, and even the spanking.

Heat races through me. It's because of the liqueur I tell myself. Nothing more.

"And how is everything else?" he asks.

I look at him. Has he read my mind?

"The spanking," he prompts.

He *has* read my mind. How is that possible?

"We told you we'd be watching you."

Still a little uncomfortable to be talking about this, especially since we're not in an intimate scene, I change positions. "Nothing like I might have expected."

"You didn't use a slow word or a safe word," Link says.

I shake my head.

"Awful?" Pax suggests. "Something you'd prefer not to do again?"

When I don't respond, he offers, "Just okay? Take it or leave it? Intriguing? Wonderful?"

I shift once more.

He flicks a glance toward Link. "I think she liked it."

"Did you, little dove?"

The experience was somewhere between intriguing and wonderful. Then again, everything I've done with them has been thrilling.

"Want to try another spanking?" Pax asks.

Every cell in my body heats and responds.

"You're free to say no," he goes on. "But if you'd like to explore a little more, stand up and take off your robe."

Movements a little awkward, I set down my glass and slowly stand, very much aware of how focused they are on me.

Since my fingers suddenly don't seem to want to work properly, I need two tries to get the belt loosened.

While Link holds his drink contemplatively, Pax slides his onto the coffee table.

"Stand in front of me," he says, voice soft but tone uncompromising.

My heart roars in my ears.

"Stop there."

Though I'm confused because I'm a few feet away from him, I do as he says.

In complete silence, he studies me, and I'm so captivated by him that I can't look away.

Deliberately he glances at the floor.

Understanding, I kneel, like I had for Link.

"Lower your head a little."

Feeling awkward, I focus my gaze on the floor in front of me.

An interminable amount of time passes, ratcheting up my tension with each passing moment.

"Breathe. Long, slow, deep breaths."

His voice is mesmerizing.

Audibly, he breathes aloud. Seconds later, I follow his pattern. Surprising me, I begin to relax.

"That's it, sweetheart."

His approval feeds a part of me that I hadn't realized was needy.

For maybe two full minutes, he leads me.

Not being able to see what's going on around me is kind of a mind-fuck, but then I forget about anything except the moment.

I'm more emotionally grounded than I've been in months. Maybe since before I fled my childhood home or even before that, when my parents had died in that horrific crash.

Pax leaves me where I am for long moments before softly saying my name.

Startled, I look up.

"So perfect. Now stand and come to me."

A wave of nervous anticipation washes over me as I do as he says.

He offers his hand and guides me into place over his lap. His legs are muscular, powerful, beneath my body.

With a firm hand on my waist, he adjusts my position.

"Tell me your safe word," he prompts.

"Red," I whisper.

"And to have me slow down or because you're uncomfortable or may need to talk?"

"Yellow."

"Very good."

Until recently, I had no idea how much their approval meant to me.

He glides a hand over my exposed skin, heightening my senses, igniting a yearning.

Pax spreads his legs a few inches, and I wiggle, trying to get more comfortable.

Not that such a thing is possible.

Then he raises one knee, jostling me forward. Desperately I touch my fingers to the floor so I don't topple off him. But one of his hands is clamped around my waist, and on some level I know he will never allow me to fall.

His touch is gentle as he soothes my bare buttocks, his fingers tracing idle patterns.

"Remember to communicate with me."

When I don't respond, he prompts me again. "Tell me you understand."

"Yes, Pax."

Gently his palm connects with my rear, an intoxicating combination of sting and warmth. I gasp.

"I want you to count for me."

Why?

"Tessa?"

Wishing I could read his expression, I finally manage, "One."

"Such a good girl." He rewards me with a gentle caress, soothing the place he just lightly spanked.

Then he does it again.

My head swims. "Two."

With every tap, Pax builds a rhythm. As he continues, he begins to increase the force a little, almost unnoticeably, and he continues to mix the slight pain with a healing touch.

As I count, I'm pulled deeper in a sensual haze where nothing exists except the moment.

When I reach ten, he pauses, running his fingers down my spine.

I draw in as deep a breath as possible given my position.

"You're handling this beautifully, sweetheart."

I close my eyes as his words go through me.

"Do you want to continue?"

I consider how to answer. My mind is swirling from the experience, and I'm trying to process what's happening, my emotions, the undeniable acknowledgment of my trust in them and their sensual dominance over me.

"Yes," I finally whisper. I'm curious, and I don't want this to end.

"My pleasure."

This time, his spank is a tiny bit harder. "Eleven," I somehow manage.

All of a sudden Link is crouched next to me. "Spread your legs more."

Since I take my time responding, Pax bounces his knees, and Link parts my thighs.

Pax goes on, his next slap sending a rush of warmth through me, leaving me teetering between discomfort and ecstasy.

"Twelve."

Link eases his hand up the inside of one of my thighs and continues until he reaches the apex.

"So fucking wet, little dove."

Even his words arouse me more.

Pax clamps my waist harder, holding me prisoner while Link explores my pussy.

Desperately I squirm against Pax's lap, wordlessly pleading with them to continue.

"Tell us. Ask for what you want," Link commands.

He slides a finger inside me, angling it to find a spot so amazing and sensitive that I gulp in air and lift my head.

"Like that?"

Oh God. "Yes."

He presses a fingertip against me and Pax spanks me again. The tiny shocks send me soaring.

"What number was that?"

As if I have any idea.

"Tessa?" he prompts.

"Lost count."

"Thirteen."

"Okay." I nod. No matter what he had said, I would have agreed.

"How many more?"

"I… Just keep going?" How long should it last? Am I supposed to say something specific?

Then I lose my train of thought as Link slides two fingers in and out of me, taking time to tease my clit as he does.

Pax continues. Between his stinging spanks and Link's demands, I barely remember to count.

I'm helpless, instinctively lifting my hips while trying to grind myself against the heel of Link's hand.

"Twenty?" I guess after Pax's hand lands once again.

"Close."

He goes on and on while Link continues to be relentless, blurring my reality.

"Remember to breathe." Pax's voice is calm, a lifeline of sorts. Maybe that's a good thing because I'm so close to being untethered.

An orgasm unfurls demandingly. "I— I can't—" Suddenly everything is too much. My breathing quickens, and I can feel the wave of awakening cresting high, ready to crash.

"Come for us, little dove."

Link finger-fucks me faster, and my world spins.

At the same time, Pax stops spanking me. Instead he rubs away the aching burn he caused.

Frantically I jerk my hips and arch my back, needing, taking.

Then I scream as I lose control.

"Such an obedient little dove."

Link eases from inside me, then he places his fingers against my lips.

"Dry them for me."

Can I refuse these men anything?

I open my mouth and suck the saltiness from them.

"Good girl." His praise is laced with gruffness.

Pax gives me another hard spank. Yelping, I kick my legs.

Since he's so much bigger and stronger, that doesn't even seem to faze him, and he helps me to stand while dizzying aftershocks make me sway.

Pax clamps his hands on my waist, holding me steady. Then Link scoops me into his arms.

"We'll let you rest," he says as he strides toward his bedroom.

Really?

"For a little while."

That's more what I expected from him.

Pax follows us into the bedroom.

While we were out for the evening, the resort staff had turned down the bedding, and Pax pulls it back a little more so that Link can place me directly in the middle of the mattress.

Each man joins me, one on either side.

"You did amazing," Pax tells me.

I look up at him. There's a blaze of pure, primal power in his green eyes.

"Are you okay?" Brushing back a strand of hair from my forehead, he studies my features.

"Yes." More than okay.

"You'd do it again?" Link asks.

"It was…amazing," I admit, to myself as much as to them.

"That's a yes?" he presses.

I nod. Every time I'm with them, I experience something new. And I can't wait to discover more.

From the living room, my phone chimes, and I sit up.

"Leave it," Link says.

"It's late," Pax agrees. "Check in the morning."

For a moment, I consider their opinions, and then I remember the evening that Natalie had called after the break-in.

I don't get a lot of calls, and since it's already after midnight, the text might be important. "I'll be right back."

Instead of trying to climb over either man, I crawl to the end of the bed.

After scooping up a discarded shirt from the edge of the mattress, I slip it on as I make my way to the living room.

Still naked, Pax is right behind me.

I dig my phone from the bottom of my purse and check the display. "Axel." I look at Pax.

With a scowl, he extends his hand. "Give that to me."

"The hell?" Link demands. Then he scowls at me. "How the fuck did he get your phone number?"

I have no idea.

Turning my back to them, I unlock the message.

CHAPTER TWENTY-EIGHT

Tessa

Congrats on your wedding, little sis.

As I'm holding the device, another message arrives.

Now they're going to kill me.

The phone slips from my nerveless fingers and clatters to the floor with a final thunk.

I knew he was in deep. But he thinks he'll be murdered?

Link turns me to face him while Pax snatches up the device and looks at it.

Without a word, he hands it to Link, who releases one of my shoulders to accept.

A tiny pulse throbs in his temple as he scans the words.

I look from one to the other. "What does this mean?"

"Little dove—"

"I asked for an explanation." How my voice is so calm I have no idea because my stomach has turned inside out.

I don't love my brother. In fact, I hate him for what he tried to do to me, but I don't wish him dead. "This isn't for real, right?"

The two men exchange glances.

"Right?" I demand again.

"We need to talk."

I shrug off Link's touch and wrap my hands around my middle. "Answer me."

"There are things you need to understand."

"Let's sit down," Pax says.

Since I'm shaking from confusion and hardly able to think straight, I reluctantly nod.

To fight off my sudden chill, I pick up the robe I'd been wearing earlier and knot the belt tightly around my waist.

Thankfully Link takes the opportunity to return to the bedroom to pull on some clothes.

My hand wavers as I reach for my drink. Then I stop. The chocolate liqueur with its milk seems suddenly unappealing. "I need something stronger," I murmur, setting the glass down untouched.

"Whiskey?" Link offers.

That sounds worse. "Wine."

Link nods, continuing across the room to pour me a glass.

Pax shifts on the couch, patting the space between them invitingly. But I shake my head. Instead I grab hold of one of the armchairs and drag it a few feet away. The physical distance mirrors my internal emotions.

Ever since the day I met them, they've kept things from me. Maybe that's because they're wanting to protect me. More likely, they trust no one.

But I won't settle for that any longer.

Link returns, offering me a generous pour of red wine. Without a thank you, I accept it.

To steady myself, I take a long sip before cradling the glass in both hands. Once Link takes his seat, I look at them, frowning from my hurt and confusion. "Tell me everything. I've had enough of your half-truths."

My harsh tone makes Link cringe and Pax wince.

The two men exchange a glance, a silent conversation passing between them. Finally Link leans forward, propping his elbows on his knees. "Axel's debts go far deeper than you realize."

That doesn't surprise me.

"It's not just gambling."

"Go on."

Link remains silent for a minute, as if contemplating what he wants to say. "He took over the business from your father."

I nod.

"And he's been working with criminal syndicates to help launder and hide money."

My wine sloshes over the rim of the glass.

"And skimming," Pax adds. "Each time he dug himself deeper, always believing the next big score would solve everything."

I fight to steady my glass. This is impossible…

My phone pings again, but Link has possession of it. "I need to see that," I insist.

Though he nods, first he reads the message. Then he shows Pax before sliding the device onto the coffee table and pushing it toward me.

You need to sign your inheritance over to me. That's the only way to save my life.

Frowning, I stare at the screen. *Inheritance?* To my knowledge, there's no such thing. I know my parents left the house to Axel, but that there's any more money stuns me.

"You didn't know about that?" Link asks.

I shake my head, and since my wine is in danger of

spilling again, I slide the glass onto the coffee table. "Did *you* know about it?" I counter.

He remains silent.

Damningly so.

Anger floods me, drowning my hurt. "And the whole thing with *Scandalicious?* Giving them an exclusive. You hired Marcella and arranged for pictures to be published so that my brother and Emiliano would find out I was married."

Again he says nothing.

"Everything you do serves a higher purpose, doesn't it? Your own."

"Little—"

"I'm nothing but a pawn to you." In some stupid, high-stakes game between powerful men.

He shakes his head. "It's not like that." Abruptly Link stands and paces to the window.

The view that had been so soothing now unsettles me.

He stares out for a long time before turning back. His expression is raw, vulnerable in a way I've never seen before.

"Look, little dove…" He sighs. "I married you to keep you safe. There's no fucking chance I would have ever let you fall into the clutches of Emiliano Sartori."

Pax leans forward, his green eyes intense. "There's something you need to understand about Link's history with Emiliano." Then he looks at Link "Boss?"

Dragging his hand through his hair, Link returns to his seat. "Sartori and I were business partners in a casino. The Casablanca."

I'd heard of the resort, a once-legendary hotspot outside of Chicago that had closed when I was a teen, amid rumors of mob activity.

"It was successful beyond what I imagined when I invested." Link's voice is tight with old pain. "But Sartori got greedy, started embezzling." He pauses, as if deciding to say something. But he shakes his head. "He ignored bills and was paying the mob for protection."

Once more, I feel as if I've fallen into a fantastical story. That seems like something that would happen in a previous century rather than just a few years ago.

"By the time my accountant figured out what was happening, it was too late. The casino was drowning in debt, and the mob wanted what was due them."

Pax picks up the story. "Link liquidated everything he owned to pay off the debts and keep the mob from coming after him. It nearly destroyed him."

My anger doesn't soften.

"And your brother owes money to Link."

I look at him. "To *you?*"

"I invested in one of his schemes."

My mind whirls.

"I called the debt. That's when he tried to sell you."

Shock leaves me numb.

"I didn't know who you were when we first met."

Desperately wanting to believe him, I search his face.

Our entire relationship—this whole situation—is so screwed up.

By marrying me, he stole me away from Emiliano. And that has made my brother even more desperate for money. And now there's an inheritance I knew nothing about.

Standing quickly, I pick up my glass and head for the bedroom I had when we first checked in.

"Tessa…"

Link follows me, and he grabs hold of my wrist, stopping me.

My jaw tight, I meet the heated anger in his gaze. With fury of my own, I yank my hand away. "I'll need the name of a lawyer. Text it to me."

CHAPTER TWENTY-NINE

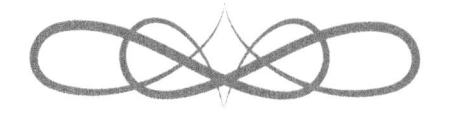

Two Days Later
Tessa

My pulse is racing as I exit the elevator and walk toward the offices of Fallon and Associates.

Of course, Torin and Mira are right behind me, their presence a constant reminder of the life I'm no longer sure I want.

When I am in front of the double doors marked with an engraved brass sign, I stop.

"Would you like us to come in?" Mira asks. "Or wait in the hallway?"

"Here. Please."

She nods sharply.

In a way, I'm shocked I'm even here. I wouldn't have put it past Link to try to stop me from leaving the house…for my own safety.

Pax is somewhat more reasonable. Though he wouldn't let me drive alone, he gave the Hawkeye agents instructions to let me go wherever I wanted.

I'm smart enough to realize he's probably tracking me and reporting my whereabouts to Link. But I'm free from his clutches for a few hours at least, and I took the time to grab a coffee on the way. Amazing how things I once took for granted now make me feel as if I'm getting away with something.

After squaring my shoulders, my heart thundering in a way that I can't control, I pull open the door.

A blond receptionist greets me with a polite smile, but I barely notice as I take in the decor. Everything about this place exudes confidence and success.

Before I can second-guess my decision to come here, a tall, striking woman in a tailored business suit emerges from an office and strides toward me.

She smiles, and she seems warm and inviting. I'm a little surprised because Drake Griffin, the attorney Link recommended I talk to, had called her a barracuda.

"Mrs. Merritt. I'm Celeste. Delighted to meet you."

As we shake hands, I catch a glint of bright green emeralds on her finger. I look a little more closely and recognize the owl design. Just how far does the Zeta society reach?

Celeste leads me into her office, gesturing toward a cozy seating area with a plush couch and two armchairs. "Let's sit here," she suggests. "It's more comfortable for conversation."

I perch on the edge of the couch, feeling small and out of place. Celeste hands me a bottle of water before taking a seat across from me. Her sharp eyes miss nothing as she studies me.

"Congratulations on your marriage," she says, her tone warm but neutral.

I try to smile, but my lips refuse to cooperate.

Celeste's expression softens with sympathy.

"Do we have attorney/client confidentiality?"

She nods. "Anything you say here—"

"Won't be immediately shared with Link?"

"Absolutely not. This is a private, privileged conversation." She's no nonsense, reassuring. "What is said between us remains between us for all time. Unless you waive your privilege."

Exhaling, I loosen the grip on my purse.

"What can I do for you?"

Her kindness undoes me. Before I know it, I'm pouring out everything I've been holding back—my brother's betrayal, running away from Chicago, Link and Pax's intervention, the whirlwind wedding, the fact I have two husbands, and the text messages that shattered my fragile sense of security.

Celeste listens intently, her face a mask of professional concern.

"I'm tired of feeling like a pawn."

She nods as if she understands completely, though there's no way that's true. "You didn't know about the inheritance your brother mentioned?"

"No." I shake my head. "I don't even know if it's real."

"Would you like me to find out?"

I appreciate that she hasn't just decided to handle it without being asked.

"Yes. Please."

She jots a note, her pen scratching against a yellow legal pad.

"And I have no idea how my brother got my phone number," I add.

Celeste notes that as well. "And your marriage?" she prompts gently. "How do you feel about that?"

I close my eyes as memories of Las Vegas rush back. The honeymoon was amazing, and there were moments when I forgot about everything else. But reality was always there, lurking in the background.

And now, after everything I've learned...

When I don't answer, she goes on. "Are you happy?"

"Happy?" My voice is sharp. And I shake my head. "I have no idea what that means." I've been overwhelmed: mentally, physically, emotionally. Everything has happened so fast that I've barely had time to think.

"Was there a prenuptial agreement?" she asks.

Her question catches me off guard. "No," I reply, shocked that Link never asked for one.

A small smile plays at the corners of Celeste's mouth, and for a moment, I catch a glimpse of the barracuda beneath her caring exterior.

"Which reminds me. I have a credit card, so I can pay your fee."

Celeste waves a hand dismissively. "This is a complimentary meeting. We'll go from there."

"But—" I start to protest.

"Don't worry, Mrs. Merritt—"

"Tessa, please," I interject.

She nods. "Tessa. Your husband will pay any bill I have."

I blink in surprise. "How can you be sure of that?"

"He's a reasonable man."

Reasonable? She must be talking about someone other than the person I married.

"To start with, I recommend we verify the existence of any inheritance, along with any details you might need. Then we'll look into how your brother obtained your number. Anything else?"

"I want to know the truth about Axel. Is he going to be murdered?"

"I'll look into it."

Part of me wants to believe Axel is trying to scare me. But I've learned the mob is real. So no doubt the consequences of not paying them back are as well.

Celeste is quiet, waiting for me to go on.

After taking a deep breath, I do. "And my marriage?"

"Legally, you have options, of course. Separation. Divorce. Potentially annulment."

My cheeks flood with heat. Isn't it too late for that?

"But I sense that's not what you're really asking," she guesses.

Celeste is right, and tears sting my eyes.

Am I ready to end this?

Since the question scares me, I shove it aside.

One thing is certain; I can't go on being manipulated, treated as if I don't have an opinion or the opportunity to make my own choices.

"Tessa," Celeste says gently, "this will come down to only one thing. What do you want?"

I open my mouth to respond, but no words come out.

What do I want?

The safety and security Link and Pax offer? The passion and connection I felt with them in Vegas? Or the freedom to make my own choices, free from manipulation and secrets?

Or maybe the one thing that matters more than any other. The one thing Link is incapable of offering.

Link

Jesus. For the first time in my life, I don't know what the fuck to do.

My thoughts racing, I pace the length of my office.

With Tessa, I'm out of my element.

Ever since she received the text from her asshole brother, she's been emotionally distant.

After pulling herself away from me in our Vegas suite, she

went into her bedroom, then closed and locked the door behind her.

The sound of running water reached me, so I guessed she took a bath. Then...I heard nothing else.

The next morning, she didn't emerge until Pax knocked on her door to let her know that we were getting ready to head home.

Though she sat with us on the plane, she angled her body to look out the window, grabbed a book, then slid in earbuds that she'd picked up at the airport.

Except for responding to questions in a cursory way, she'd been totally silent.

Once we were back home, she returned to the bedroom I'd given her the first night she arrived at my house.

Arrived? My conscience taunts me.

More like she was taken there without her agreement.

But if the situation replayed itself? I'd make the same decision all over again.

A knock on my door pierces the storm clouds gathering fury in my head. I stop pacing long enough to scowl.

Without waiting for an invitation, Pax enters. "Boss." He closes us in and drops into a chair in front of my desk.

"Where is she?" I demand.

For a moment, he is silent. "She's in a meeting."

I scowl. "Who with? Griffin?"

Drake Griffin is the hotshot attorney I recommended when she demanded the name of a lawyer. He's a cutthroat as well as a friend. I would have expected him to give me a heads-up about the consultation. Maybe we should have a discussion about loyalty.

"Celeste Fallon."

Pax's words fall into the silence. "Celeste?" I couldn't possibly have heard right. "The fuck?"

Celeste Fallon is a fellow Titan, and she's on the organization's steering committee. To most of the world, she appears to run Fallon and Associates, a PR firm that's been in her family for over a hundred fifty years. But the truth is, her specialty is crisis management. The ruthlessly intelligent attorney makes any problem go away—but the cost is astronomical.

Pax shrugs. "As we're finding out, our wife has a mind of her own."

"How the hell did she find Celeste?" If Griffin gave her the recommendation, I'll fire his ass. "Goddamn it."

"Mira and Torin are with her."

I glare. He knows this is about more than her physical safety. If I could, I'd keep her locked up in the house, at least until I've dispensed with her brother.

The problem is, that wouldn't help.

Tessa is turning out to be a problem I can't solve with money or influence. Our relationship isn't a hostile takeover I can strategize my way through.

She's left me feeling more powerless than I've ever been.

Harnessing my anger and frustration, I cross the room to drop into my chair. The leather creaks as I scrub a hand over my face. "She's going to file for divorce." The words burn like acid in my mouth.

"We don't know that," Pax counters. Though he's calm and thoughtful as ever, there's a hint of doubt in his voice.

"What the fuck else is she meeting with Celeste about?" The edge in my voice is sharper than I intend. "She's barely spoken to us since Vegas."

Vegas. Christ. When we were there, I'd caught a glimpse of the future I wanted. The three of us, happy. A real family, unlike the one I'd grown up with.

The memory of Tessa's laughter, the sight of her walking down the aisle to pledge herself to me, the way she looked at us both with trust and desire, the image of her on her knees, in our arms… Now I have nothing left but memories and a dream, and even that is slipping away faster than I can hold onto it.

"Might be about Axel," Pax says.

"Something we are handling."

"By ourselves. Without her input."

I clench my jaw so I don't fire back and kick him out of my office.

Pax stays silent for a long time, and the tension grows and thickens between us. And I'm going mad wondering what the hell she's discussing with Celeste.

Finally Pax leans forward. "You need to talk to her, Boss. Really talk. Open up."

I turn my chair to face the windows.

This office is a testament to my ambition and success. My empire. But what the hell good is any of that right now?

"She was right in what she said." His words are slow and deliberate. "About being a pawn."

I jerk my gaze back to him.

"She needs to know why we've been controlling this."

"The fuck you talking about?"

Pax unflinchingly meets my fury. He's the only person who would say any of these things to me.

"You're becoming him, Link."

The mention of Warren Merritt, my father, jolts me with hot, familiar anger.

"The man you swore you'd never be."

His words are a grotesque blow.

I've spent my whole life fighting my father's ghost, only to end up exactly where I never wanted to be. Controlling. Distant. Unemotional.

And just like him, I've driven away the only woman I've ever cared about. "I just want to keep her safe."

"At what cost?"

I want to rage, tell him to fuck off.

But I can't argue. The memory of my mother walking out, turning her back on me because she was unable to bear my father's suffocating control any longer, lances through my mind.

Pax's phone buzzes. He checks it, then flicks his gaze back up. "Tessa just left Celeste's office building."

"Is she going home?"

"It doesn't appear so."

CHAPTER THIRTY

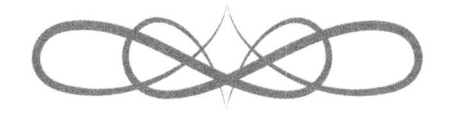

The Next Day
Tessa

"You have news for me?"

After we shake hands, Celeste gestures for me to take a seat.

This is our second meeting in less than twenty-four hours.

I perch on the edge of the sofa, my hands tight on my purse. Ever since she messaged me early this morning, I've been a nervous wreck.

She offered to chat on the phone, but I didn't want to risk either Link or Pax overhearing my conversation.

Still, getting away from the house wasn't easy.

I understand their protectiveness, especially since Axel's texts are coming faster and more furiously, but being under constant surveillance is wearing me down.

Today Torin and Mira are off, and that leaves me with Arielle, the agent who'd been with me in the bridal room at the Bella Rosa. Since Pax isn't comfortable with me just having one agent, I wouldn't be surprised if he followed us.

Still, when I glanced out the back window of the SUV, I hadn't seen his motorcycle.

Celeste takes a chair. Then without further pleasantries, she says, "You're going to be a very wealthy woman when you turn twenty-five."

"I'm..." *Speechless.*

Honestly I didn't expect my inheritance to amount to much.

Before the information has fully sunk in, Celeste goes on. "What do you know about your parents' home?"

"Axel met with the lawyers. When he came back, he told me that the house was mortgaged, and that my dad's business was pretty well bankrupt when...when the accident happened." I clear my throat. "Evidently he made some bad decisions."

"So you'd be surprised to learn the house was fully paid for and in the clear when they passed?"

"It was..." My ears start to buzz. "I..."

"And that the business was on solid ground?"

I grip my purse harder, as if my life depends on it. "What are you saying?"

She pulls a file folder from beneath her ever-present yellow legal pad. "Did you sign this?" She extracts a document and slides it toward me.

I study the blue ink. It's close to my signature but not exact. "No."

"It's a second mortgage."

Stunned, I drop the paper, and it flutters to the table. "I know nothing about it."

"Fraud," she suggests.

"And you said my father's firm wasn't bankrupt?"

"Quite the opposite."

I'm sick. How many betrayals do I have to go through?

"There's something else you should know." Her voice is calm and careful.

Trying to gather my composure, I sit back.

"Link has been in touch with the lawyer overseeing your trust."

Of course he has. I shouldn't be surprised, but somehow I still am.

Frustrated, I squeeze my eyes shut.

"As your spouse, he has a right to do so." She waits for a moment before adding, "He wants the funds to be transferred to a different management company."

Fury rises in me. "Merritt Sovereign," I guess.

"You're correct."

For the next fifteen or twenty minutes, Celeste explains options to me, including the terms of the trust. I can apply for funds for living expenses and education. Anything beyond that must be approved. "I have the means to support myself?"

"It will all depend on the definition of living expenses and what's included. If you wish to live independently, we'll also request funds from your husband."

My heart twists into a hard knot.

"This is a lot to take in."

I'm reeling, hardly able to piece anything together.

"Any questions for me?"

"The fund manager. Is he doing a good job?"

"As far as I can see, Julie is doing an excellent job of looking out for your interests."

Julie. I like that my dad chose a woman for me to work with.

"Management fees are higher than I'd like to see, but not out of line with industry standards." She pauses for a moment. "I believe Merritt Sovereign is higher."

I'm not quite sure what all that means, but I'm determined to find out.

"I'll text you her phone number. You should get acquainted. If you like her, you can continue to work with her. I'll also send you the information for your parents' attorney."

"Thank you."

"Take some time to think about all of this. Call me when you'd like to meet again? Of course, I'm here if you have further questions. And if you should want to make any moves, we can."

Dazed, I stand and say goodbye. When I reach the door, I stop and turn back. "What about Axel's trust? Did he have one?"

She nods. "He did."

"It's gone?"

"As far as I can tell. I haven't taken a deep dive into his finances."

With his gambling issues. I know the answer.

She's quiet for a moment. "Tessa… I don't normally give advice."

For the first time, I smile. "But…?"

"Your brother had an inheritance, a house that was paid off, a business that was solvent. He's had more than enough chances. If you sign over your trust, he'll be back in the same financial situation again soon."

Celeste is right. Yet he's still my brother, despite everything.

Back in the SUV, I try to sort through my crazy emotions. I'm frustrated and angry with Link. I'm furious with my brother. My dad worked his whole life to take care of us. Even after his death, he'd done that. And Axel screwed it all up.

Would I be selfish to keep the funds my dad set aside for me? Especially considering the cost to Axel?

Not quite ready to return home, I ask Arielle to swing by the coffee shop, and since the afternoon is steamy, I order us both a frozen concoction. Then I splurge and add cake pops to the order.

"Oh God," she complains when we drive through to pick up the order. "I so don't need this."

"Neither do I." I grin as I place the beverages in the cup holders.

"You didn't need to get me anything."

"Are you kidding? You need the caffeine. Your job is hard." And probably boring as hell. Trying to stay sharp, prepared for danger, even when nothing ever happens.

"Thanks," she says, wrinkling her nose at me. "But now I'll have to hit the gym after my shift."

I stick my straw through the whipped cream and stir it in. "Wouldn't you anyway?"

"But I usually work out for an hour, and now I'll have to make it two."

We both laugh, and I appreciate the break from my worries.

At that moment, a motorcycle roars past us, and I instinctively glance over.

Pax.

No doubt.

"Did he follow us from the house?"

"Who?" She never takes her gaze off the road.

But she hadn't blinked when the bike blazed by. Her light shrug tells me all I need to know.

When we turn into the neighborhood, I remind her that I'm going to visit Natalie later in the day. David's out of town, and she's invited me to see their apartment.

Girl time is exactly what I need.

"When do you want to leave?"

"Five."

"Got it." She nods. "Text me the address, and I'll have it programmed in."

I grab my unfinished drink and cake pop, then let myself into the quiet house.

After our return from Vegas, I insisted on having the codes to the alarm. Link was a little reluctant, but Pax eventually relented. After all, every time a door or window is touched, a notification is sent to his phone. I'd never get outside without him knowing.

Relieved to be alone, I head upstairs to change into jeans and a comfy shirt.

Since we got back from our honeymoon, I've been spending plenty of time in my room, reading and watching movies on my laptop, looking at local colleges...avoiding my husbands as much as possible.

This afternoon, I call the fund manager and my family's attorney and make appointments to talk to them tomorrow. Then, feeling somewhat more empowered, I drop onto my bed and once again look at local colleges.

All the information from Celeste makes me think.

If I hadn't been forced to drop out of school when I ran away, I would still be there. Now I'm determined to go back. I want to know more about finances, about business. If I keep the money my parents left in trust for me, I don't want to waste it.

The big question is, where do I want to live?

Should I stay in Houston?

If not, where would I go?

Returning to Chicago isn't an option.

And the truth is, until Axel leaves me alone, I'm probably trapped with Link and Pax.

I check out a few colleges that are nearby. University of

Houston looks interesting, but it may be more money than I can afford. But what if I got a job?

As if Link will allow that.

Frustrated, I sigh. How long is my life going to be on hold?

But as Celeste said, I do have options. Right now, it doesn't feel that way.

I look at the local community college. For now, I could enroll in some online classes and get started soon. They offer an associate's in business. With the classes I've already completed, I can earn that quickly.

Resolved, I exhale.

One thing feels settled, even if the rest of my life is still upside down.

The alarm on my phone rings, and I realize I'm running late.

After grabbing my purse, I slip on a pair of sandals.

As I walk down the staircase, I hear the deep rumble of male voices.

Crap. Is Link home early?

If he is, I can hope he's in his office so I can get out the door without him seeing me.

The tension between us is thick and uncomfortable, and I've barely been able to sleep. Even though I hate the tension between us, I won't back down.

As I near the kitchen, my heart sinks. Both men are there.

The worst possible scenario.

"Going someplace, little dove?" Link's voice carries across the room.

God, I wish he wouldn't call me that. It's a reminder of what we had, and the wedge that has driven us apart. Now that I'm this close, I recognize the truth. Staying away from him is slowly killing me inside.

Link is standing near the door, blocking the exit. His gaze roams over me, and I feel exposed, vulnerable.

"I made reservations for the three of us for dinner at Maestro's," he says, his tone casual, but I hear the strain of tension in his voice.

"Is that your idea of an invitation?"

He winces.

"I hope you and Pax enjoy yourselves. I have other plans."

"You have—"

"Other plans." I try to get past him, but he captures my shoulders. His touch sends a white-hot jolt of awareness through me.

"Stay," he murmurs, his voice low and persuasive.

Gently he moves his fingers in a soothing, sensual way that would have been my undoing at one time.

Despite myself, my insides start to melt. I long to collapse against him, surrender, forget any of this has happened.

But at what cost?

With effort, I bring up my arms between us. Then I widen them to dislodge his grip. "I'm going to be late."

"Mira and Torin are going with you?" Link's eyes narrow.

"Arielle," Pax answers for me. "Mira and Torin have the day off."

"The fuck?" Link demands, his jaw clenching.

Since I don't have the energy to deal with Link, I leave Pax to answer the question.

"I don't like this," Link insists.

"And I don't like the fact my husband is trying to move my money around without my permission." I bring up my chin. "The fund manager is doing a fine job. The cash stays there."

"Look, little dove—"

"You'll excuse me. I'm running late." After I key in the code on the alarm, the door releases. Quickly I open it before I can change my mind or Link tries to stop me again.

Arielle is waiting in the SUV with the engine running. As I slide into the back seat, I exhale, feeling like I've escaped a trap.

Rain begins to fall as we drive to Natalie's apartment. The weather matches my mood—gloomy and dark.

Natalie greets me with a warm hug. As we settle onto her couch, she says, "First things first. What are we doing about dinner? I'm starved."

"Want to order pizza?" I offer. The ones Pax got for us were amazing.

"Order?" she repeats. "You mean we're not going to have those cardboard things that we used to get at the grocery store?"

I grin at the very recent memory. Still, I no longer feel like the same person. "My treat."

"In that case, I want extra pepperoni and double cheese. Oh, and whatever they have for dessert. Something cinnamony or chocolatey."

"You got it." I look up the place and call them while Natalie pours us some wine.

Outside, thunder crashes, and lightning streaks past the window. I'm doubly glad we're staying in. And I'll have to tip the delivery person double. Being out in that weather sucks.

"So spill," Natalie says, handing me my drink, then dropping back onto the couch next to me. "What's been going on?"

I take a deep breath. "Where do I even start?"

"How about with your brother?" she prompts. "He leaving you alone?"

"I wish." I run a finger along the rim of my glass. "Axel's been texting me nonstop." A chill goes through me. "He says that my marriage signed his death warrant."

"What the actual hell?"

"Now he wants me to sign over my inheritance to save his life."

Natalie's eyes widen. "An inheritance? Are you serious?"

Thunder rumbles, and I jump.

After forcing out a breath, I take a sip of wine to steady myself. "Apparently so."

"You didn't know?"

"No idea." Over the next few minutes as driving rain beats against the window, I fill her in with everything I've learned since meeting Celeste. "Link knew about it. He's been trying to move the fund over to Merritt Sovereign. He talked to the fund manager, claiming spousal privilege."

Natalie's expression darkens. "You're not going to let him?"

"No." I shake my head.

"Good. Now tell me you're not giving it to Axel after all he did."

"Honestly I'm not sure what to do. Celeste advises against it."

The doorbell rings.

"Must be the pizza," Nat says, jumping up.

I follow her to the door, digging in my purse for cash to tip the driver. Nat swings the door open.

The delivery person has a hood up because of the weather, but as he raises his head, he tosses the hood back.

My heart thunders to a stop.

"Hello, little sister."

CHAPTER THIRTY-ONE

Tessa

Axel shoves the pizza box forcefully at Natalie, pushing her off balance.

Time slows, each second stretching into an eternity as my brain struggles to understand what's happening.

Our dinner crashes to the floor as his lips curl into a sneer. "I'm here to collect what's mine."

"Tess," Natalie whispers, gripping my arm hard enough to leave bruises.

But the pain is distant, secondary to the rising panic that threatens to choke me. I don't have to protect just myself; I have to protect my friend who doesn't deserve to be trapped in my mess.

With trembling fingers, I reach into my purse, praying I can reach my phone without Axel noticing. Just one button. That's all I need to press.

I look into Axel's eyes. The brother I used to know has vanished completely, leaving nothing but a desperate stranger corrupted by greed. "You need to leave."

He lunges, closing his arm around my wrist, yanking me toward him with brute force. I cry out, more in shock than pain, and Natalie screams.

"Let her go!" Natalie yells, trying to pry Axel's fingers from my skin.

But he's too strong. With a vicious shove, he sends Natalie stumbling back. Her head hits the wall with a sickening thud.

"Nat!" Frantically I twist around to see if she's okay.

The momentary distraction is all I need to grab my phone, and I manage to jam my finger against the number two.

"You're going to sign over that trust fund, and then maybe—just maybe—I'll have a chance of getting out of this mess alive." He yanks a gun from his waistband.

My blood turns to ice.

"Do as you're fucking told for once, and no one has to get hurt."

Frantic, I dig my heels into the carpet.

I can't—won't—go without a fight.

"Drop your weapon."

Arielle.

Her voice is cold and steady.

Axel's grip tightens as he spins us both around, using me as a human shield. His sour stench burns my nostrils.

"Back off," he warns, his voice shaking. "Or I swear to God, I'll—"

"You'll what?" Pax's calm, measured tone knifes through the tension.

My eyes lock onto him as he steps into view, his presence filling the small entryway. Relief floods through me, even as fear for his safety twists my stomach into knots.

"Pax." I whimper, hating how weak I sound.

His eyes meet mine. Silently he reassures me that everything will be okay.

Then his attention shifts back to Axel, his expression hardening.

"You'll want to let her go." Pax is calm, his voice deceptively gentle. There's coiled, lethal power in his stance. "This isn't going to end well for you if you don't."

Axel's laugh is hollow, tinged with hysteria. "End well? Don't you fucking get it? If I don't get that money, I'm dead anyway."

"And you think taking Tessa is going to solve that?" Pax takes a single step closer, his hands raised in a placating gesture. "You won't get far. Link will tear the world apart to get her back. Is that what you want? To spend the rest of your life—however short it might be—looking over your shoulder?"

"You have no fucking idea what it's already like."

"I understand better than you think," Pax counters. "But this? This isn't the answer. Let Tessa go, and we can talk. We'll figure this out."

Axel tightens his grip, and he shoves the gun against my temple. I hold my breath, scared out of my mind that the slightest movement might set him off.

"You don't want to hurt her," Pax says. "She's the only hope of getting the money."

My brother's grip wavers.

"That's what you want, isn't it? The money?" Pax is calm and measured. "Link has plenty. Maybe he can forgive your debt to him. Take care of Sartori for you. That's what family is for. Right?"

Axel pulls the gun away, but I'm still in front of him, and his arm is tightening on my throat.

In that moment, Pax's gaze finds mine.

His eyes are dark and intense, like they had been in our Vegas suite. Deliberately he flicks his glance to the floor.

Terrified, I blink.

He wants me on my knees.

Calling on all my courage, I give him the tiniest hint of a nod, telling him I understand his order.

"Now."

In one fluid motion, I bring my foot down hard on Axel's instep. He howls in pain, and I go limp. The full force of my weight makes him lose his grip.

What happens next is a blur.

Arielle and Pax move with lightning speed, disarming Axel.

In seconds, they have him face down on the floor, and Arielle is zip-tying his hands behind his back while Pax keeps him pinned.

"You both okay?" Pax calls out.

In an instant, Natalie is next to me, helping me to my feet and guiding me toward the kitchen.

When we're there, we fall into each other's arms, gulping in massive amounts of oxygen.

"Oh my God, Tess."

"I'm so sorry this happened to you," I tell her.

She steps back but holds my shoulders. "Jesus, Tess. The hell? You were the one with a gun to your head."

Maybe the adrenaline has completely worn off because I start to shake.

"I think we need wine."

The bottle is on the counter, and I glance at it, but then I can't help but look into the living room.

Along with Inamorata, a swarm of police officers have arrived. Right behind them is a man in a suit who takes charge.

The unknown person shakes hands with Inamorata. "We've got it from here."

"Thank you, Detective."

The man hooks his thumb toward one of the cops and nods at Axel. "Get him the hell out of here."

Moments later, heavy metal handcuffs are clamped around Axel's wrists, and he's pulled to his feet and hustled toward the door.

"Tessa!" His eyes are wild as he looks over his shoulder at me. "Don't let them do this to me!"

My emotions are a tangled web of relief, anger, and grief, and I feel as if I'm in a nightmare I can't wake up from.

"Mom and Dad wouldn't want this!"

Because he won't go willingly, two cops have to drag him away.

Even when he's been gone for long seconds, he is still screaming my name.

The wails echo in my head, and I squeeze my eyes shut against them.

Minutes later—or maybe hours, I've lost all sense of time—Pax appears in the kitchen doorway. Without a word, he crosses the room and pulls me into his arms. I melt against him, inhaling his familiar scent as tears tumble down my cheeks.

"I've got you," he murmurs, his lips pressed against my hair. "You're safe now. I promise."

I cling to him, letting his strength anchor me as the full weight of what just happened crashes over me. My own brother held a gun to my head.

Moments later, Pax checks on Natalie. "Can I call David for you?"

She shakes her head. "I'll do it. He's out of town on business. I hate to bother him."

"He'd want to know," Pax assures her. "Let him know that Arielle will be spending the night with you."

"I—"

"Not optional," Pax interrupts. "I want to be sure you get some rest."

She looks at me, and I shrug helplessly. How well I know what it's like to try to argue with either of my men once they've made a decision.

An EMT, apparently on Hawkeye's payroll, arrives to check Natalie and me over. We both say we're fine, but Pax insists we both be examined. "David will want to be sure you're okay."

Natalie wrinkles her nose, then nods.

"As for you…" Pax looks at me. "If you don't get checked out, Link will take you to the hospital."

I sigh. Even though he's not here, I'm swept into the storm that is Link Merritt.

Natalie and I sit next to each other on the couch.

The EMT perches on the edge of the coffee table in front of Natalie. Someone—a Hawkeye person, I guess—removes our wineglasses and cleans up the mess left by the pizza box.

"You hit your head?" the EMT asks.

"Back here." She winces as she touches it. "It's a little sore."

He presses lightly around the area, then says, "I'm going to touch a little harder. Let me know if you feel any sharp pain."

After a moment, she tells him, "It's not too bad. Just sore."

"Good. That's what I want to hear." Then he shines a small flashlight in her eyes. "Now look straight ahead and follow the light with your eyes."

After a few moments, he switches off the light. "Your pupils are reacting normally, which is a good sign. How are you feeling otherwise? Dizziness, nausea, or blurred vision?"

"No." Natalie shakes her head. "Just a little…rattled, I guess."

"Totally normal after what you've been through. I'm going to check your vitals now, just to make sure everything else is where it should be." He pulls out his stethoscope to listen to her heart. Then he wraps the blood pressure cuff around her arm.

As the cuff inflates, Natalie glances at me. "I really do feel fine."

I have no idea what I'd do if she'd been seriously hurt.

A few moments later, he's done. "Everything looks good. I'm not seeing any signs of a concussion, but I want you to take it easy for the next twenty-four hours. No heavy lifting, no strenuous activity."

"Wine?" she asks. "I could drink a gallon."

He grins. "That's never advised. But a glass should be okay. I recommend some ice for the bump. Frozen bag of peas, if nothing else."

"I'll do that."

"Even though there's no concussion right now, I want you to monitor for delayed symptoms…a sudden headache, dizziness, changes in your vision, that kind of thing. If that happens, you need to get checked out."

"Got it," Arielle assures the man.

The EMT turns to me.

"I really am fine," I tell him.

Pax's gaze locks on mine. "Check her out."

"Any dizziness, headaches, or nausea?"

The same thing Nat just went through. "No. Nothing like that."

After checking my pulse, he pulls out his stethoscope.

Pax is right next to me, arms crossed.

A few minutes later, the EMT confirms everything I knew. "Heart rate and blood pressure are normal. No signs of anything concerning, but Agent Gallagher is right to be cautious. Stress can have an effect on the body."

Even though I didn't hit my head, he pulls out his flashlight again.

I blink as the light passes over my eyes, but it's over in a second. "Pupils are reacting normally," he confirms, standing up and offering his hand to help me up. "Everything checks out."

I stand, feeling relieved that it's over. "See, Pax? I'm fine."

The EMT turns to Pax. "Same caution I gave your friend: if you feel any dizziness or notice anything unusual over the next few hours, call us."

Pax finally unfolds his arms. Despite the reassurance, his eyes still hold concern.

As he leaves, Link rushes in, accompanied by Torin and Mira.

I see him before he sees me, and I take in the tense set of his shoulders, the barely contained fury in his eyes as he speaks in low, urgent tones with Pax and Inamorata. When his gaze finally lands on me, his face changes entirely.

"I'll go call David." Nat gives me a quick hug and leaves the room.

In three long strides, Link is sitting next to me, and he cups my face between his strong hands. "Are you hurt?" he demands, his voice rough with emotion.

"I'm fine." Despite myself, I stay where I am, inhaling the scent of his confidence and drawing comfort from his strength.

He places his forehead against mine. For a moment, the anger and tension between us vanishes, leaving me with the undeniable connection that drew me to him in the beginning.

"Let's go home." His words are soft, and so is the way he strokes my cheeks, tracing the tracks of my earlier tears.

"I need to make sure Nat is okay."

He sighs his impatience but to his credit, says nothing.

I go in search of Nat and find her in the bedroom. "David changed his flight. He'll be on the first flight tomorrow morning."

"If he's ready to leave now, I'll send a private plane," Link says.

I whirl, and Nat glances over my shoulder at him. I had no idea he followed me.

"You will?" she echoes.

"Pretty luxurious," I tell her.

"You're serious right now?"

"I am." He places his hands on my shoulders. "If I were traveling, I'd need to get home as soon as I could."

"Honestly I don't know what to say."

"Yes," I urge, turning to face her. "Let him." I mean, after all, the man seems to have more money than he knows what to do with.

"In that case, thank you."

"Where is he?" Link asks.

"Los Angeles."

I stand next to my friend as Link releases me to pull his phone from his pocket. He hits a number, then speaks in a clipped, no-nonsense tone. "I need a plane. Los Angeles." He glances at Nat again. "Give me his name and the time he can be ready to depart."

Within minutes, David's on his way to the airport in a car Link has also provided.

Now that it's time to leave, I don't want to walk away from Nat. "I'm so sorry," I start, but she cuts me off with a fierce hug.

"We're both okay. It's over."

I'm not sure why, but I glance to Link for confirmation. "Is it?" *Really? Truly?*

With Torin in front of us and Mira bringing up the rear, we make our way outside and into the SUV. Even though the evening is mild, the moment I'm in the seat with the door closed, I begin to shake.

Delayed shock?

Moving to sit next to me, Link shrugs out of his jacket and tucks it around me. Then he drapes his arm over my shoulders, holding me tight.

"You're safe."

"Am I?" What about Emiliano? And what will happen to my brother?

I shiver. Axel's cries will haunt me forever.

When we arrive at the house, my energy has gone. Part of me wants to head upstairs to take a bath, but my legs won't cooperate. Instead I slide onto one of the bar stools while Link says goodnight to our bodyguards. I'm guessing Hawkeye agents never truly get a day off.

"Sparkling water?" Link offers, the emeralds in his cufflinks glinting in the overhead lights, reminding me once more of who he is.

"Wine," I respond.

"I'm not sure that's recommended."

"The medic said that Nat could have one. And she bumped her head."

With a tight nod, he uncorks a bottle of red.

"Just stick a straw in it and hand it over."

Of course, he ignores me and instead pours two glasses of wine and slides one across to me.

"Axel's been arrested. Do you know the charges?"

The roar of a motorcycle and the flash of the headlight through the windows distracts me.

Pax.

Less than a minute later, he's inside, the alarm set again,

and he tosses his jacket over the back of the chair next to mine.

"Wine?" Link offers.

Pax shakes his head and heads to the refrigerator. He grabs a bottle of beer. After using a metal tool to remove the cap, he sends it spinning onto the countertop.

As if trying to make sure I really am okay, he sweeps his gaze over me. "I'm sure you have questions."

About a million of them.

"They can wait for the morning."

I shake my head. If I go upstairs now, there's no way I'll be able to sleep.

"Then let's get comfortable.

Still wrapped in Link's jacket, glass in hand, I follow them into the living room where I curl up onto the couch. Since I'm ready to start shaking again, I grab a small blanket from the back of the couch and pull it over my legs.

Link places his glass on the mantel, then lights the gas fireplace.

Mesmerized, I stare at the flickering flames, trying to lose myself in them.

Both men take seats across from me, and I'm grateful they're giving me space.

Pax takes a long, well-earned drink from his bottle. "Your brother is going away for a very, very long time."

I have no reaction to the news. He's the only remaining member of my family, yet he's betrayed me over and over again.

After placing his bottle on an end table, Pax leans forward and props his elbows on his knees. "When we found out that he was trying to sell you, we read Hawkeye and Inamorata in on the information. They've been working with law enforcement, building a case. We believed an arrest was imminent, but tonight accelerated the time frame."

"You said he's going away for a very long time."

He nods.

"What does that mean?"

"With everything we've uncovered so far, he'll be facing a lot of charges. He'll also be prosecuted under the federal racketeering statute."

After taking a sip to settle my nerves, I breath out. "Emiliano is still out there."

"He was just taken away by the FBI. RICO charges of his own."

Since my hand is trembling, I set down my wine.

"If he is smart, he'll plead guilty. If he gives up anyone else in the organization, he'll need witness protection to survive more than twenty-four hours."

I shudder.

So it really *is* over.

All of it.

Including my reason to stay married.

CHAPTER THIRTY-TWO

The Next Day
Link

"The actual fuck is wrong with you?"

I glance up. I've been so obsessed with thoughts of my wife that I didn't notice that Pax entered my office.

Without an invitation, he closes the door and crosses the room to drop into a chair facing me.

"Make yourself comfortable."

He ignores my sarcasm.

"She deserves the very best you have."

I scowl. "The hell does that mean?"

"Stop being so damn selfish and think about someone other than yourself for once."

Fuck you.

Since the day I met Tessa at the Rusty Nail, my whole life has revolved around her, from giving her hundred-dollar bills for tips, saving her from Axel and Emiliano's clutches, showering her with every worldly good that I can, including a fairy-tale wedding and now, a new car to replace her old heap of shit. There is nothing else I have to offer anyone.

"She needs compassion."

In frustration, I toss my pen onto my desk. God knows I'd given everything I was capable of last night, which included my restraint. I'd kept my mouth shut, and that required considerable self-control.

When Pax notified me that Tessa's brother tried to abduct her, I died a thousand deaths.

I should have refused to let her leave the house yesterday, should have insisted she take a dozen agents with her.

When I finally saw her at Natalie's apartment, sitting there on the couch, pale, seemingly lost, my whole world collapsed.

I wanted to shake her senseless for scaring a decade off my life. But more, I yearned to cradle her, carry her home, fuck her hard enough to chase away her demons and the ache inside my soul.

Once I knew she was okay, anger raged through me.

I'm terrified to think about the possibilities had Pax not followed her to Natalie's place.

Though I wanted to tear Ariella limb from limb I believe Pax when he says she followed all protocols.

She had stopped the delivery guy when he exited the elevator and verified he was wearing clothing that matched the name of the restaurant Natalie had ordered from. Axel's hoodie had been up against the weather, and the pizza boxes were damp from the rain.

Not only that, she'd made him lift the lid to ensure the pizza was in there.

The moment she realized something was wrong, she'd acted swiftly.

I took some measure of comfort from the fact Tessa had

the foresight to push a button to summon Pax. She trusts him, if not me. "We could have lost her."

"Keep this up, and we still will."

Rage makes me grind my back teeth together.

"You need to let her in."

To my cold, dark heart? We both know I don't have one. My father saw to that. What little bit that was left shattered the day I placed a single red rose on top of my mother's casket.

My father led me away, and I stopped to look back the moment they began to lower her into the ground.

My tears finally fell, and my father brutally pinched my ear. *"Don't fucking cry, boy. You're not a goddamn infant. You're a Merritt."*

"Showing emotion doesn't make you weak."

Pax knows me better than anyone else on this planet… realizes what he's asking. More than anyone, he fucking knows I can't give her anything more than I already have.

"You're about to lose the best thing that ever happened to you." He smacks his palm against my desk. Then he uses the momentum to stand. "To us. And I fucking resent you for that."

He strides to the exit, then stops and faces me.

His eyes are dead cold.

When he speaks, his voice is flat, condemning. "I ought to lay you out flat myself. Something has to get through your fucking thick skull."

Once more, he slams the door, making it rattle, the sound hammering through my head, echoing with finality.

He's gone, and so is Tessa, at least emotionally.

But I've given her everything I possibly can.

I know it's not enough. *I'm* not enough.

Never will be.

I pick up the whiskey glass that I've been nursing all day. I hurl it at the wall.

Shards splinter everywhere, just like the pieces of my life.

Now what the hell am I supposed to do?

Tessa

"What do you think of this one?"

Frustrated by all the options, I blow out a breath and look at Natalie.

Several days have passed since the awful incident at her house. Since she's such an amazing friend, she is spending her day apartment hunting with me.

So far, we've visited five different places. Although they are all nice, serviceable, none of them feel right.

"Tessa?"

"It's…" We're standing in the small living room of a unit close to downtown, and they're starting to blur together. "Fine, I guess."

Each place that we visited, she picked up papers with floor plans and lists of amenities and tucked them all into a portfolio.

She's way more organized about this whole thing than I am.

Choosing where to live is a tough decision. One I'm not sure I even want to make. Maybe that's why I can't decide.

"This one is close to transit. Makes it easy to get to U of H."

There's nothing wrong with this sample, and it's right in my budget, which means the finishes are nothing special. But it's so much better than the place Natalie and I used to share.

I wander to the window and pull back the blinds. The

view is of other apartments in the complex. The good news is there is a pool and a workout room, not that I will use either.

"Is there something bothering you?"

Natalie is far too perceptive.

With a sigh, I wander back toward her and drop onto the couch.

She sits next to me, her large hoop earring glittering.

"This place is fine," I say.

"Fine?" She raises an eyebrow.

"This will sound ridiculous…"

"Try me."

I search for the right words. "It doesn't feel like home."

"I understand that."

"Do you?" I hope so, because I'm not even sure exactly what I mean. The truth is, I haven't had an actual home since my parents were alive. After they passed, I had believed that the house belonged solely to Axel. He repeatedly told me that and said he was doing me a favor by letting me live there.

At least right now, when I am at Link's, I feel mostly like a guest.

Part of that is my own fault, I'm sure. I have absolutely no doubt they would welcome me back into bed with them if I showed the slightest interest. But to save myself and my wounded emotions, I've refused to do that.

Since the night of Axel's arrest, my mind has been numb.

Despite that, I keep moving forward. Celeste and I have talked every day. I've had multiple meetings with the family attorney and my trust fund manager. Following Celeste's advice, I hired a real estate agent to put my parents' house on the market. No doubt the sale price will only cover the cost of the second mortgage. If we're fortunate, I'll have enough to cover the real estate fees.

I plan to fly back to Chicago soon to go through my

parents' belongings. I don't want anything, except for my mom's Christmas ornaments. Some of them I bought for her. And never seeing them again would break my heart.

Once I've got those, I'll bring in an estate sale company to get rid of everything else.

Then I'll never return to my home state again.

Axel keeps trying to call, but I refuse to talk to him. Any necessary communication can go through lawyers.

Before my conversation with Nat can continue, a couple more people walk through the door, accompanied by an apartment representative. Quietly she tells me that if I want the last available one-bedroom unit, I may have to act quickly.

"I understand." But I'm not ready to sign a contract.

Why, I'm not sure.

"How about a coffee?" Natalie suggests as we walk out into the sunshiny day. "We can head to the Heights. Maybe wander around while we're there."

With the number of places that Link dragged me to before our wedding, I'm not sure I will ever enjoy going shopping again.

"Or maybe we can have an early dinner? All this has made me hungry."

"Sounds perfect." I haven't been eating well, and even my new clothes are starting to get a little too big on me.

"I know just the place," she says.

Twenty minutes later, we park in front of a small, local restaurant near her apartment.

"David introduced me to this place, and it's become my favorite."

According to the sign and the decorations on the windows, I'm guessing the food is Italian.

"Carb lovers heaven." She grins.

"Sounds perfect." Comfort food is exactly what I need.

"The lasagna is to die for. But David loves the fettuccini alfredo."

We walk in, and she's greeted by name and swept into a hug by the woman she introduces as the owner.

Mouthwatering scents fill the air: fresh baked bread, maybe herbs, and bubbling cheese. Suddenly I'm hungrier than I realized.

As we're sliding into a booth across from each other, Natalie orders each of us a glass of house red wine, along with a dozen garlic knots to share.

"I'll be right back," the owner promises.

"Come here often?" I tease.

Natalie blushes. "If David didn't keep me so…busy, I'd already need to buy a whole new wardrobe." She giggles.

Moments later, our drinks are delivered, and we each have a menu in front of us.

Natalie peeks at me over the top of hers. "Save room for the dessert trio."

"Oh?" I scan to the bottom. "Oh my God. No."

"Cannoli, tiramisu, and torte caprese."

Which, according to what I'm reading, is a decadent rich, flourless chocolate-and-almond cake.

"I'm going to be in a coma at the end of this meal."

"That's the plan." She grins. "You've been thinking too damn much. Did you decide on your entrée?"

I'm thinking the dessert and garlic knots should be more than enough food. Then my gaze stops on my favorite dish of all time. Gnocchi. Pasta and potatoes all in the same delicious bite.

Now I'm convinced. Within an hour, I'm going to be in a food coma.

The appetizer is delivered, and once we've placed our orders, we both sit back with our glasses of wine.

"I can't thank you enough for going with me today."

"Are you kidding me? I love this kind of thing. House hunting. Seeing different interiors, decorating styles. I've become addicted to home improvement shows on television. My favorite takes place in New Orleans. There's a contractor on it who is so yummy. Part of me watches just to see his muscles ripple. Mason Sullivan. Have you seen it?"

"No." I transfer one of the garlic knots onto my plate. "But now I'm tempted." I take a bite, and the rich, buttery flavor explodes in my mouth. "Oh dear Lord."

"Warned you!" She shoots me a triumphant grin.

"Did I die and go to heaven?"

"You'll definitely think so by the end of the meal."

We both laugh.

After a few sips of wine, I start to relax a little more. "I'm surprised David still lets you be friends with me."

She rolls her eyes. "He understands it's been an unusual time. But I definitely think he enjoyed flying on a private airplane and that suite at the Bella Rosa."

I'd also enjoyed some of the perks that went along with knowing Link. But they're about to be a thing of the past for me.

"I'll be honest, I was a little surprised when you told me you were looking for apartments. What's really going on?"

I shift a little uncomfortably. "What do you mean?"

"You're different than you were at your wedding. Even though you were dealing with a lot, you seemed more relaxed and confident."

I wrinkle my nose. "You know me too well."

"That's what friends are for."

This is all so complicated, even to me.

"Did you fall in love with them?"

Love? My breath whooshes out, and I put down my glass.

"Is that why you're struggling?"

Maybe it is. "Pax is so uncomplicated. If I had met just

him, things might have been easier. I think I could have been very happy with him."

"But there's Link."

She's made a statement, instead of asking a question.

"Yeah." I nod. "He's so complex. Emotionally distant." Anger and frustration seem to be the only emotions he's comfortable expressing.

"That's not enough," she guesses.

How can I be happy living with someone who can never feel the same way about me as I do about him?

"It's draining you?"

She lets the question hang between us, waiting for me to go on. Eventually I do. "Look at you and David. You're just so easy together. So perfect. So right."

"With him, I wear my emotions on my sleeve." She shrugs. "But he says he appreciates it. He doesn't have to guess what I'm thinking or feeling. After what I went through with my ex, that's refreshing."

My parents were madly in love. At times, their relationship was so close that they shut out the rest of the world. I don't want something that intense, but to feel loved and not just controlled? That's the dream.

"Is that why this decision is so difficult?" Nat guesses. "You don't want to leave, but you can't imagine staying with the way things are?"

I nod. "That's it."

Our food arrives. Though I'd been starving, the conversation and my realizations, have made my appetite fade.

She stabs into her lasagna, and steam rises. "If needed, David and I will help you move."

"You've already done so much."

"Friendship." She raises her fork as if saluting me. Then she takes a bite and sighs completely. "I hope they have this in heaven."

Her happiness helps my mood, and I try the gnocchi. She's right about the food. "I think I need to live close to this restaurant," I say.

"That's the main reason I'm never moving."

We both laugh.

While she talks about a movie she and David went to the previous night, my thoughts wander.

Since I'm limited on how much I can withdraw from my account, I'll need money. Maybe Marge will let me have my old job back. She can be flexible with hours, and I can work them around my studies. Maybe I can even start babysitting again.

Since Natalie warns me again to make sure I have room for dessert, I save some of my entrée to take home with me.

Of the three small plates that are delivered to the table, the torte is my favorite. "I'm serious about finding an apartment around here," I say as I polish off the last crumb.

She laughs. "We could have a regular girls night here."

"I'm in."

The visit with Natalie and being spoiled by the restaurant owner was exactly what I needed, but by the time I arrive back at my car, I'm more miserable than I'd been at the beginning of the day.

Even though I no longer have a bodyguard with me, I suspect Pax keeps an eye on me. And I wouldn't be surprised if he still had an agent hovering somewhere in the background.

At Link's estate, I let myself in through the back door.

No one is in the kitchen, so I quietly place my leftovers in the refrigerator. And maybe if I'm quiet enough, I can sneak up the stairs without anyone realizing I'm home.

An image of my first night in the house flashes back. I'd locked the door that night, but in the morning, my belongings were in the room.

A hundred times over the last few days, I've glanced over at the lock, but it has never moved.

Shoving back the memory, I move through the kitchen.

Near the staircase, I freeze.

Link is standing there, his face stark, eyes bleak. His shirt sleeves are rolled back, and there's a shadow on his face.

I have never seen him look like this. Uncertain, haunted.

Frowning, I ask, "Is everything okay?"

He's silent. The tension thickens and grows.

"Link?" My heart misses a few beats. Then my stomach plunges.

"Do you want a divorce?"

CHAPTER THIRTY-THREE

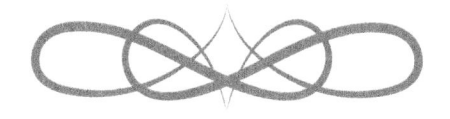

Tessa

A divorce? I frown. I've been thinking about it. But I never expected him to be the one to bring it up. "Link…"

"Answer me."

My emotions lodge in my throat, and I choke on them.

"You've been out looking at apartments."

So my guess was right. Even if I don't have Hawkeye bodyguards assigned to me, Pax still isn't taking any chances.

"Look, Tessa…"

Tessa. Not *little dove.*

He scrubs his hand over his face. "You don't have to leave."

There's no way I can continue to sleep under the same roof as Pax and Link.

"Even if you can't be with me—with us—you have a home here."

But I don't. Not really. I have a place to sleep while wondering what they're doing. And I spend a lot of my time holed up, trying to avoid them.

"You can have the guest house."

"The…" I'm shaking, and I don't know how to respond.

"I know you've been talking to Celeste. She had to have asked about a prenup. Since we don't have one, that means that whatever you want, financially, I will pay."

Wrapping my arms around me to ward off a chill, I shake my head. "You don't know anything about me." This—my attraction to him, the fact I care so deeply—has nothing to do with money. In fact, that may make things even more difficult. "I don't want anything of yours."

"You deserve it. I know I turned your life upside down."

Without giving me a choice.

"Every court in the land would agree with that."

"Link." Frustrated as always when it comes to him, I suck in a breath. "You're not listening."

"Then fucking talk to me. Say something. Anything." His voice cracks, and I steel myself against the way I'm melting inside.

"I don't want to be manipulated." Even though tears are stinging my eyes, I continue. "I don't want anyone telling me what to do."

"You have the trust fund."

I wave that off. "I won't be able to claim that for years. But there are provisions for my education and some living expenses." Which he no doubt knows because of spousal privilege. "I'm thinking about getting a part-time job, maybe back at the Rusty—"

"Over my dead body."

"Shut the fuck up."

Stunned by the forceful interruption, I turn toward Pax. I had no idea he was there.

"Stay out of this," Link bites out.

"The hell I will." His stance is wide, his eyes blazing with barely restrained threat. Tension cords his muscles, making them bulge. "Shut the fuck up before I shut you up. Tessa is making her own decisions."

"Goddamn it."

I turn and run up the first few steps, but then Link's voice freezes me where I am.

"Tessa, please."

There's anguish in his tone,

"Please hear me out."

Despite myself, I remain in place.

"I am a flawed, fucked-up human being."

Fighting to remain steady on my feet, I carve my fingers around the banister in a death grip.

"The truth is…"

Slowly, slowly, I turn.

Link looks broken, defeated in a way I've never seen him before.

Clearing his throat, he starts again. "The truth is, I love you. I don't fucking know how to act."

"About goddamn time," Pax all but growls.

My knees wobble. I can't possibly have heard right.

"I don't deserve you, little dove. Don't deserve a second chance." He swallows deeply. "But I can't let you go without a fight."

"You…?"

"I love you." His voice breaks.

"Keep going," Pax clips. "While you still have the chance."

"My father…" He stops.

Everything inside me urges me to go to him, to run my fingers across his furrowed brow to soothe his emotional pain. Instead I force myself to stay where I am.

"Link," Pax warns.

"I was five. Kindergarten. It was close to Mother's Day. The teacher had us all make gifts for our mom."

I remember doing the same thing. Cards. Paper flowers. Decorated plant pots.

"On Mother's Day morning, at breakfast, I ran upstairs to my room to get her gift, and I gave it to her. She smiled and thanked me." He gives a half smile. "I got teary and kissed her on the cheek, and I told her I loved her."

His words are halting.

"My father dragged me outside and beat me."

No. Losing my grip, I sink down onto a stair. My heart breaks for the boy he'd been.

"Merritts don't show emotion."

Weakness.

"The last time I almost cried was the day of her funeral. I was thirteen. After placing a rose on her casket, my father pulled me away. I stopped to look back." He swallows deeply. When he goes on, his voice shakes. "She was in that box. All alone." He pauses for a moment, and Pax nods at him. "My dad warned me not to cry. But because there were people around, he settled for pinching me and reminding me who I was."

A Merritt who wasn't allowed to be human, even at his own mother's graveside.

"After everyone left, he beat me."

Tears stream down my face. "Oh, Link."

He scoffs. "The irony is, my dad cared for my mom. He was scared of something happening to her. So he showed love in the only way he knew how."

God. It makes so much sense.

"He suffocated her."

I understand Link so much better now. And Pax as well. He knows Link's secrets and has remained by his side. That kind of loyalty means something.

"I won't blame you if you can't forgive me."

"I…"

He shakes his head. "There are no guarantees. I know I'm controlling. But you mean more than anything to me. I can promise I will always try to be the man that you want. That you need. That you deserve." His face twisted with raw anguish and honesty, he drops to his knees. "I promise—I vow—that I will die trying to be someone worthy of you."

Giant sobs rack me.

He's shredded my heart.

I run to him, lower myself to the floor, and wrap him tight.

He grabs me hard, as if he'll never let go, and he gulps giant breaths of air. I sob into his shoulder, soaking his shirt, shedding tears for the boy who'd been emotionally crushed and for what we've come so very close to losing. "I love you, Link Merritt. You dictatorial, know-it-all—"

"Bastard," Pax supplies

Grinning, we both look at him.

"Little dove, say anything you want. I'll take it."

I place my palm alongside his face. "I love you. Link. I love you. Now and forever."

We both hold on tightly, desperately.

Minutes later, Pax helps us up, and the three of us embrace.

"I was afraid I was going to have to beat some fucking sense into you." Pax's voice has lost its edge, and I'm grateful for that.

Link nods. "As long as you did it before she got away from us."

"For damn sure."

All three of us joined together, Link looks at me. "Please say you'll be my wife—*our wife*—now and forever."

"There's one condition."

"Name it."

"I want to renew our vows."

He frowns. "We just—"

"With the word *love* in there."

He nods. "Of course."

"We've had something official. I want something meaningful, just for us."

Both men grin.

"Link knows how to organize events," Pax says.

"I'll make it happen. Within a month?"

"Yes. It's okay with you, Pax?"

"More than," he assures me.

Everything inside me melts.

"Little dove..." Link tucks a strand of hair behind my ear.

"I've missed you," I whisper. Then I look at Pax. "Both of you. More than words can say."

"I need you more than oxygen."

"Take me?" I ask. I want to make this real, to feel them inside me.

Neither man needs a second invitation.

Link removes my shirt so fast that buttons pop off. Simultaneously Pax unfastens my jeans and pulls down the zipper.

Laughing, happier than I've ever been, I kick off my heels.

Maybe this is why I couldn't find an apartment. I secretly wanted to be here, with them.

With frantic movements, they finish stripping me, their strong fingers tracing familiar paths over my skin. I shiver with anticipation, and my heart thunders. I've craved this, missed this—their touch, passion, possession.

Link captures my mouth in a searing kiss, his tongue sweeping in to claim me. Everything he demands, I happily give.

Behind me, Pax presses against my back, his hands

roaming over my hips, my thighs, before sliding between my legs to cup my mound.

I moan into Link's mouth as I buck my hips against Pax's hand.

"You're already wet," Pax murmurs.

Yes.

I need this.

Link breaks the kiss, his breath ragged. "I want you over the back of the couch." It's an order, but the words are hoarse with desire.

Gently but firmly, Pax guides me into the living room.

Are there any limits to the new ways they want to claim me?

I have to lift onto my tiptoes to bend myself over the couch. And because I know they won't be easy with me, I dig my fingers into the soft leather.

I look over my shoulder, watching as Link swiftly removes his clothes, his body lean and toned. Pax's movements are efficient as he undresses to reveal his massive chest and muscular arms.

Both so different. Both so perfect.

Link's cock is large and throbbing, seeming to arrow toward me. "You're going to take me. All of me."

I nod. I'll die unless he enters me.

He places his hand on my back to hold me down, and Pax reaches between my legs, fingering me, making me squirm, making me ready.

He pulls away, and then Link takes me with a single, powerful thrust, filling me completely.

I scream his name, digging my fingers even deeper into the couch.

"Look at me." Pax fists a hand in my hair as he turns my face in his direction.

They've trapped me, keeping me helpless.

With his free hand, Pax masturbates himself, his enormous cock getting even bigger. The thought of him filling me...

I'm on the edge, my body tensing around Link as he relentlessly makes up for lost time.

"You're mine." He presses his palm harder against my back, grounding me.

"Yes."

"I love you." Driving deeper, Link slams into me.

The physical and emotional domination is too much, and I scream his name as I come hard, my body convulsing around him.

He groans, slowing his thrusts, and then pulls out. "God, you're spectacular." He circles around to face me, his cock glistening with my pleasure. "Stroke me, little dove. Feel what you do to me."

I'm hardly able to keep my balance, but somehow I manage to wrap my hand around him.

"Do it," Link commands.

I start, and then I feel a thrill as he pulses in my hand, hot and hard.

Pax moves behind me. As always, he ensures I'm ready before bending his knees slightly to enter me. Instinctively I tighten up, bracing myself for his invasion.

"Relax," he coaches.

Will this ever become easier?

Inch by inch he pushes in, stretching me, filling me beyond belief. I gasp, my hand faltering on Link's cock.

"Keep going." Link covers my hand with his, setting the rhythm.

How could I have forgotten how truly amazing making love with them is?

Pax pulls out slightly, then drives in deeper, sending waves of pleasure through me. He repeats the motion, each thrust bringing me closer to the edge again. But just before I tumble over, he pulls away.

I whimper at the sudden emptiness. "Pax!"

Link releases his grip on my hand. "Stop stroking me."

The moment I release Link, Pax scoops me up and carries me deeper into the living room. Link tosses a couple of blankets onto the coffee table. Then Pax positions me on all fours, his fingers digging into my hipbones.

"You're going to suck Link off while I fuck you from behind, sweetheart."

How can he expect me to think while he's inside me?

Link kneels in front of me, cock jutting against my face.

He reaches forward to play with my breasts, rolling my nipples between his fingers. I moan, feeling a response pull deep inside me.

I could let him do this forever. Instead he guides himself toward my face. "Open your mouth for me." He places his cockhead on my tongue, and I swirl around it, tasting myself on him. "Show me how much you want this cock."

Pax begins to enter me again, and I suck Link's dick into my mouth.

"Good girl." Link's words are a sensual purr of approval.

"This pussy is mine." Pax forcefully thrusts, pushing me forward onto Link's cock. Being filled from both ends is overwhelming. I choke on Link's impressive length, and he grabs my shoulders as he groans deeply.

Pax's pace quickens, his hips slapping against my ass. "You'll always belong to us."

Their words— their possession—sends me spiraling out of control. I come hard, gagging and crying. But Link is relentless. His body tense, he continues.

Finally, long moments later, he spills in my mouth, leaving me desperately trying to swallow every drop.

Pax thrusts several more times. Then, with a groan, he

pulls out. His hot release streams onto my back, and he rubs it into my skin, marking me.

I'm theirs.

Maybe always have been.

Exhausted, I collapse and roll onto my side.

Pax lifts me into his arms and carries me upstairs to Link's bedroom. *Our* bedroom now.

They lie down beside me, their bodies warm and solid against mine. I'm sandwiched between them, exactly where I want to be.

"I love you," I whisper.

While Link echoes my words, Pax kisses my forehead. "I love you, sweetheart."

I don't consciously fall asleep, but I must have drifted off because when I open my eyes, I'm on my side and both of my husbands are gently exploring my body.

Pax circles my nipple, then he lowers his hand to stroke my pussy, spreading the wetness that's already gathering there.

Behind me, Link is pressed against my back, his arm wrapped securely around my waist. "Ready for me?"

"Yes."

Within moments, he's easing into me and moving his hips in a slow, steady rhythm.

This isn't the fierce, demanding sex we had earlier…it's gentle and connects us together emotionally. It's lovemaking.

I sigh as I respond to their touch.

Pax captures my mouth, his lips giving instead of demanding. His tongue teases mine, and he continues his slow movements on my breasts.

Gently Link places a kiss at the tender spot on the back of my neck. Though his beautiful cock fills me, his movements are measured, designed to build my pleasure gradually. He's not chasing his own release. Instead, he's nudging me toward mine.

Pax releases my mouth, and I reach back to touch Link's hip, urging him closer.

Maybe guessing I'm ready to climax, Pax teases my clit again.

As Link continues to stroke, Pax increases the pressure on my sensitive flesh, moving in smaller, tighter circles.

Suddenly Link begins to thrust faster, and he pushes deeper. My men are in sync, working together to bring me pleasure.

"Come for us, little dove," Link murmurs. "Show us how much you love this."

Pax captures my mouth once more, swallowing my moans.

I'm right there, teetering on the precipice, and then with one more thrust from Link and a final stroke from Pax, I tumble over.

My orgasm washes through me in waves, and my body clenches around Link's cock. He groans, burying his face in my neck as he finds his own release.

Pax breaks the kiss. "You're incredible." He releases my clit to cup one of my breasts.

I lie still, feeling safe, loved, and cherished between these two men who have become my world.

After sliding from inside me, Link helps me onto my back. "We didn't think about birth control."

I go still.

Frantically I try to think about the timing. "I don't think it's the right time of the month," I say. Hope. "We should be okay."

"We're all in this together," Link promises. "Whatever your dreams are, you'll never have to give them up. Pax and I should both be competent at childcare."

I see fear in Pax's eyes, and I can't help but grin. This giant, strong bodyguard who has faced incredible danger all over the world is scared of an infant?

"If we need a nanny, childcare, a second housekeeper to help us, we'll make that happen."

I nod, relieved. "I want kids," I assure them. "But I'd prefer to wait a little while."

"Understood." Link nods. "Selfishly we don't mind having you to ourselves for a while."

"And give Pax a little time to adjust to the idea of fatherhood?" I tease.

"You'll pay for that."

Within seconds, squealing, I'm scooped from the bed and thrown over his shoulder. I'm laughing and frantically kicking, as he strides into the bathroom and dumps me onto the counter.

I start to scramble off, but Link's there, blocking me in place.

"I think you should be a good girl and take your punishment without complaint."

Punishment? It's a good thing I'm sitting because there's no way my body would be able to support me.

As I peek around Link's imposing body, Pax sets the water temperature, testing it with his hand before crooking his finger at me. "Come here, sweetheart."

Link helps me down, and I'm shaking as I make my way into the glass shower unit. It used to seem enormous. Now it feels small and tight with the three of us inside and me not knowing what to expect.

"Hands on the far wall." Pax's voice is rough with command, making my thoughts fracture.

Each motion feeling awkward, I do as I'm instructed.

"Hands higher. Press your beautiful breasts against the tiles."

They're cool, and goose bumps chase up my arms.

"Legs farther apart," Link adds.

"And stick your ass out as far as you can."

Their orders are coming at me so fast that I'm beginning to lose track of what they're saying.

"You don't want us to have to repeat our instructions," Link warns.

God help me.

Quickly I do as I'm told.

Pax leans close to me, and I inhale his sense of determination. "Look at me."

I turn my head slightly to meet his gaze.

"Tell me your safe words."

He expects me to be able to communicate? "Yellow for slow." I swallow. "Red for stop."

"Good. And where are you right now?"

Scared. Curious. "Green."

He nods. "You know what this is?" Then he lifts his hand to show me something he's holding.

My mouth dries. "Uh…" I expected him to use his hand. "A bath brush."

What is he going to do? Use the bristles between my legs? Or use the back side to spank me? Or worse, both?

"Stings more if the skin is wet." Link's words are conversational as he takes down the showerhead.

After turning on the water and checking the temperature, he drenches my rear.

In silent protest, I wrinkle my nose.

Then he stands to one side and sets the spray to pulse and directs it between my legs, finding my pussy, making me gasp.

For balance I spread my fingers even farther apart.

"Ask for a spank," Pax says against my ear.

He's so beastly. "Please. I'm ready." The first is always the worst.

Link brings the water closer to me, ratcheting up my pleasure. Helpless, needy, I moan. *"Yes."*

As I hoped, Pax uses the back of the brush and taps my rear as a warmup.

I exhale, relaxing into trust as he lands a second on my other butt cheek.

He continues, alternating sides, each a little firmer than the last. The sting builds, but the pleasure from the pulsating water on my clit balances it out, creating a dizzying mix of pain and pleasure.

"Where are you, little dove?" Link asks, adjusting the showerhead to change the pattern.

"Still green," I gasp out.

"Still green, *Sir*," he corrects.

Sir? He expects me to call him that?

Tensing, I wait for Pax to go on, but he doesn't.

"Say it."

Can I? Will I?

Link moves the water away from my aching pussy.

I need this...everything we're doing.

"Still green, *Sir*." The word rolls from my tongue easily, naturally. It feels so right.

"Fuck, yes."

Pax lands another strike, this one harder.

Simultaneously Link increases the water pressure, the spray pounding against my clit. I moan, bucking my hips back, wordlessly demanding more.

Behind me, Pax continues with the bath brush, creating a delicious sting that radiates across my skin. The combination of the water and the punishment makes me throb with need.

"You're doing so well." Link's voice is thick with desire.

He leans in, capturing my mouth in a searing kiss, his tongue mimicking the pulsating rhythm of the water.

As Pax lands the implement again, I whimper into Link's mouth, my body shaking. He slowly ends the kiss, his eyes dark with lust and something deeper—love.

"We've got you," Pax says, his voice steady and reassuring. He spanks me again, the bath brush hitting a particularly sensitive spot, and I gasp, digging my nails into the tile.

"Doing okay?" Link asks, his gaze locked onto mine.

I nod.

Link adjusts the showerhead yet again, the stream now relentless against my clit.

I arch my back, and Pax delivers a hard strike.

"Your ass is so red."

The bath brush clatters to the floor, and then his hand is there, soothing the ache, his fingers slipping between my cheeks to tease my tight hole.

"You're so close, little dove," Link murmurs, his voice a low growl. "Come for us. Let go."

Pax presses a finger into my back entrance. The pressure is too much.

A climax crashes through me in wave after wave of intense pleasure. I scream, my hands slipping as I fight to stay upright.

Link hangs up the showerhead, and warm water cascades over us. He wraps his arms around me, holding me tight as I ride out the storm. Pax's arms join his, their bodies pressing against mine, supporting me, their cocks hard against my skin.

As my breathing slows, I become aware of their hands, gentle and soothing, stroking my back, my arms, my thighs. I surrender to their touch, my body sated and limp.

"Such a good girl," Link whispers.

"So beautiful," Pax agrees, his voice low and deep against my ear.

I attempt a smile. But there's no doubt I feel cherished. And loved. This was everything I could have hoped for. "That was…remarkable."

"Good thing you liked it," Pax says.

Link leans forward and finishes with, "Because we're just getting started…"

EPILOGUE

Five Weeks Later
Tessa

Slowly, aware I'm alone, I open my eyes.

My husbands have let me sleep in, and I appreciate their thoughtfulness.

With a satisfied yawn, I stretch.

Last night, we'd ordered in, and they'd taken turns feeding me while I was blindfolded. Then they'd taken me upstairs to my old room, one that they've turned into a dungeon.

I'd suggested we could use the guest cottage for that, but Link insisted that it's mine to do with as I wish. So I've turned it into a bit of a sanctuary, part study space, part feminine retreat. Natalie helped me choose furnishings and bookcases, and we've spent the last few Saturday afternoons shopping for items to fill the shelves.

Last weekend, David was out of town, so I invited her to come over, and we watched silly romantic comedies, things our men would never be interested in.

Since she left late, Pax drove her home, and a Hawkeye agent delivered her car to her.

If this is marriage, I'm happy.

When I found out I wasn't pregnant, I made an appointment to get on birth control, and the three of us decided we'd talk occasionally about when we might want to have kids. For now, I want to enjoy the three of us being a family and finish my education.

I'm considering something in finance as a career, maybe advising other women about their money so they're not as clueless as I am.

Natalie thinks that's a great idea. She's considering real estate, and she wants me to be on her team as a mortgage broker. Every time we're together, she brings it up.

Our dreams are so different from where we started at the Rusty Nail.

Axel has finally stopped messaging. With my blessing, Pax and Link are following his case, along with the prosecution of Emiliano. But I want nothing to do with any of that.

I fought Link hard for my independence, and it turns out there are things I actually prefer him to handle.

He's been wonderful, letting me adjust to my new life. But he's asked if I'm okay serving as his hostess at a party this holiday season.

As long as all I have to do is memorize names and be gracious, I'm fine with it. Though I did negotiate for a spa day at the Uptown Sterling before the evening's festivities.

If he wants to spoil me, I'll let him do it on my terms.

The aroma of freshly brewed coffee reaches me, finally dragging me out of the warm bed. With another yawn, I pad to the bathroom for my silky robe and knot the belt as I walk down the stairs.

Sunlight is streaming through the large windows, which means it's later than I originally thought.

I adore weekends because both men adjust their schedules so we have some family time. Though they both generally work on Saturdays, they go in late. But I appreciate them leaving the house because it gives me time to catch up on my studies.

In the kitchen, there's a box of bagels on the counter, along with a to-go cup from my favorite coffee shop.

Pax must have slipped out early. I smile at the thought of him—this strong, stoic man—braving lines at two stores to make me happy.

Link is dressed in a white shirt with the sleeves turned back oh-so sexily. He's seated at the island, his laptop open in front of him, and he's scrolling through what I assume are emails.

He looks up as I enter, and he allows his gaze to meander down my body, reminding me of everything we'd done in our dungeon last night. He smiles, and I blush, looking down.

"Morning, little dove."

Even now, the way he says that makes my heart flutter.

"Morning."

"No adverse effects from your spanking?"

"None." Though when I slide onto my chair, I wince a little. "Well, maybe one or two."

"Let me look."

I open my mouth to ask if he's serious, but he immediately arches an eyebrow in what I now think of as his Dom look.

Without sighing, because that might earn me a reprimand, I slip off my seat, turn my back to him, and lift the hem of my robe as I bend over.

He doesn't just look; he uses his hands, even parting my buttocks. "Link!"

"You've got a couple of tiny marks. I'll get the arnica."

"I'm sure I'll be fine."

He flips the robe down. "Did I ask your opinion?"

I hold my sigh until he's out of the room entirely.

Then, grinning, I pick up my coffee.

The stuff they brew would be fine, especially since they keep hazelnut creamer in the refrigerator for me. But this is a wonderful treat.

When he returns, he tells me to put my hands on the counter, and he massages the cream into a couple of tender spots. "Thank you," I say when he's done.

"Self-serving," he admits, capping the tube.

"Need to make sure I'm ready for tonight and tomorrow?"

"Exactly." He gives me a long, lazy kiss that makes me hungry for him right now.

When he releases me, I take my seat again, and he returns to his. Then I enjoy another sip of my amazingly strong, sweet drink. If my guess is right, Pax added an extra shot of espresso to my order, and I glance at the printed ticket on it. I'm right. But then I catch the name on the label, Princess Tessa.

Grinning, I hold the cup tight. "Where's Pax?"

"On a call." Link closes his laptop to give me his full attention. "What are your plans for the day?"

"After my bath…"

"Smart. I ordered more Epsom salts for you."

"For who?" I counter, remembering what he'd said about being self-serving.

He grins.

"I'm going to spend the morning studying. I have a test coming up next week. Then I'm meeting Natalie for lunch."

Link nods. "I'm going to head into the office for a bit."

Then, no doubt, he'll hit the treadmill or get some other form of punishing cardio. Assuming he hasn't already done so.

Just then, Pax enters the kitchen. He's wearing a fitted black T-shirt and jeans, his muscles bulging slightly as he moves. The man is so delicious, and I can't believe he's mine.

"Morning, sweetheart." He drops a kiss on my forehead.

"I thought maybe you'd changed my name to princess."

"Fits."

"Thank you for getting breakfast."

He shrugs, as if it's no big deal. "I had a meeting with some of the guys at Hawkeye this morning. I figured I'd pick up some bagels on the way back."

I look between the two men, grateful for the life we're building together. "Are we going out to dinner?" It's becoming a bit of a tradition.

Link glances at Pax before answering. "How about seven? Maestro's? That should give us all enough time to get our work done."

I appreciate that he doesn't always make assumptions. He's not perfect, but more often than not, he catches himself and tries again. "Sounds perfect."

As we sit there, the three of us enjoying our breakfast and catching up, I want to pinch myself. This is what my version of happiness looks like. I have a family, people I cherish, men I'd do anything for.

Even though we all have things to do and places to be, we somehow end up back in bed for a quickie that leaves all of us satisfied and anxious to reunite in a few hours.

"No masturbating," Pax warns before he heads out the door.

I blink. Until now, I hadn't even considered it.

"If I ask, and you lie, you'll blush." He lifts one shoulder. "Dead giveaway."

Frowning, I protest, "You're diabolical, Agent Gallagher."

"I mean it. Keep your hands—and any toys—away from

our pussy, or you'll have a difficult time sitting for a couple of days…"

Because I'm thinking about the night ahead, I struggle to focus on my studying, but I enjoy my time with Natalie immensely.

By six thirty, I'm wearing a dress, and I have on heels.

I've taken the time to put my hair up, and I've added a necklace and earrings that Link bought for me.

As I walk down the stairs, I see both of my men sitting in the living room, glasses of whiskey in hand. Bonds, no doubt. Only the best for my men.

When they catch sight of me, they stand.

The way they treat me, with such courtesy and respect, always makes me want to swoon.

To think how close I came to losing it all…

"Join us," Link invites.

When I do, they both kiss me.

"You look exquisite, little dove."

"So do both of you." Link is dressed perfectly, as always. Pax has on a suit jacket, but no tie, and his first couple of buttons are unfastened.

Suddenly I'm voting to stay home instead of going to a restaurant.

"We have a surprise for you this evening," Link adds.

I shake my head. "You'll turn me into a spoiled brat."

"If you're in any danger of that, we'll give you a much-needed spanking."

No doubt that's true.

Pax reaches into a pocket and pulls out a small, metal piece that resembles a teardrop with a base at one end.

Suddenly I realize it's a butt plug, and I sink onto the couch. *No. No, no, no.*

"I don't think we need to explain," Link teases.

My gaze lands on a small bottle of lube. They can't mean... "You want...?"

"We do," Link assures me.

"The less fuss, the better." Pax's voice contains a hard, no-nonsense quality. "We'll give you choices. You can bend over the back of the couch, drape yourself across Link's knee, or get on all fours on the coffee table."

Dressed like this? None of the above.

When I clamp my lips, Pax nods. "Over Link's knee it is."

Link takes a seat in an armchair.

In moments, I'm off the floor and over Link's lap. My breath whooshes out of me, and I can't even protest when the two of them somehow manage to lift my dress and lower my panties, dropping them to my ankles.

"You don't want to make us late for our reservations," Link warns.

His thighs are strong beneath me, and he clamps an arm around my waist to hold me solidly in place.

"Kicking will earn you a spanking," Pax informs me matter-of-factly.

When I test him, he proves his point, making me yelp.

"Reach back and spread your ass cheeks for me, sweetheart."

I'm drowning in embarrassment.

When I don't act quickly enough, he gives me a second spank.

"Show us that tight little hole."

Instinctively I tighten my buttocks.

"Tessa." A third, much harder spank lands.

We all know I have a safe word, but I don't use it. I'm not even a little bit tempted.

Moving slow—testing him?—I open myself for him.

"Such a pretty sight. And after we take you tonight, it will no longer be a virgin hole."

My heart stops.

How do they expect me to make it through the night knowing they plan to fuck my ass? Taking a finger is hard enough.

He lubes the metal and begins to press it in.

They've taught me to bear down when they tease me there, and I do so now. Surprising me, it slides in easily enough, but it takes me a moment to adjust to the coldness and the intrusion. "Will it…stay?"

"Unless you push it out," Pax replies.

"Which would make us both unhappy. And result in us putting it back in you at the restaurant."

Gasping, I try to lift my head to see if they're serious.

But I already know they are.

Link helps me to stand, and I pull up my panties and straighten my dress. Having the plug inside me is not awful, just strange.

I squirm and wiggle all the way to the restaurant, and when we're shown to our favorite table and have champagne in front of us, Pax glances at me. "Sit flat on your ass."

Until he gives me that instruction, I hadn't realized I'd been leaning slightly to one side. "But it will go in more."

Both men flash me wicked grins.

Since I know there will be consequences if I disobey, I reluctantly comply.

"Much better."

Link's approval is almost worth the discomfort. Almost.

Throughout the meal, I'm a little lost inside my thoughts.

Over coffee and dessert, Pax's voice cuts through my fog to capture my attention. "Sorry?"

"I was asking if you played with yourself this afternoon."

My eyes widen, and I frantically look around to see if anyone overheard us.

"I asked you a question."

"No, Sir." God. How did that word slip out in public? "I didn't."

"Such a good little dove." Link all but purrs his approval.

The drive home seems to take a handful of minutes, even though I know that's not possible. For once, I'd like to delay the inevitable, but every light seems to turn green as we approach.

Pax barely has the car in Park before Link is out and opening my door, offering his hand to assist me. My heart races with each step we take toward the house.

Pax closes the door behind us, and after the alarm is set, the entire space seems supercharged with tension.

"Our bedroom," he commands, his tone leaving no room for argument.

Reluctantly, my legs feeling heavy, I lead the way. As I walk up the stairs, I'm acutely aware of their gazes on me, their eyes burning into my back, my hips, my legs. Each step sends a shiver of anticipation mixed with nervousness down my spine.

Once we reach the bedroom, Link takes control. "Stop where you are," Link instructs.

He continues past me, and when he turns to me, his eyes are dark with a hint of dominance that sends a shiver down my spine. He begins to undress, his movements deliberate and controlled. I watch, mesmerized, as he reveals his toned body, the muscles honed from years of discipline and control.

Behind me, Pax moves closer, his fingers sure as he slides my zipper down. Pressing a kiss to my shoulder, he eases the dress off, letting it pool at my feet. I step out of it, breathless as Pax unhooks my bra and slides my panties down. I'm left standing in just my heels and the jewelry Link had given me.

Link, now naked, comes to stand in front of me. His cock is already hard. He reaches to cup one of my breasts, his thumb brushing over my nipple, making it pebble. "God, little dove. You're perfect."

Near me, Pax finishes undressing.

Then the heat and strength of his body presses against my back, and his rigid cock nudges against me.

"Now, little dove..." Link voice is part soothing, part firm. "Bend over, grab your ankles, and spread your legs. Show us that pretty plug."

With a deep breath, I do as he says, and I grip my ankles tightly. Cool air brushes my exposed pussy and the plug that's snuggled into my most private place. I'm on display for them, completely vulnerable.

"That's our good girl," Link murmurs.

I hear the rustle of his movements, and then his warm hands are on my ass, gently spreading my cheeks apart.

"Such a beautiful sight."

Pax echoes his sentiment with a low groan. "You have no idea how stunning you look, sweetheart. Seeing you like this, submitting to us... It's more than we could have ever asked for."

There's a gentle pull on the plug, and I gasp as nerves spark to life. Link traces the rim where the cool metal meets my skin, making my knees shake.

"How does it feel?"

"Strange," I admit. "But...okay."

In an instant, Pax removes the plug. I gasp at the sudden emptiness, and I tighten my butt cheeks.

"I'll be right back, sweetheart."

He disappears into the bathroom, and in the distance, water splashes.

Link helps me to stand up, and he trails his touch down my body, finding my clit and circling it lightly.

We haven't even started, and my body is already on fire.

Pax returns, his cock hard and ready, a bottle of lube in his hand. "I'll be the first to fuck your tight virgin hole."

"Bend over for him," Link tells me as Pax coats his fingers with the lube, then presses one against my tight hole.

Link teases my clit, his touch featherlight and teasing, distracting me.

Pax presses his finger in slowly. It's a little uncomfortable, but as Link increases the pressure on my clit, I'm filled with an intense pleasure.

"You're doing so well, little dove," Link murmurs, never stopping his delicious torment.

Pax adds a second finger, stretching me farther. I gasp, and I latch onto my ankles for support.

Link's touch becomes more demanding, his fingers moving faster, making sure I can't focus entirely on what Pax is doing.

"Almost there, sweetheart," Pax says, his voice rough with desire. He adds a third finger, and I whimper.

I'm impossibly full.

"Keep breathing," Link advises. His touch keeps me grounded, his fingers working their magic.

Pax pulls out, but before I can react, he captures my hips in his firm grip, holding me in place as he presses the head of his cock against my anal whorl.

There's no way I can do this.

He gives me time to adjust, but his cock feels so different from his fingers: harder, unyielding. There's no way I can do this.

Link leaves me for a moment. Lost, I cry out.

Water runs again, and when he returns, he has a small vibrator in his hand. He kneels in front of me, his fingers finding my clit once more as he turns on the vibrator and presses it against my pussy.

Waves of arousal wash through me. As Pax surges deeper, taking my ass, my discomfort is overtaken by pleasure.

"Fuck. You feel so good, sweetheart." Pax groans, his grip on my hips tightening.

"And you look so beautiful, taking him like that," Link adds, his fingers moving faster, the vibrator pressing harder against me.

"Oh God!"

As Pax begins to move, his thrusts slow and steady, I shout his name.

Sensation after sensation bombards me.

Link doesn't let up. His touch is relentless, driving me higher, outside myself.

Finally I scream, the world spinning as an orgasm rushes through me.

Pax's thrusts become faster, harder, his groans filling the room. With a final, deep thrust, he comes, his body shuddering against mine.

As Pax pulls out, Link turns off the vibrator, his fingers gentling, bringing me down slowly. I release my ankles, my body trembling with the aftermath of my orgasm. Link scoops me up, carrying me to the bed and laying me down gently.

"You were incredible, little dove," he murmurs, his lips brushing against mine.

"Let's shower," Pax suggests a short time later.

In there, they wash me, tenderly taking care of me.

After they dry me, they help me back to bed.

These men have completely changed my life and given me something perfect in return.

Until them, I had no idea it was even possible to be this happy.

Link makes sweet love to me while I stroke Pax. Shockingly he begins to harden again. How is this even possible?

We make love again, and afterward Link bathes me between the legs. "You know I love you." Then he pulls me back against him.

Moments later, Pax's warm, strong body is protecting me from the other side. "You're ours, sweetheart. Always."

I'm snuggled between them, my body sated, my heart full. I've never felt more loved, more cherished. As we drift off to sleep, I know that this is where I belong.

Forever...

◊ ◊ ◊ ◊ ◊

Are you ready to be Captivated again?

When you never planned to get married, and now you're being forced to marry a billionaire and his morally gray partner...

Will you say yes?

DISCOVER THEIRS TO POSSESS NOW

Stay updated on my latest releases, exclusive content, and special offers. Join my newsletter and be the first to know about new books, sales, and more!

As a thank you, you'll receive a free full-length novel featuring your favorite characters.

SIERRA CARTWRIGHT NEWSLETTER
https://www.sierracartwright.com/subscribe/

And more! How about the very best deals on all my books?

Visit my online store for exclusive discounts, bundles, and special editions you won't find anywhere else. Plus, buying directly from my store helps support my work and allows me to continue bringing you the stories you love.

SIERRA CARTWRIGHT STORE
https://www.sierracartwrightbookstore.com

***DISCOVER THEIRS TO LOVE**, a tantalizing Titans Captivated story...*

THEIRS TO LOVE

EXCERPT

Rylee

Alone, I sip my drink through a straw.

But I can't resist another peek in the mirror.

The men are walking toward the bar. Probably to take a couple of empty seats at the far end.

But they don't change directions.

And then... They approach. There's no doubting their intention.

As if by prior arrangement, they move in, standing at the end of the bar.

The dark haired one on the left scares the hell out of me. He reminds me of a panther, sleek and graceful and slightly terrifying. Very real feminine intuition screams a warning to flee far and fast while I still can.

The other gentleman—if either can be called that—has a gentler presence, or at least less threatening. His gray eyes hold kindness. Then he blinks, and that emotion is gone, replaced by a cool, calculating gleam.

Had I only imagined kindness? Maybe a trick of the light? Or just my fanciful imagination?

Then the man on the left speaks. "We've been watching you."

God, his voice is hypnotic. As deep as it is rich.

He leans in just a little closer. His eyes captivate me. Almost amber and predatory. I try to look away but I'm helpless, trapped within his compelling gaze.

"I see your necklace."

Without thinking, I touch it.

"Is it a collar?"

I shake my head.

"So you're not under a Dominant's protection."

"No…" I struggle with how to finish my sentence. Instinct urges me to address him formally, but protocol doesn't demand it. Right now, despite his overwhelming and Dominant air, I have no connection to him. And thirty seconds from now, he'll likely turn on the heel of his very expensive shoes and walk away.

"How remiss."

"I'm sorry?"

"If you were mine, I'd have you collared, and you'd never be left unattended for anyone to approach."

My world spins, and my breath seems to freeze somewhere in my diaphragm. *If I were his...?* The idea is absurd. Something out of a fantastical fairytale. For someone else who isn't me.

"And you're here to scene." He inclines his head, indicating my wristband.

Where is this conversation going? Are they toying with me? The blond doesn't seem like the type, but the other... I wonder if he has a cruel side.

"We haven't met."

The blond has spoken, shattering the building tension.

Relieved, I direct my attention toward him. Anything to escape the gravitational pull of his friend.

"Everett Parker." He extends his hand.

His voice is soothing, like a cool evening rain, and his grip is reassuring. "Uhm...Anne." Have I really stumbled over my scene name? Absently I wonder if his name is also made up. It suits him.

"My pleasure...*Anne.*"

"Ours." The other man cuts into the conversation. *"Our* pleasure."

Courtesy dictating that I also greet him, I give him my full attention, something he seems to command as well as demand.

"Drake." He's bolder than his friend. Instead of the politeness I expect, he lifts my hand and kisses the back of it intimately, in a way that has my wayward heart galloping toward happily ever after. No man has ever treated me this way.

"Is this your first visit?" Everett seems to be the one with the greatest social skills.

I can't help but smile.

"Was that funny?"

"Sorry. Just reminds me of the pickup line. 'Do you come here often?'"

Everett grins. "I'll give you that. It was a pickup line of sorts. And not as smooth as I hoped evidently."

His honesty disarms me, and I respond in kind. "I come here every once in a while with my friend." I'm not sure if I would have the courage to attend by myself.

"And you have been known to enjoy a scene?"

"It's amazing stress relief."

"And has it been a tough day?"

Day? Dozens of them—in a row. "Year." I'm not sure where the admission comes from. Maybe because this whole situation is surreal. I might not ever come back now. Which means I'll never run into this pair of dangerous, charming men again.

Drake, obviously over the easy chitchat, changes the direction of the conversation. "Have you ever played with two guys before?"

To cover my shock, I take a drink of my soda. "No." Most times I don't play with anyone. But the idea secretly thrills me every bit as much as it terrifies me.

"Anne, I'd like to thoroughly Dominate you while Parker here plays with you and paddles your ass."

I freeze.

Everett winces. "What my Neanderthal friend means is—"

"I meant what I said, Parker."

Does he always refer to his friend by his last name?

Then Drake leans forward, smelling of masculine determination. He fingers my necklace then places his finger alongside my carotid artery where my pulse flutters like a butterfly. "I want to thoroughly Dominate you and ruin you for any other man."

I resist the impulse to pinch myself. If this is a dream, I suddenly—maybe stupidly—don't want to wake up.

Still, a nagging, incredulous part of me refuses to be silenced. I vowed not to be any man's plaything ever again. Last year, I'd believed Peter loved me. His awful comments to me when I found out otherwise nearly destroyed my soul. *"You're the kind of woman men fuck, not marry."*

I need to be sure this isn't a horrible game to them. "You can't mean this."

"On the contrary. I've never been more serious in my life."

"Why me?"

Everett responds. "Are you kidding me? You're beautiful."

With a small laugh, I shake my head. I believed that kind of smooth-talking lie once. Never again. "Even if I believed that, there's no shortage of gorgeous women here tonight."

Most who wouldn't hesitate for one second to agree to what either of these men suggest.

Drake doesn't seem to have the same patience as his friend. "Do you see me—us—looking at anyone other than you?" He leans in just a fraction of an inch closer, and his presence overwhelms me. "You were watching in the mirror."

So much for my clandestine skills.

"Deny it."

I remain silent.

"You know we were watching you."

My friend Juliana had said as much, even while I'd remained oblivious.

Everett shoots Drake a quelling glare, not that it seems to have any impact. "We'd enjoy—very much—spending some time pleasing you."

For another few moments, I debate. The night could be amazing if I keep my heart on a short leash. Playing with them doesn't have to mean anything. But still we need boundaries. "It's just for tonight."

"For a start." Drake's counter is immediate, as if he's anticipated my response.

Before Peter, I'd have never been capable of what I say next. "Then I'm afraid I'll have to decline. Thank you for your interest."

"Thank you for your interest?" Drake snarls.

Everett, however, smiles. "The lady is making a simple request."

"She's being insulting." Though he responds to his friend, Drake doesn't take his gaze off me.

Is he feral?

I shiver. Drake, whoever he is in real life, is definitely not the kind of man to cross. Wondering who this new, bold version of myself is, I respond in kind. "If you're offended, you're welcome to go find someone else to scene with." *Hell's bells.* My voice shakes with emotion I'm trying to hide.

"I know what I want." He continues to invade my space.

Numerous dungeon monitors—obvious from their navy T-shirts with DM in great big gold letters—are spread throughout the club, watching every interaction. Security cameras are prevalent as well. It'd take less than two seconds to get rid of Drake and Everett.

"But if the scene goes as well as I intend, then I'd like the opportunity for us to pursue this further."

That he dulls the sharp claws he's flashed at me means something, and I exhale.

"Drake would simply like the opportunity to see you again if you're agreeable."

"I can fucking speak for myself."

"Perhaps." Everett shrugs. "But not well."

Once again, the less unnerving man makes me smile.

"Give us a chance?"

Drake looks at his companion. "Asshole."

Everett's grin is quick and easy. "Dick."

Are they partners or foes?

"What do you say, Anne? Will you forgive Drake's lack of tact and agree to give us a couple of hours of your time?"

ABOUT THE AUTHOR

I invite you to be the very first to know all the news by subscribing to my very special **VIP Reader newsletter**! You'll find exclusive excerpts, bonus reads, and insider information.

For tons of fun and to join with other awesome people like you, join my Facebook reader group: **Sierra's Super Stars**

And for a current booklist, please visit my website.
http://www.sierracartwright.com

USA Today bestselling author Sierra Cartwright was born in England, and she spent her early childhood traipsing through castles and dreaming of happily-ever afters. She has two wonderful kids and four amazing grand-kitties. She now calls Galveston, Texas home and loves to connect with her readers. Please do drop her a note.

ALSO BY SIERRA CARTWRIGHT

Titans
Sexiest Billionaire
Billionaire's Matchmaker
Billionaire's Christmas
Determined Billionaire
Scandalous Billionaire
Ruthless Billionaire
Forbidden Billionaire

Titans Quarter
His to Claim
His to Love
His to Cherish

Titans Quarter Holidays
His Christmas Gift
His Christmas Wish
His Christmas Wife

Titans Sin City
Hard Hand
Slow Burn
All-In

Titans Captivated (Ménages)
Theirs to Hold
Theirs to Love

Theirs to Wed
Theirs to Treasure
Theirs to Corrupt
Theirs to Possess

Titans: Moretti Mafia

Vengeful Vows
Savage Vows

Titans: Reserve

Tease Me

Hawkeye

Come to Me
Trust in Me
Meant For Me
Hold On To Me
Believe in Me
Surrender to Me

Hawkeye: Denver

Initiation
Temptation
Determination

Bonds

Crave
Claim
Command

Donovan Dynasty

Bind

Brand

Boss

Mastered

With This Collar

On His Terms

Over The Line

In His Cuffs

For The Sub

In The Den

With This Ring

Collections

Titans Series

Titans Billionaires: Firsts

Titans Billionaires: Volume 1

Titans Billionaires: Volume 2

Billionaires' Quarter: Titans Quarter Collection

Risking It All: Titans Sin City Collection

Yours to Love: Titans Captivated Collection

His Christmas Temptation: Titans: Quarter Holidays

Hawkeye Series

Undercover Seduction: Hawkeye Firsts

Here for Me: Volume One

Beg For Me: Volume Two

Run, Beautiful, Run: Hawkeye Denver Collection

Printed in Great Britain
by Amazon